Pride Publishing

Single Books
Grayality

GRAYALITY

CAREY PW

Grayality
ISBN # 978-1-80250-962-5
©Copyright Carey PW 2022
Cover Art by Kelly Martin ©Copyright July 2022
Interior text design by Claire Siemaszkiewicz
Pride Publishing

Published in 2022 by Pride Publishing, United Kingdom.

Pride Publishing is an imprint of Totally Entwined Group Limited.

GRAYALITY

Dedication

"It is a risk to love. What if it doesn't work out?
Ah, but what if it does."
Peter McWilliams

This novel is dedicated to my husband Joe for proving to me that love knows no gender. This novel is also dedicated to my friends Becki and Kathleen for inspiring me to pursue my dreams as an author.

Chapter One

Pate

How did I get here?

The question engulfed me as my eyes cringed and my guts tensed up as Oakley and I flew down the highway going seventy-five miles per hour. All I saw were miles of flat earth, lazy summer cows and the occasional rolling hill extending off into some unknown horizon. It looked distant and hopeless.

I was twenty-six years old and going nowhere. The only thing that I'd ever known for certain was that I wanted to be a man. I spent most of my high school days and early twenties working endless shifts at whatever hourly wage job would have me. I also worked small tutoring jobs, helping high school drop-outs study for their GEDs, or helping kids in the neighborhood get through high school trigonometry. Luckily, I got a steady gig as a bartender in East Atlanta that offered full-time benefits and insurance, something I had thought was an elusive dream. It took years of sacrifice and slaving away to scrape together enough funds to pay for my hormones and, eventually, my top surgery. Of course, kids typically stay on their parents' insurance until their mid-twenties (thanks Obama!), but I was not welcome at home anymore and didn't want to bug my parents for their insurance card. So I had to do it on my own.

I performed well in high school and later in college, maintaining a four-point-oh average and getting enough scholarships to help me fund my bachelor's degree in English education. However, when I realized that I was transgender, college just wasn't a priority anymore. I dropped out after two years to work full-time and earn more money for treatment.

Now, my current transitioning journey had been halted. I'd been taking hormones for more than two years and had top surgery ten months ago. I had no more funds to pursue the full transition, the coveted bottom surgery. I was now more visibly a man, but I was a man with no job, no more money and no support, except for Oakley.

Oakley and I met in the first grade. He was the typical "rebel" southerner who wore death metal shirts and played lead guitar in a death metal band. Oakley was my first everything. First friend, first real boyfriend (good ol' ninth grade) and first sexual experience.

Oakley had a slow start into adulthood. He came close to marrying a girl he met after high school. Her family owned a dry-cleaning business, and they let Oakley manage one of their stores. A few years later, the girl got pregnant, and it seemed that Oakley's future was set. For someone so rebellious, here he was getting married, having babies, buying a home and working in the family business. *What a sell-out,* I thought. A few months before the wedding, the girl told him that she had been seeing the drummer in his metal band and that the baby was the spawn of their passionate, clandestine romance that occurred often in the backseat of his truck while Oakley was tuning his guitar. Oakley never fully recovered.

Here we are, years later, Oakley childless, and me breastless.

A few months ago, Oakley's grandmother was diagnosed with breast cancer. She was having a double mastectomy done in Seattle and would be returning to her ranch in a small town in Eastern Montana. She needed someone to take care of her and provide transportation for medical appointments. She offered Oakley free room and board, homecooked Granny meals and a beautiful, skyscraper-free skyline. Her only caveat was that she wanted Oakley to enroll in the local university and hold a part-time job. Since he had spent his childhood and adolescent years taking many trips to Montana for snowboarding and skiing, Oakley claimed that he was ready for a change and that the South just wasn't where his soul belonged. Too afraid to embark on this new Pacific Northwest adventure on his own, he talked his grandmother into letting me move with him.

Neither of us grew up in urban, crowded, skyscraper jungles, but we were products of endless major highways with exits every five to ten miles that glowed under golden arches and gas station beams. As Oakley's 2004 Pontiac Sunfire flew up Highway 2, my eyes frantically searched for lights, gas stations, food and civilization, only to see nothing more than flat earth and cattle ranches every time our car passed over a hill. *I think I will need to develop a strong bladder.*

"Are you sure that there is a town on this road?" I asked, more to myself than Oakley. "And why the fuck is it so cold? It's freakin' July!" I shoved my hands into my armpits in futile hopes of warmth. All my clothes were packed tight into old suitcases and garbage bags in the trunk, and I was sporting a tight-fitting black tank to show off my petite but toned biceps. But when our little Sunfire pulled into the dark, shady gas station along the Montana and North Dakota border, my face was met with a slap of icy cold wind and droplets of rain, sending a piercing shiver up my spine. I checked the weather on my phone. It read forty-five degrees.

"I've never actually driven here. We've always flown in from Billings in the eight-seater plane. Trust me, it will look better when we reach Cloverleaf," Oakley calmly assured me.

Rising up from the conservative Southern trenches that had filled my belly with a large, hardened rock, I had learned to keep my mouth shut and my head down. As my eyes scoured the landscape of dilapidated derelict buildings and closed businesses when our car arrived in town, my heart wasn't optimistic that Cloverleaf was going to be the place for me to thrive. As I looked closely at a man climbing out of his gargantuan four-by-four truck, I could just make out the ruggedness of his dirty hands with bloody cracks, his stiff, muddy boots that were probably black underneath all the dirt, and his deep forehead wrinkles from the hours in the blazing sun and frigid wind. Even if men here accepted me as a man, I didn't know how I would interact with this form of masculinity. Instead, I gently caressed my soft, delicate, feminine hands.

I wasn't a man's man, yet in some ways, I was. I'd always been athletic. I played sports in elementary and middle school before quitting to work during high school. I was never talented, always preferring to support the good players rather than put myself out there, especially with the form-fitting uniforms that showcased my bouncy breasts when I ran. However, sports offered me a good excuse to exercise and stay fit in an attempt to avoid developing female curves.

Even after I started working, I still jogged three miles daily and lifted weights to make everything as lean and tight as possible. It took about a year and a half for the testosterone to thin me out like a man. As I ran my hands along my thigh bones that were hugged by my runner's muscles, then along my abdomen where I could now feel the subtle crevices that nearly formed a complete six-pack, I finally adored my body. Years of working out and restricting my diet still left a hovering, protruding belly of fat that stuck out, and round hips that insisted on telling the whole world that I was a woman and never allowed me to have the body that my exercise efforts and heart cried out for. I scratched between my legs, waking up from my physical admiration as my genitals reminded me that I was still only half a man.

"You'll be fine. There's still a lot of pretty girls around here. And we'll be hot stuff because we're new and exotic," Oakley sang as he rubbed his septum bullring piercing, causing his shirt sleeve to rise, revealing his array of skull tattoos.

Oakley and I were similar guys. We both had small, skinny physiques that prevented us from appearing like tough, dominant masculines, so we chose to paint our bodies with as many skulls, horror tattoos and gag-inducing piercings as possible to prove our masculinity in another kind of "tough" way. After all, I didn't think that truck-driving ranching man who I saw at the last town was "man enough" to stick a needle in his septum or through his penis, as Oakley bravely did a few weeks ago. Yet, I felt that our masculinity was always dismissed because it didn't follow stereotypical displays that involved driving trucks, getting dirty or flexing muscles. On the other hand, maybe it was all in my head.

"How do you suggest that I date around here?" I asked, throwing my hand up at the ocean of perpetual brown fields. "It would only take two seconds before everyone here knows I'm a freak."

"You're not a freak."

"Yeah, well, say that to all the other men without vaginas." I crossed my arms.

"I think there are a lot of women who wouldn't care. Women are more open with their sexuality," he argued.

"But then you add the no job, no money, no car—"

"We'll get jobs," he interrupted me. "There's always hourly work around here. That's easy. You can save up for a car. And we're going to college, so our financial situation is acceptable."

"Are you really into the college thing?" I challenged.

"Are you?" Oakley turned his eyes sideways to search for any dishonesty.

I heaved in a gulp of air as I looked away from him and focused my gaze on a worn-down Misfits sticker on his dashboard.

"What?" he urged.

"It's just a waste of time," I grumbled.

"You're a good teacher. You're going to be a good teacher—"

"No one is going to hire or accept a trans teacher in schools. Even if I get certified and hired, if I am 'discovered'"—I made quotation marks with my fingers—"it's over. And even if it's not, I don't want to put up the fight, you know?"

"Why not?"

"Because I'm not trying to be some transgender freedom fighter." I sighed. "I just don't want anyone around here to know about it, okay? Like don't tell *anybody*."

"Granny knows," he reminded me.

"Besides Granny."

"Okay."

Chapter Two

Oakley

All my life, I've been straight. Even in elementary school, I loved watching the pretty girls run around in their dresses with their long hair. The admiration wasn't sexual, of course, but it was attraction. I wanted to be near them, to touch them and to hear their high voices laugh and giggle. When I entered middle school, I hit dating full on, bouncing from girlfriend to girlfriend and accruing days of sweet memories that involved holding hands and receiving small pecks on my mouth that sent shivers of excitement up my spine. Then there were the love letters that were passed around so that I could absorb the splendor of middle school love literature during my algebra class. There was always something to look forward to even though there was minimal action. The innocence of junior-high romance and the lingering unknown kept me coming back for more.

I always knew that I favored black-haired girls. So, when I met Patricia, a.k.a. Pate, it felt like love at first sight. Patricia had this long black hair that frizzed up in the unforgiving humidity of the South, causing it to appear even thicker, like a wild lion's mane. Her skin was the palest that I'd ever seen, without a single blemish, just white and smooth like milk, and next to her black mane, her skin glowed even paler. Then there was the *gothicness* that emerged in high school. Patricia always dressed in black, mostly with black T-shirts of bands like White Zombie, Misfits, Rancid, and the occasional eighties New Wave band. Patricia always had a strange fascination with eighties New Wave that still baffles me to this day. At age fourteen, she was the most beautiful little gothic rock girl that I'd ever seen, making her exactly what I craved. Much to my surprise, she agreed to be my girlfriend.

I dated Patricia for four glorious months that culminated in both of us losing our virginity. Patricia was always an outgoing, social person — at least at that time — so I was mesmerized by her timid, vulnerable nature as she grimaced and moaned when I slowly and caringly broke her hymen. My heart swelled with a rush of emotions as I absorbed the indescribable gift that she had bestowed on me. I told her that I loved her that same day, and I meant it. In retrospect, I wonder if Patricia was just going through the motions of trying this sex thing out and discarding her virginity label even though Pate assures me that the experience was important for him, too. But what I was supposed to think when I realized that I had sex with a man?

I wasn't grossed out so much when Patricia told me that she wanted to become Pate. Patricia and I had a unique relationship. Despite only dating for a few months, we continued our physical relationship all through high school. Patricia would spend hours at my house, squeezing her body tight against me, leaving my cheek slightly wet from the moisture in her breath as her forehead leaned lightly against mine. Kissing and the occasional sex was just natural for us. We were best friends who experienced everything together, and even though my love for her at the time was never returned the way that I wanted, I savored the intimacy.

Patricia had just started her second year of college when she came out to me as trans. One night, we lay curled up in my bed, consuming glasses of homemade black Russian. Patricia always enjoyed learning about new mixed drinks, and there was usually an open bar at my dad's house. I gently kissed Patricia around her left ear and moved my lips slowly down her neck. She closed her eyes. Patricia usually closed her eyes. She never wanted anyone looking at her, and I think she believed that closing her eyes somehow shielded her from my eager gaze. I sat up and firmly pulled her body down and curved it into me, kissing her harder and grabbing her breasts. Pushing her backward, I yanked her T-shirt and bra up, exposing her delicate white breasts and dull pink nipples. I loved the way nipples felt in my mouth. They were so soft but firm. My eyes shot up to examine her reaction only to find her staring blankly up at the ceiling as if she were getting a shot in the doctor's office but didn't want to watch it happen. Patricia always looked that way during sex if her eyes were open.

Patricia sat up suddenly, and her shoulders heaved up and down slightly. I heard a sniffle.

"Are you okay? What's wrong?" I sat up next to her, putting my arm around her. Pat had been struggling with depression for the past six months or so, which she had spoken to me about, yet I wasn't sure what was going on. I just knew that she was sad. But I hadn't seen her cry before.

"What's wrong?" I asked again, softer this time. I didn't want her to think by any means that I was upset about the disruption in our lovemaking.

"I don't *know*!" She started crying loudly, and the anguish that pushed the *know* out of her mouth was a despair that I had not heard in a voice before. I turned my body slightly away from her, searching the room to find something to stop her pain. I frantically combed through my thoughts for comforting words, but my mind blanked. Instead, I gently placed her bra back in its position, even carefully sliding her breasts into the wire cups. She moved her arms to let me pull her shirt back down.

"Sometimes I wake up at three a.m.," she sobbed. "*A lot* of times, I wake up at three a.m., but I just lie in bed until ten, eleven, twelve—wishing that I didn't have to wake up."

I hugged her tighter.

"I don't want to live anymore."

"I *want* you to live, Patricia. I love you."

"I know. I don't know why I feel this way. I just *do!*" She pulled her knees forward, leaning her head against them.

My heart tightened and my throat dried up as I watched her cry. When she glanced at my eyes, I could see the tiny red blood vessels drizzled along her green pupils, and her cheeks were blanketed with a rosy flush underneath splotches of tears. Honestly, I was more in love with her than ever at that moment.

"What can I do?" I asked, placing my chin on her head.

"I wish I was a man," she whispered.

I questioned my hearing. *She must have said, 'I wish it would stop, man.' Something like that.*

"I feel like if I am up for killing myself, then maybe I should just do anything, you know? Just take any risk because it doesn't fucking matter if the other option is death."

I was lost. Instead, I stared at her.

"What do you think?" Her crying had subsided, but the sniffles remained.

"About what?" My cheeks felt red.

"About...becoming a man?"

What? I looked down, feeling my brain freeze up.

"Would you still be my friend?" She placed her hand on top of mine.

"Like..." I had no idea what words were safe. "Are you...one of those trans — trans — trans-sex people?"

"What's that?" she asked.

* * * *

Pate

Not many people talk about trans people unless they know someone or are experiencing it themselves. It just doesn't arise in most conversations. Transgender people seemed like these faraway beings that I didn't understand and who were a lot braver than me. Trans people faced violence, discrimination, bullying, and even in some severe cases, rape and murder. I was just some white, coddled, middle-class suburbanite who had never been in a physical fight and whose pathway in life seemed for the most part, easy. *How can I be one of those people? Don't these things happen to other people? Not me?*

After my disclosure to Oakley, I decided to see a psychologist, which was affordable on my parents' income since I was enrolled in college at that time. Yet when I walked into the small corner office and sat my body into the oversized, cushy couch, I didn't know what to say. Part of me just wanted to continue sinking deep into the crevices of that couch as the therapist's eyes peered into me. *What if he thinks I'm lying? That I am doing all this for attention? Maybe he'll just say that I am depressed and psychotic.*

I told the doctor my thoughts, thoughts that I had shared many times with others who had never grasped the true meaning behind my words. I went through a tomboy phase in childhood like many girls, yet there were things that differed. When I was nine years old, my parents told me to wear undershirts to cover my small nipples that sometimes poked out. They weren't really bras, but they *were* bras, and my future milk jug development became real. I watched movies, and in every movie, I studied the women's breasts. Some women exposed their cleavage and seemed happy to have breasts, while other women attempted to cover their breasts with T-shirts, yet there was no denying those two mountain peaks that protruded, exposing what I saw as a feminine curse. This notion haunted me throughout my childhood.

When I started puberty, there was no denying it. My nipples turned into agonizing, hardened rocks as if my body were forcing this female onto me and ensuring that I was going to suffer the entire way through it. I wore baggy clothes, but there was no hiding them. Sometimes my mother would make those obnoxious motherly comments that "your boobies are growing," and I would cringe in embarrassment. Examining my two older sisters, both equipped with D or double-D cups, I felt doomed.

Then I got my period, another relentless, brutal punishment onto my body. I now had to buy tampons and pads and familiarize myself with this female world that men would never know. Having a period meant that I was always casually checking between my thighs when I stood up, making sure that no red stains had emerged to engulf me in humiliation. Not to mention when I started having sex, I'd assume I was off my period only to stare in horror as the guy pulled out a blood-stained penis from my vagina. For me, being a woman meant always being embarrassed by my body.

When I started puberty, the emotions came. I found myself spending hours in my room alone, crying for no specific reason, and most of all, feeling isolated. I never felt that I belonged with my circle of friends. While I had boyfriends, I always felt like I was not exciting like other girls. Most of my friends in school were boys, and over time, they felt comfortable talking about their sexual encounters. I listened to stories of girls who took showers with them. Girls who could have sex all day. Girls who let them cum all over their bodies. When I had sex, I just lay there. It wasn't because I didn't like the emotional intimacy of it. I just didn't know how to be a woman in bed. At the same time, I didn't know how to be a man, either. So, I faked orgasms. I pretended to enjoy exposing my breasts, and I pretended to not feel violated or humiliated when men sucked on them. In reality, I hated being naked.

With the advent of emotions from the hormonal turmoil of puberty and adolescence, I sat in my room blaming God, whom I still believed in at the time. *Why did he make me, a man, be born as a woman?*

The idea stayed with me, and sometimes when I was smoking weed with friends and morphed into my philosopher role, I asserted to everyone that I was a man whom God placed in a female body to punish me for something my soul must have done. I always laughed when I said this, and it wasn't until I sat in the therapist's office rehashing it that I realized the true weight behind those words.

But I'm not transsexual?

I sat in his office for six months talking about wanting to be a man, yet reluctant to do anything about it, including admitting to myself that I was transgender. Telling my parents, who were Republicans and not as hip with the new generations and new gender roles, seemed impossible. Hell, just telling anyone seemed so impossible. *How did all those other transgender people do it? They make it look so easy. It won't be easy for me.*

One afternoon when I was bored and didn't feel up for schoolwork, I turned on HBO. They were showing a movie called *Transamerica*. The movie was more a dark comedy but followed a transgender woman on her journey to have bottom surgery, the last stage in her transition. In one part, she had to go home to her parents' house and even ask them for money to help her get back to California for her surgery date— otherwise, she would have to wait another year. Studying the character, Bree, I was intrigued by her mixture of confidence and insecurity. Here she was, living her life full-time as a woman, yet she still had all these fears and insecurities. My favorite part was when a Native American man showed romantic interest in her, which obviously contributed to her feeling like a woman. *What it would feel like to have a woman or gay man hit on me...*

When I decided to walk through the door, I leaped. Still weirded out and still getting over the end of our sexual relationship, Oakley stood by me. When my mother called me a freak and wanted to have me institutionalized on the claim that I was suicidal and "out of my mind," my dad told me to move out or seek professional help. Neither were thrilled when I informed them that I had been seeing a therapist, and I produced a letter from him acknowledging that I had gender dysphoria and had been approved for hormone therapy. Defeated, I was just told to get out.

I quit school and moved in with Oakley and his dad, staying in their basement, even though Oakley and I still liked to sleep cuddled up together. At least, we did until I started changing.

Chapter Three

Oakley

The drive from Georgia to Montana took forever, and I doubted that my little car would plow through it. Even when we pulled into Cloverleaf, Pate didn't look too thrilled. Pate wasn't big on support groups and trans-friendly organizations, but he did occasionally make use of the ones around Atlanta whenever he claimed that he "needed to be around other trans folks." Here, he wouldn't have any safe place to go, but I couldn't fathom not having Pate around me. While my romantic inclinations had faded, I was still drawn like a magnet to his soul. I believed that he felt the same with mine.

Granny lived a few miles from town on a small ranch. She rented her land to other ranchers for their cattle, in exchange for tending to a few of her own cattle that she mostly kept around to slaughter in the wintertime. My uncle lived in Flathead and would travel back and forth helping her maintain the ranch since he was the future inheritor.

We weren't far from the front door before the aroma of salmon patties, homemade French fries and biscuits danced up my nostrils. *Yes, she hasn't lost her Southern cooking!*

The main door was open for us, so I opened the screen door, knocking to alert her to our presence. Granny walked in from the kitchen. She had had her double mastectomy about three weeks ago but was still recovering. She looked good but frail and tired.

"You shouldn't be up and cooking, Granny." I half scolded her because I was starving. I carefully embraced her, avoiding squeezing too hard. I could tell she was sore.

"My friend came over and helped me put it together. I just had to heat it. How was the drive? Long?" she asked as she walked into the kitchen, which was our cue to follow her. She already had the food laid out on the table. I had called her when we were close to give her ample time to prepare for us. She sat down and motioned to the fridge. "Help yourself to anything to drink. I cook, but I don't wait on people."

I grabbed a Coke, and Pate motioned for a water. Pate had not met Granny yet, but Patricia had.

As we sat down, Granny's eyes fixed on Pate as if she were purposefully searching for remnants of Patricia. Pate began eating, placing his focus on the food, but I knew he noticed.

"So how are you feeling?" I inquired. "When do you start chemo?"

"In a few weeks. They want me to heal more first. I need my strength." She brushed a few strands of her thin gray hair out of her face. Her eyes stayed on Pate.

"Where are they?" I asked.

"Billings."

"That's a drive. Let me know the schedule so that when I register, I can make sure that my classes don't interfere," I told her, but her eyes remained on Pate.

"Is there something that you want to ask me?" Pate muttered, slowly looking up from his plate and clinching his jaw.

"So...do you have a penis now?"

"Granny!" I snapped.

"I don't mean anything by it. I just don't know what all you've had done."

"No." Pate pushed another mouthful of food into his mouth.

"Are you going to?" Granny continued to pry while rubbing her fingers along the table.

"I don't know. I don't have the money," he replied.

"You were so pretty as a girl. I thought you and Oakley would get married and have some pretty babies. You two would have pretty babies—"

"Granny," I inserted, "Don't—"

"It's okay." Pate said gently holding up his hand to me. "Yes, I was a pretty girl. Now, I am a handsome man."

"You still look like a girl. You have that baby face." Granny finally started eating a piece of biscuit.

Under the table, I squeezed Pate's thigh. Pate was more than aware that he looked ten years younger and feminine in the face. He desperately wanted facial hair but little had emerged, and he was very insecure about it.

"So, if you don't have a penis yet, aren't you still a woman?" Granny pushed between bites of biscuit.

"Does not having breasts mean you're not a woman anymore?" Pate stated more than asked, and his green eyes laid right into Granny's. My throat fell into my chest.

Granny was mid-mouthful when Pate made the comment, and the silence was agony.

Finally, Granny smirked. "I guess you're right."

Granny had an upstairs loft in her house that had been converted into a bedroom. When Pate and I walked upstairs, we found two twin beds with heavy winter comforters over sheets squeezed so tight on the bed that only a grandma could do it. There were small refinished gray nightstands beside each one and one large chest of drawers. Some racks were placed along the wall for us to hang our clothes and two large black bean bags sat next to a small table in front of a thirty-inch flat screen television. Two folding TV tables were leaning against the wall with two small chairs if we needed a makeshift desk for homework.

"She made it pretty cozy in here," Pate remarked as he set his bags down. "Where's the bathroom?"

"There's a half bath at the bottom of the stairs on the left. If you want to shower, then you'll have to use the main bath beside Granny's room."

Pate sat down on the bed, pressing his fists into the mattress to test its sponginess. "Did I go too far?" he asked, still focused on his mattress pressing.

"No, Granny's cool. She loves you."

He smiled. "Sounded like she loves *us*."

"That, too, but she'll understand." I started unpacking some clothes. I was exhausted and ready for a long shower and maybe a few hours of playing *Zelda* on my Nintendo Switch.

"Oakley, what do you think will happen here?"

"What do you mean? Like, will Granny die? I hope not."

"No. I mean, you didn't just come up here for Granny. What are you hoping for?"

"I really don't know." I sighed and shoved my shirts into the top drawer.

"Oakley!" Granny yelled from the bottom of the stairs.

"Yes!" I leaned over the stair railing.

"So...are you two gay?"

* * * *

Pate

Coming from Georgia, Eastern Montana is a major culture shock. Being transgender, it is a culture shock. Identifying as bisexual, it is a culture shock. Hell, it's just a culture shock.

After high school, I lost my sociability. I was never a large crowd person, but I enjoyed my close-knit group of freaky goth kids on the weekends, listening to metal music, getting stoned and watching *Willy Wonka and the Chocolate Factory*. After high school, it was just me and Oakley and the occasional boyfriend. I always wanted to date girls, but I was afraid of being written off as a lesbian. I didn't mean to insult lesbians, but instead of seeing me as a man who liked women, getting called a lesbian just placed another misunderstood feminine label on me. Thus, while I had engaged in some sexual experimentation with girls in high school, I had never gone all the way or pursued a serious relationship with one. Since I wasn't interested in getting married or in having sex in my female form, I only had brief relationships, which felt more like going through the motions than authentic attempts at establishing something long-lasting.

So, socially, this small town in rural Montana suited me just fine. It was relieving to not sit in traffic for hours to drive across town and to not have to wait in line for anything. It was also nice to not have to go into crowded stores or worse, crowded men's restrooms.

When I first decided to come out, I joined a few FTM (female-to-male) support groups on Facebook. It was nice to have a safe space to ask awkward questions. The restroom question was a common one. It was difficult to try to explain to non-trans people why the act of urinating or pooping in a public restroom was such a challenging milestone that created a lot of anxiety and sometimes fear in many of us. Like many, I asked when other people decided it was time to change restrooms. Some were brave enough to venture pre-transition or no-transition (keep in mind, not all trans people transition). Some waited until they showed more masculine qualities. Others asserted that they knew it was time when women reacted uncomfortably to their presence in the women's room. For me, I started using the men's room six months after starting T (testosterone).

Now, I had been spoon-fed the myth for many years that men didn't talk in bathrooms. The concept of congregating in bathrooms in groups was always a female thing. Hence, I felt sure that if I kept my head down and did my business, it wouldn't be the traumatic event that my head made it out to be. During my second time going into the men's room, I felt okay. After all, people always told me that I should own it. As I walked into the tiny gas station restroom which contained only one urinal nestled right smack beside the one stall, I already wasn't thrilled to see a man at the urinal. One of my illogical fears was that men would hear that I peed sitting down and would confront me, even though that had never happened to me. However, when I walked into the restroom, the man at the urinal flipped around and hollered, "Good morning!" Dumbfounded and too scared to say anything for fear that he'd notice my feminine voice, I just nodded and went into the stall.

On another occasion, I was patiently following my bathroom routine in which I quietly peed a little, then stopped to avoid the noise of peeing sitting down. Several men had come and gone from the restroom, and I always let my pee explode freely whenever a toilet flushed or a sink ran. I sighed in relief as the last man left, hoping that I would be alone to pee in peace. Suddenly, a loud, excitable voice emerged entering the restroom. The man went directly into the stall beside me, which was my cue to just give it up and try another gas station restroom, a common dilemma for some trans folks with public restroom anxieties. Just then, the man yelled, "How's it going in there?" followed by an awkward laugh. He said something else, but by that time my pants were pulled up, and I was getting the fuck out of there!

Oakley and I both found jobs at the local Walmart in Cloverleaf, making using public restrooms more of a daily ordeal, but doable. Fortunately, I had already legally changed my name before leaving Georgia, as well as my gender on my driver's license. Thus, I avoided any awkwardness of presenting as a man with a female name and ID. But I could tell that people suspected Oakley and I were gay. While I was still learning about my masculinity and figuring out the man I wanted to be, I still upheld many of my female mannerisms, which I supposed would be more characteristic of a stereotypical gay man. In a way, I was relieved. It meant a lot of people would leave me alone.

What I loved most about Montana was Granny's barn. It had been cleared out recently by Oakley's uncle, and I had brought along all my surround-sound stereo equipment. I wanted to create a large space where I could dance. Ever since I was in elementary school, I had loved to dance. Sometimes we would drive up to one of the Atlanta clubs, not to pick up women, but to dance. Typically, women, and sometimes men, would immediately dance with me, which Oakley claimed proved that one, I was good, and two, women liked me.

Granny was fully supportive of my use of the barn, especially because it kept the music from disturbing her. Oakley and I both agreed that it was a good place to smoke pot, a pastime we both planned on continuing, even in Montana.

After setting up my surround-sound system and cleaning up the floor, it was only a question of which song would serenade these walls and my body with the emotional power that woke within me whenever I danced. In a new place where no one knew the dead me, I selected *Mr. Roboto* by Styx. The words about throwing away one's mask and having others see the speaker's true identity swelled my heart, and I let it lead me all around the barn floor and occasionally, on top of the beams. I was in awe of the way my new, lean body seemed even more made for dancing. This barn alone made moving here worth it. I spent hours every night in that barn, the one place where I could be myself.

Chapter Four

Oakley

I barely finished high school. I completed my work and passed my classes, but school was not my focus. I was perfectly content with my persona as a D student who was also a damn good metal guitar player. The future was elusive to me but wasn't a stressor, either. I was a hard worker and always managed to find jobs. Work was more about paying bills and hanging out so that my energy could be devoted to my music. I formed a band with a few friends from high school and a few guys they'd recruited along the way. We practiced three times weekly in the singer's basement and sometimes in my dad's garage. At least a few times a month, we played a gig at local breweries and small clubs around Atlanta. It wasn't stardom, but I was happy. I just wanted to write and play music on my guitar.

However, it wasn't enough for my bandmates. Either their jobs became more demanding and lured them away with promotions or higher pay, or they married and had babies. While we still played, it was more of a pastime for them. Eventually, I was the only one writing new material, and they weren't up for learning it. I found more joy in playing by myself. I even purchased a basic acoustic to see if I could manage as a one-person band, but I never played anywhere.

When things fell apart with Carly and the baby, I was done with Georgia. Browsing my Facebook feed, I envied my classmates who had moved away and posted pictures of long white beaches that lurked outside their doorsteps or skyscrapers lit up like Christmas trees surrounding the horizon of their selfies.

When Granny offered for me to stay with her, the concept of some faraway, mysterious, exotic town in Montana was so alluring that it intoxicated me. I was ravenous for any change. I didn't care what it was. My life was isolating, boring and predictable. I was heading into my late twenties with hardly any life-changing experiences to mold me into the person I was meant to be. This future me hovered underneath my skin, itching to get out but stifled by the mundanity of Georgia. Anything new would be good.

Granny and my parents wanted me to go to college. They worried that I would not have enough to do in Cloverleaf and felt that a college education would expand my options so that whenever I left Montana, I could go anywhere. That latter part enticed me enough to agree, and Pate had always been a good student, so I talked him into doing it with me. Fortunately, he had not finished all his general education classes at the University of Georgia, so even if we chose different majors, we could still take classes together.

Pate and I sat at Granny's kitchen table on Pate's laptop exploring our degree and class options. Pate was tending to a simmering pot of chili on the stove while I was buttering some garlic bread to soak it up with. Pate always liked to cook even though I always felt that cooking was such a feminine stereotype that he would want to avoid it. But Pate seemed adamant about not letting gender-stereotyping define his masculinity. After all, he concocted a mean pan of Southern-style chili, thanks to spending time with his own grandmother who had died eight years ago.

"What are you thinking?" I inquired as I jumped up to shove the bread into the oven to brown. "They got a lot of education options. What was your major again at UGA?"

"What's the point?" Pate shrugged. "I'm never going to teach in a school. Do you know how society treats trans people already? Then you throw schools in the mix where parents can enforce whatever transphobic, homophobic shit they want and push schools to follow their backward ideals. I'm not doing it." He aggressively pushed the laptop back and slumped back in his chair.

"But you're good at that stuff," I pleaded, pulling the laptop close to me.

"Forget it."

"Okay. What about liberal studies? Or health promotion? You like exercising and dancing."

His interest in exercising was enough to jolt his body back forward, and he clicked on the program sheet link for health promotion. I studied his green eyes as they moved up and down the screen.

"Well?" I asked.

"Okay," he muttered.

Sighing, I realized that Pate was just as stuck as me, and it was comforting not to be alone in my indecisive, nondirectional adult pit. I grabbed the laptop and clicked back to the automotive technology program. "I think I am going to do this one."

"Looks good for you. You basically rebuilt your car."

"You mean I repaired my cheap car." I corrected him with a wag of my forefinger.

"Well, I'm not good at that stuff." Pate laughed as he got up to check the chili. "What classes can we take together?" he asked as he stared down at the stew pot.

Pate was very anxious about ensuring that we had classes together. Growing up, Pate was intimidatingly confident and popular among our little freakish group in high school. But transitioning had changed him, both for the good and the bad. It drastically liberated his dancing. He moved freer and lighter without the bouncing, awkward breasts on his chest. He seemed at peace when he ran along Granny's ranch. Pate often said that he couldn't explain it, but he was only at peace when he was in motion.

Immediately after coming out, Pate developed extreme social anxiety. He withdrew from almost all social situations, including hanging out at band practice. He immediately escaped if anyone ever came over, often hiding outside my dad's house or walking up and down the street until the threatening visitor left. I figured it was all in his head until he started hormones, and his brain just went bonkers. He was tense, forgetful and sad at one moment and just flat and dead the next. Sometimes at the end of the day, he just sat staring at the TV but not watching it. His dull eyes peered somewhere beyond the screen to some mysterious place in his psyche. It wasn't his first bout of depression, but it was the scariest.

Since top surgery, Pate had improved a lot, but his social anxiety still drowned him when places got too crowded, and in public restrooms. He was nervous about classes in small-town Montana, assuming that others would be able to discover the female that he had so desperately tried to dispel. I assured him all the time that he passed and that many dudes had slightly higher voices. None of my affirmations eased his tensions.

"Did you take writing at UGA?" I asked after seeing that everyone had to take writing classes.

"No. Funny enough, I avoided it." Pate had always been a good writer and loved reading, especially poetry. He was always secretive with his work, so avoiding a writing class where his work would be read then critiqued didn't surprise me.

"What about science?"

"No."

"Cool. We can take writing and science." I smirked, pleased that we would definitely have several classes together. I also didn't want to take all my classes alone. "What about biology?"

"Sure."

"We can go register tomorrow." My voice froze as I realized that I sounded more confident—and eager—than I was. I had no clue if I could pass a college writing class or biology. Academics seemed hard.

"Sure," Pate concurred as he stirred the chili.

* * * *

Pate

Years ago, attending college would have tightened my stomach in excitement. Instead, walking up to the registrar's office at the university filled me with dread and uncertainty. At the same time, I didn't have anything else to do. The last years had been filled with doctor's appointments, therapist letters, court dates, surgeon consultations, breast cancer screenings and so on. My funds were bled dry, and when I researched bottom surgery, fear and doubt stopped me from planning that pursuit. The procedure was ridiculously expensive and required several surgeries and long recoveries. I was also fearful of the results and that I wouldn't be satisfied. Worst, I feared that I might lose the intensity of my testosterone-infused orgasms, a side effect of transitioning that was fucking awesome.

We had already completed the paperwork and been accepted before we made the long journey from Georgia. Somehow, as we walked inside the building and past the classrooms, the reality of returning to school and being out in public sank in. I was desperate to see what the restrooms looked like so that I knew what I was getting into when I had to pee. *God, I hope they have more than two stalls!*

Oakley went to register first, and I decided to browse the hallways—and sneak a peek at the men's room. Passing by a bulletin board, I explored all the corny college fliers that decorated it. Fliers about study habits, getting enough sleep, time management and stress reduction through mindfulness. Through my peripheral vision, I sensed someone beside me. The smell of honeysuckle, a Southern familiarity, crept into my nose, creating a burst of nostalgia.

Careful not to move my head, I glanced sideways to see her. She had curly dark brown hair down to her waist that she had pulled back with a clip that only captured half of it, allowing the messy curls to fall sporadically along her face and shoulders. She was shorter, thank God! Standing only five foot seven, I had accepted being a short dude but would cower away if a girl was taller than me. I didn't need that insecurity. Her skin was darker than my pale, peachy color, but it was smooth like mine. Her body was shorter and rounder than mine, and she carried her weight in all the right places, creating a perfectly curvy hourglass figure. Her sundress accentuated her small waist and full hips.

"Do you see anything on here about apartments? People looking for roommates?" Her eyes met mine. They were a deep golden-brown highlighted with black mascara, that curved up at the outer corners.

"N-n-no," I stuttered. *She spoke to me!*

She turned her eyes back to the board. She moved her body closer, standing on her tiptoes for some of the higher fliers.

Say something! I cringed at my failure to generate conversations. I just knew I wanted to say something to her. I wanted her to stay.

"Need an apartment?" I mumbled, acting like I was browsing the board for something specific.

"Do you know a place renting? I need roommates or something cheap." She moved her body to face toward me and the corners of her mouth rose slightly in a smile that revealed dimples on her round cheeks.

"No, I'm not from here," I responded with a slight laugh.

"Where are you from?"

"Georgia."

"*Really?*" Her eyes sparkled and her grin grew wider. "I can hear the accent. What made you come here?"

"I'm staying with a friend. His grandma is sick, so he's helping out."

"So, you tagged along?"

"Kind of."

"That's cool." She smiled.

"Are you from here?"

"Yeah, I am. Born and raised in Cloverleaf." She wasn't looking at the board anymore.

"Do you like it?" *Why the fuck am I asking her if she likes it? She just said she's lived here her whole life. If she didn't like it, she'd move. What a stupid loser! She can probably tell I'm off.*

"I guess. I'll probably move to Missoula or Billings when I graduate. There's more jobs. It gets boring here sometimes. I'd like to live in the bigger city. Are you from a city in Georgia? What cities are there?"

"Just Atlanta. The rest is suburbs or small towns mostly. I grew up outside the city, but close enough to hang out there often."

"That's cool. So, are you just starting here? What's your major?"

What the fuck is my major? God, my stupid brain. My pits were getting wet.

"Health promotion, I think," I responded. I forced my eyes to meet hers, knowing that I should look people in the eyes to show interest, especially girls. "What's yours?"

"I'm not sure. I am just taking general education courses." She gave a slight laugh. "I guess I need to figure it out soon, so I don't keep wasting time."

"How long have you been in school?"

"Oh, I'm just starting! Like you!" She giggled. "Maybe we'll have classes together. What are you taking?"

Shit, maybe she's only eighteen, I guess. Is this illegal?

"Writing and biology, for sure."

"Cool! I'm taking both of those! We can study together. What's your name?" Her body was now flat-on facing me with her shoulders leaning forward. Her eyes never seemed to leave mine, but I stared down frequently, trying to hide. *If she is still here, she might like you, right?*

"Pate."

"Oh, is that a Southern name?"

"Sure."

"I'm Maybelle." She offered her hand to me. It was decorated with silver rings with black stones in them and her wrist bracelets jingled. I liked the noise. I took her hand and squeezed it.

Oakley came up behind me, jumping on my shoulders, unintentionally swinging me into the board. "What's up, motherfucker!"

"This is my friend that I'm staying with. Oakley. He's taking writing and biology, too. This is Maybelle."

"And Maybelle is taking writing and biology," he stated rather than asked, rubbing his chin as if he had caught us engaged in some secret.

"Yeah. Are you from here?" she asked Oakley. *Fuck, now her attention was on him.*

"No. My granny lives a little outside of town. I'm a Georgia boy. Can't you tell?" Oakley grinned.

"I like your accents! They're so cute." She giggled.

"Why, thank you, darling," Oakley schmoozed. He was so much better at this than me.

I stepped slightly back, realizing that Oakley had seized the conversation and was likely going to score.

"Why don't we all hang out sometime?" Oakley proposed, nudging me in the side. I glanced at his face only to catch a fleeting wink. "What's fun to do here?"

"I don't know." Maybelle rubbed her chin. "I usually just hang out on the ranches or in the mountains with some friends. Drinking and stuff. I think we're driving out to the mountains this Friday night if you guys want to come?"

She called us "guys."

"She's looking at you, man. Do you want to go?" Oakley nudged me.

"Yeah." *My freaking one-word answers. I'm like an ape.*

"Cool." She took her phone out of her pocket. "What's your number?" She was looking at me with those amber eyes.

I gave it to her, and she punched it in, causing my phone to ring.

"That's me." She put the phone back in her pocket. "You can save the number in your phone. Just give me a call maybe around twelve or one on Friday, and we'll decide how to meet."

"How many people will be there—" I stammered before Oakley cut me off.

"We'll talk to you, Friday." Oakley grinned.

Maybelle smiled and turned to walk away. Oakley hollered, "Hey, do you always go out with strangers?"

"No," she yelled over her shoulder, then she turned around, walking backwards. "Just cute Southern boys." She headed down the stairs.

She called me a boy.

Chapter Five

Oakley

Camping and nature were not my idea of fun on a Friday evening. I just imagined a long chilly night surrounded by the vicious Jurassic mosquitoes that attacked with no mercy during the Montana summers along with flies, snakes and whatever other creature dwelled out there. Also, I wasn't one for strangers. But I was proud to see Pate talking to a girl. Usually a girl would look at him, and he'd just stare down the whole time, muttering one-word answers if she attempted to get his attention. He claimed his shyness and social anxiety paralyzed him. What I saw was a cocky, abrasive asshole ignoring pretty girls who were desperately attempting to get his attention.

Pate was better looking than me — than most men, which I am sure would bother them if they knew he was trans. His cheeks had sunk in, highlighting beautiful cheekbones. His skin was still pale, but his thick black hair — now short — accentuated his full facial features. I was the same height as Pate and stockier in build. I had exercised at local gyms in Georgia, but I wasn't as committed as Pate was about obtaining his ultra-lean physique surrounded by large, curvy muscles. My hair was a thinning light brown mess that couldn't decide if it wanted to be straight or curly, so it just stuck up in the most awkward places. I grew it long. I kept it short. Nothing looked good. I just wore hats. My skin was rough and freckled, not smooth and milky like his. So it both amused and annoyed me when I saw girls checking him out only for him to ignore them, even though I knew he wasn't doing it on purpose.

When I saw him talking to Maybelle and even making eye contact, I knew something was different. But I also knew his punk ass wouldn't make a move. Thus, there we were on a Friday night, sitting in the Walmart parking lot waiting for Maybelle and her friends so that we could follow them to their camp spot.

"I won't be able to pee," Pate mumbled, fidgeting with the air conditioner vent.

Pate was so anal about the peeing thing. I spent the whole morning offering to watch out for him or even make an excuse for us to walk away so that he could go, but instead, he consumed three liters of water that morning, then refused to drink anything else the rest of the day. He ran into Walmart three times while we were waiting, to use the restroom so that he wouldn't pee for hours. Yet the anticipation seemed to make him want to pee more.

"I told you. I'll go with you," I emphasized to him, rolling my eyes.

"To the bathroom? What will *that* look like to everyone else? They'll think we're gay."

"You care if she thinks you're gay? Don't you like men anyway?"

"So I should just discuss my bisexuality with a group of strangers in rural Montana — people that I will have classes with? That's *exactly* how I want to start my life here."

"We'll say that we're taking a walk," I suggested.

"What if one wants to join us? What if she wants to join us?"

I shrugged. "We'll say that we're getting something from the car."

"Why would both of us need to go? What would we bring back?" Pate continued to argue.

"Pate, you're overthinking this. Everyone is going to be drinking. They're not watching every move we make."

"That's it!" Pate opened the door and leaped from the car. "I'll go in and get beer. That way, we can go to the car to get more booze."

"What if they bring a lot? What if we never run out?"

Pate stared at me, horrified.

"Go get some sodas or juice," I told him, realizing this might never end. "Something they may or may not have with them. That way, we can say that we're thirsty and that we want our own drinks."

Pate shut the door and leaned down against the open window. "You think that would work?"

"Yes. Go get your shit with your pee-induced anxiety." I flipped my hand up at him, waving him along.

They arrived while Pate was in the store. Maybelle was riding in the passenger seat of a large black pick-up truck. There was another large, but older, gray pick-up behind her. I waved my hands outside the car and she saw me. She jumped out of the truck. She was wearing pink shorts that were more like underwear with their length, but they showed off her tan legs. She sported a loose red tank-top with a shiny gold heart in the middle. Her curly locks were in a ponytail pulled tight under a Grizz cap.

"What's up? You guys made it." She leaned forward assertively and peered over, looking for Pate.

"He went inside."

"Oh. How long you've been waiting?"

"Just a few minutes." Actually, we were there for an hour so that Pate could go in and pee ten thousand times before leaving. "Who are your friends?" I gestured toward the trucks.

"Kelly and Foster are in the truck with me. Bullet, Bubba and Jimbo are in the other truck."

My gut tightened, and I peered back at the gray truck. I knew Bullet. No one visited Cloverleaf without knowing Bullet.

"Do you want to ride with us? Your car is kind of small," she offered.

"No, we'll drive."

"You sure?"

"Yeah." All I needed was to send Pate into a heart attack if we were not protected in the privacy of our own vehicle. Also, it was our excuse for him to pee, and it was my escape if this turned sour.

Pate was walking to the car, and I saw his whole body flinch before he then awkwardly but deliberately proceeded closer. Maybelle giggled and took off running toward him, nearly leaping into his arms—he barely caught her. I laughed, imagining what a tense rock his body must have felt like when he caught her.

Maybelle took his hand and dragged him, stammering, to the car, stopping a few feet from the passenger door.

"Ride with me. You want to?" She pulled his hand up so that their hands were at the same level as her chest.

"I can't. Oakley doesn't like riding alone," he told her. When I glanced over, he was grinning, but still looking down.

"Okay. But you can sit with me at the park, right?"

"Sure."

Maybelle kissed him on the check and jogged over to the trucks. "Follow us!" she yelled as she hopped inside.

Pate slowly got back inside the car. "I'm not sure about this," he said with a nervous smile on his face.

"Well, she obviously likes you. She can't be more forward, man."

"I don't know if I'm ready." He fidgeted with his fingernails.

"You've been single for five years. You're ready. I'm not toting you around everywhere because you can't get a life."

"We always go everywhere together," Pate insisted, snapping his head up at me.

"I want to find someone, too, you know? I can't always babysit you."

We followed them along the highway toward the mountains. Pate was silent, staring out of the window, but I sensed that he was experiencing a mixture of excitement, arousal and fear. I was proud of him for going, but I was also worried.

"So, I have to warn you." I looked at him until he returned eye contact. My look extinguished the cheer from his eyes.

"What?" he asked reluctantly.

I proceeded to tell him about Bullet.

Bullet Banks was the classic image of the large, aggressive, cocky asshole. He stood around six foot four with dark, sun-scorched skin from working in the ranches and hay fields all his life. His eyes were large, black, evil circles underneath two thick eyebrows. He spent hours bodybuilding when he wasn't working, but I knew that he did it for power and intimidation rather than for health reasons. Bullet was an avid bully who would chase someone down until he beat the shit out of them to show off to his asshole friends or potential female fans who thought violent masculinity was sexy. He was an outspoken racist and homophobe who never spoke two sentences without an array of various slurs interwoven between his words. The whole town seemed to fear him even though he was only twenty-two years old. He'd gotten a football scholarship after high school for the University of Washington but returned home after one year. Rumors were that he sexually assaulted a girl, though it was never proven.

Granny had told me many stories about the Banks family. Bullet seemed to be the love spawn of the most unsavory people in town. His great-grandfather went to prison for shooting a Cree man by "accident." His father philandered around, getting several women pregnant before shooting himself one night after a drinking binge. The rumor was that he had raped the mayor's daughter and feared the ramifications. His mother had nine children from four different fathers and various health problems causing her to live on disability. Most people claimed that she sold meth from her house. Bullet's siblings were spread out from prison to institutions to the military, which was considered the only employer who would take them.

Bullet was different. His size, scary arrogance and pleasure from intimidating others commanded respect. He was built for football, which earned him a great deal of popularity compared to the rest of his family. Despite leaving a trail behind him of black eyes, broken bones and bruised ribs of his victims, no one seemed to care as long as he played football. When he got his football scholarship, everyone thought that he would be the jewel in the dysfunctional family, as well as the town. Instead, he just came back an expelled potential sex offender.

I didn't want to discourage Pate, but not preparing someone for Bullet would be completely unethical.

"Okay," Pate mumbled.

"I just wanted you to be prepared. This guy's a fucking prick. Who knows how he'll act if he's drinking, too?"

"Do you think she's friends with him?" Pate asked.

"I don't know. I guess we'll find out. But just know, he'll probably say things about gay people and faggots, as he calls them. So just ignore him."

"Okay."

I smiled slightly at Pate, and his eyes met mine with an assured grin. I didn't want to tell him that I was scared.

* * * *

Pate

I didn't put much thought into Bullet. I had already been in situations where people talked shit about gay or trans people around me. *What if he senses that I'm off? That I'm...different?* I knew if I overthought it, things would be worse because it might cause me to act more awkward. I decided to stay calm and just avoid him, if possible.

We pulled into a park with some picnic tables around a little stream. I inhaled with relief knowing that we weren't going to sit around a campfire on the ground in the middle of the forest. While I grew up in a small-town-vibe suburban community, I was not an outdoors person, especially when it came to peeing.

Everyone exited their vehicles. Kelly and Foster grabbed a few coolers from the back of their truck. I saw three tall men climb out of the gray truck. One of them hovered way above the others. He was wearing a blue T-shirt that hugged his large build tightly with an unbuttoned flannel shirt and loose jeans. He had a baseball hat with an eagle and a USA flag on it. He looked like a Bullet.

We followed the crowd to a set of picnic tables. Kelly removed some beers and handed each of us one. Oakley shot a glance at me, and I could feel us both grimace on the inside as we realized that we would spend the evening drinking Bud Light, one of the most tasteless, boring beers ever made. Oakley was a connoisseur of beer and liquor, and I didn't see any reason to drink alcohol unless it was to savor its distinct taste.

We took the cans and opened them while still standing awkwardly as we watched everyone else goof around.

"Sorry, dudes! I'm Jimbo." A taller, chubby but cheerful guy extended his hand out to us. When I touched his hand, the calluses almost scraped some skin off my delicate palms. My insecurities rose into my throat. All these people were outdoorsy. Here we were the two pampered suburban goth kids from the East Coast. I feared we had made a mistake.

Jimbo pulled Oakley slightly forward when he took his hand. "Whoa, dude! Check out that nose ring. Did that hurt?"

"A little, but not bad," Oakley said casually.

"You guys must like needles and pain with all them piercings and tattoos. Where you guys from?"

"Georgia," Oakley answered, glancing at me as if to urge me to speak.

"Well, that's a hell of a long way away. How'd you get to Montana?" Jimbo nearly inhaled his beer and hollered at Bubba to pass another.

As Oakley explained Granny's situation, I surveyed the scene, searching for Maybelle. She had walked over to the water, taking her sandals off and poking her feet into the cool stream. Bullet was playing as if he would push her in, and she giggled and dodged him like two little kids flirting on the playground. My anxiety intensified, but my mind went to the way she had leaped into my arms back at the parking lot. I decided to venture around the area to check out the surroundings…or to avoid conversation.

Social anxiety can be an internal monster inside a person's head. It starts with tension rising in the temples then pressing into the skull, clouding the ability to think or act, let alone engage in conversation. My stomach knotted up and my hands shook lightly. My cheeks grew warm when I wondered if anyone would notice what a pitiful wreck of a dork I was. I had thought men were more confident, but it just wasn't working out for me that way.

"Hey, you."

I turned. Maybelle was standing behind me.

"Do you want me to show you around? Take a walk?"

"Sure," I said.

We walked around a sheltered picnic table area, following the stream in the opposite direction from her bout of flirtation with Bullet. The area was peaceful, shady and cool without the sunlight shining directly on us. The heat in Montana was different than the unforgiving humidity of Georgia that felt like a gargantuan snot-ball had engulfed the area.

"You don't talk much, do you?" she asked.

"I'm kind of shy," I stammered, but I forced my eyes to meet hers. *It's important to make eye contact.*

"Are you guys going to be here for a while? Or are you thinking just a year or semester?" She took a little dandelion from the earth and started twisting it with her fingers and snorting the aroma into her nostrils. I was enamored by her childlike innocence.

"I think we'll stay until we graduate. We don't really have any other plans." I kept trying to glance at the water or at the trees to evade the desire to just stare at her.

"How old are you?" She twirled the dandelion stem in her fingers while gazing at me, sending a few shivers down my spine.

"I'm twenty-six," I replied. I wanted to move closer to her, but my fear held me back.

"Really? What took you so long to go to school?" She grinned, apparently intrigued.

I guess she likes older men... Go with it. "I went for a while, but personal shit happened." I shrugged, casually picking up a dandelion myself.

"Like what?" She sounded concerned, but there was no way that I was going to tell her the whole story.

I sighed, tossing the dandelion out into the water. "My parents kicked me out. I couldn't afford to go anymore." *Oops, maybe that was too much information.*

"Really?" Her eyes widened in respectful amazement. "What did you do to make them do that?"

I gulped. "I decided to be myself. It conflicted with their values or something. My parents aren't open-minded." I sucked at giving people simple responses.

"So, they kicked you out for having tattoos and piercings?" Maybelle also tossed the remains of her dandelion into the lake. "That's fucked up. I still live at home with my parents for now — at least, until I find an apartment. But I don't know what I'd do without them if they disowned me or something. Do you not even talk to them?"

"No, I don't want the negativity," I insisted, holding up my hand. Sadly, that was true. My relationship with my parents was over.

"Cool," she said.

She thinks I'm some bad boy now. How the hell am I going to live up to that image?

"I hope you like my friends." She smiled, giving me a small wink. "We've been hanging together since high school. Jimbo is my cousin, and Bubba's mom is friends with my mom. It's a small-town thing."

"How do you know Bullet?" The question rushed out of my lips before I realized that it made me sound almost possessive. She gave me a coy stare like she had noticed that *I* had noticed.

"He's my ex-boyfriend."

Silence filled the air except for the calming burble of the stream. I was staring down at my toes, so I forced my gaze upward. I stopped walking and turned my body to face her.

"Ex-boyfriend?" I inquired, trying to force some assertiveness into my words. *Or should I be nonchalant? Why must there be a fine line between being confident and an asshole?*

"We broke up about two months ago." Maybelle gazed outward along the large trees and the breeze gently caressed her hair. My efforts to appear confident, charming or asshole-like weren't even registering.

"So, you two are still friends?" I hesitated.

"Yeah, I was kind of like this cheerleader in school when he was playing football, so we were like this popular couple. Then we tried the long-distance thing when he went to Washington, but it didn't really work out." She looked sad for a moment. "Then he came back, and we tried again."

"But it didn't work out?" *Ugh, I sound too desperate.*

She sighed. "If you knew Bullet, you'd understand." She finished her beer. "Want to get another beer?"

"Sure." I turned so that we could walk back to the table, but she grabbed my shoulder.

"No, stay here. I want to hang out with you." She skipped away back to the table. My thoughts informed me that *she* was the assertive and nonchalant one. I was the gibbering idiot.

We spent an hour sitting on a patch of grass near the stream. Maybelle told me about her life. She came from a middle-class family. Her father worked in real estate, selling properties to wealthy retirees that wanted to settle in western Montana, so he wasn't home often. Her mother was a nurse at the local hospital. She was the only child, making her the "princess" of the family.

Her father doted on her, buying her clothes, keeping her hair dyed and highlighted and ensuring that her nails stayed long and glossy. Even though he traveled and stayed on the western side of the state most of the time, she never hesitated to call him for anything. Often, she got her way.

"I don't know what to do in school because I never had to *do* anything!" She laughed.

I smiled. It was easier to listen to her story to avoid mine.

She turned to me and bit her lip. "What kind of girls do you like, Pat?"

"Pate," I corrected her.

"Oh, Pate. That's a strange name."

"It was my grandpa's," I told her.

"Oh. I like it. It's kind of sexy."

Sexy. The word mystified me. People threw the word around all the time. *"This guy is hot and sexy." "That girl looks sexy in that dress."* I never knew what that meant. The only time that I could become sexually aroused was if someone could make me feel relaxed with them or if someone could make me feel like a man. I still didn't understand what that even meant. Sexual arousal from a name or just someone's appearance was strange. I couldn't get naked without knowing that I was safe with someone. For the past few years, sex hadn't been an option.

"Well?" She set her eyes on mine and rested her palm gently on my thigh, sending a shiver up my spine.

I stared, mouth open, at her hand. "What?"

"What kind of girls do you like?" She giggled.

"Oh...I don't know," I stuttered, nervous. Our conversation had turned more personal, and I knew I was blowing it.

"You don't *know*?" She snorted. "How do you *not* know? Do you like girls?"

"Yes! Oh course!" I shifted my weight nervously.

"Then *what kind?'*

"This is your subtle way of flirting with me?" The words sneaked out of my mouth, and my cheeks flushed red. But I had grown up as a girl. Like Maybelle, I was also rather popular in high school with my long black hair, porcelain skin and athletic figure. However, growing up, my grandma had insisted that girls never call boys or "chase boys."

"Boys chase girls. It isn't natural for girls to pursue boys. It makes them easy," Grandma would claim.

Knowing that I was attracted to boys and believing that my plight in life was to be a woman, I patiently waited to see Grandma's theory play out. By the time I was in the seventh grade, I concluded that if I were to wait for a boy to take a risk and ask me out, I would remain celibate for the rest of my life. I didn't know what culture the boys I knew came from, but they certainly didn't come from Grandma's culture.

Thus, I was in a position in which I had to make moves on guys without directly doing it. Boys seemed to feel that rejection equated to torturous ego slaughter. Like Maybelle, I inquired what girls they preferred, or I asked if they liked certain characteristics that were often my characteristics. Or I would do the subtle, "Too bad we won't see each other again until Monday" — an approach to encourage them to ask me out for the weekend.

Now I was the timid, scared mess and Maybelle was the confident girl who was nudging me to act or forever hold my peace.

Maybelle looked down and twisted blades of grass along her fingers and pink fingernails. "Maybe..." she whispered.

I sucked some air into my lungs before answering her question about my type of girls. "I like anyone who likes me."

"So, you're desperate?" She laughed, snapping a blade of grass.

"No! That's not what I meant." I gently slapped myself in the side of the head.

"Sounds pretty desperate to me." Her elbow jabbed into my side, causing me to squirm.

"No, I mean...I don't like games. I want someone who accepts me for who I am. Someone honest."

"That's a strange answer, Pate." She rubbed her chin. "Are you used to being rejected or something?"

The irony in her question was that I had *never* been rejected. As a girl, no boy had ever turned me down, and for the most part, I was the one who ended the relationships. As a guy, I was too afraid to discover the burn of rejection. My heart tightened with a new wave of empathy for all those boys that I had ever labeled as wusses because they forced me to make a move. At the same time, none of those boys had a vagina.

"I've never been rejected. I just don't like fake people," I stated.

She nodded in agreement. "What about appearance? What's your type?"

The truth was that Maybelle *was* my type. I loved shorter girls with round hips and some extra weight on their torso. I guess perhaps I was fascinated by the same qualities that I hated in myself as a girl—the large breasts, the plump hips and round bellies. Or maybe I felt that I needed the curvy, feminine figure in the girls I pursued to make me feel masculine.

"I like girls who look like you." I gave her a slight smile and nudged her with my elbow.

"That's a cop-out answer!" She giggled.

I blushed. "It's true."

"You're tiny. You probably think I'm fat." Maybelle rolled her eyes, turning her head away.

"No, you're not fat. You're very pretty."

"I think you're very pretty, too." She pinched my cheek.

"Guys aren't pretty," I corrected her.

"Handsome, then." Maybelle stared down at her palm that was still resting on my thigh. Every now and then, she moved her fingers to remind me that her hand was still there.

I placed my hand on top of hers and deliberately rubbed my thumb back and forth.

"What makes me handsome?" I asked.

"Your features. You have big lips and big eyes. Oh, and you have good skin. A lot of guys around here have rough or acne skin. Yours is really soft." She lifted her palm and turned mine over so that our palms were together.

I wasn't sure what to feel. The exact traits that she found handsome in me were the exact traits that I felt made me feminine.

"Do you want to kiss me?" she suggested more than asked, lifting her head up and scooting her body toward me.

I leaned forward and pressed my lips against hers. She opened her mouth slightly, allowing my tongue and hers to mingle. I opened my eyes to find hers closed. We kissed for several minutes. Her palm moved to my hip, and my hand squeezed her side. When she pulled away, stars were exploding from my gut. I didn't want my hand to leave the tiny jelly roll along her side that I continued to pinch lovingly.

"Let's walk back over. We've been gone too long. Don't want to be antisocial." Maybelle laughed as she stood up, extending her hand to help me. I took her hand and held it, brushing the dirt and grass off my pants with the other.

Chapter Six

Oakley

The mountain trip ended without any incidents from Bullet. However, I couldn't help but notice the way that Bullet stared at Pate throughout the evening. Bullet asked a lot of questions about Pate, too. He queried where he worked, how much money he made and if he was single. During the entire inquisition, Bullet's eyes never left the spot by the stream where Pate and Maybelle sat. His curiosity about Pate was concerning.

"Maybelle is his ex-girlfriend," Pate told me on the ride home.

"Seriously?" I gasped.

"Seriously."

"Fuck." I hit the steering wheel with my fist.

"He didn't say anything to us. Plus, we're going out without him," Pate said.

"Where are you going? You know this is a small town."

"Her friend Kelly wants to go to Billings for the weekend before school starts. Maybelle wants me to go."

I swerved. "You're traveling alone with her on the first date?"

"No. I'm traveling with *you*, and she's traveling with Kelly."

"Wait. You set me up with Kelly? I thought she was dating that Foster dude?" I swerved again trying to process the weekend that Maybelle and Pate already planned out for me.

"No. She *is* with that dude. Maybelle is going with her friend. And I want to see Maybelle, so I need you to go as *my* friend." Pate stared at me with his arms crossed.

"I get to tag along with a girl who has a boyfriend and a girl that you are trying to score with? That is *exactly* how I envisioned my weekend."

"We're going to Billings. You can meet girls there," Pate suggested while holding his palm up.

"Girls who live in Billings. That's like three or four hours away."

Pate turned around and slouched deep into the seat. "I need you to go with me. I can't go alone," he said quietly.

I sighed and glanced at him. He was staring down, sad and disappointed.

"Okay, I'll go."

* * * *

"So...you gay?" Granny blurted out during dinner a few days later. We were consuming Granny's famous corned beef and cabbage that melted through the mouth and into the soul.

"Huh?" Pate's mouth dropped open, causing some food to drop back on his plate.

"You sound gay if you are dating a girl. Y'all want some more tea?" Granny went to the fridge to obtain her highly sugared Southern specialty.

"Um…" Pate looked at me, but I had no suggestions. His sexuality was a mystery to me. "I guess I'm bi."

"Bi? What's that?" Granny plopped back down in her chair.

"Bisexual."

"Bi…sexual. Because you have a vagina?" Granny raised her eyebrows in curiosity while jamming her fork into the corned beef.

I just stared down and inhaled my food, abandoning Pate.

"No," Pate explained patiently, setting his fork down on the table. "It doesn't have anything to do with that. It means I like men and women."

"Really…how does that work? You mean you have a boyfriend and a girlfriend, too? You think you're *that* popular, huh?" Granny teased.

"No! It means that I don't care if I date a boy or a girl. I'll date either."

"Have you dated a girl before?" Granny came across as intimidating and pushy, but it was just her way of figuring people out.

I knew that Pate had been with girls. He was a beautiful girl in high school and seemed open and confident in his bisexuality. As soon as lesbians, other bisexual girls or just bi-curious girls got wind that he was a potential dating partner…well…he got more action than I did.

"Yes, I have," Pate answered Granny calmly and pushed his empty plate away. "Do you want to hear about it?"

"What the fuck!" I yelled, shooting my bulging, embarrassed eyes at him.

"Hey!" Granny slapped the table with her hand. "For all you know, I may die soon, and I've seen and heard a lot of different things in my life. But lesbian sex is missing."

I covered my head with my hands as Pate detailed his escapades while maintaining a sense of decorum about himself. Pate described the softness of girls' lips and the way they often trembled slightly when his hands moved around their body the first time. I hadn't kissed Pate since he started testosterone. I wondered how men's lips would feel different than girls'.

I had kissed Pate many times, but somehow, kissing him as a man seemed different. Something in my mind told me that it shouldn't matter. I should be able to just kiss him like before. Then I saw the budding mustache and curly beard hairs forming, and I panicked. So I just wrote it off as something we did in the past, when Pate was Patricia.

"Are you satisfied now, Granny?" I asked, as I stood up to clear the table. "Can we please talk about something different now other than being gay or lesbian sex?"

Granny and Pate giggled.

"I guess the young'un can't handle it," Granny joked, slapping Pate on the shoulder.

"Apparently not," Pate agreed.

* * * *

Later that night, we both snuggled up in my bed to talk. Snuggling had never ceased in our relationship. It felt too good to have someone pressing up against my body, letting me absorb their warmth and listen to their internal noises as my head rested on their chest. There were no expectations or complications involved. It was just peaceful.

"Do you really like Maybelle?" I asked as he played with my hair.

"Yeah. I guess it's been a long time since I even considered dating anyone. I'm nervous."

"Are you going to tell her?"

"How can I?" Pate sighed, hopeless.

"She'd find out eventually."

He stopped touching my hair and got quiet. I sat up. "It can be dangerous around here, you know? She's pretty known around town. If she claimed that you tricked her or something…"

"What do you want me to do?" Pate threw his arms up. "I either tell everyone here that I'm trans and deal with—who knows what? Or I don't tell them and then they find out, and I'm fucked there, too!"

"Why don't you just have the surgery?" I pleaded, throwing my arms now.

"Because I don't have any money! What am I supposed to do? Stay celibate and a recluse?"

"Do you just want to be openly trans?"

I knew that my questions were frustrating him, and he got up and went to his bed. I just couldn't imagine being only part-way. I would have waited until I had all the money needed to get it all done at once. Then no one would ever know. Being a dude without a dick, let alone a dude with a vagina, was just too weird.

"I'm sorry," I said as I turned out the light.

He didn't answer.

* * * *

Driving to Billings that following Friday, I was relieved that Pate wasn't the typical nervous wreck that he usually was whenever we went out in public. Instead, he seemed confident in his loose, worn jeans and Joy Division shirt. He wore one-inch gauges with steampunk gears in them. I surveyed my outfit. I was wearing tighter jeans with a black Megadeath shirt. Even though we were dressed similarly, part of me felt that Pate was more attractive than me. When he was my girlfriend, I had never once worried that his presence would draw attention away from me. No one saw girls and assumed that they were bisexual. But Pate had slimmed down, and with his muscle tone from dancing and running, he looked more like a famous rockstar than me. Here we were, driving to Billings for him to spend the weekend with his new potential girlfriend who seemed to have laid claim to him immediately. And the fucking dude hardly talked!

"We're not going to get there until close to nine," I told him.

"It's cool. There's a bar at the hotel. We thought we'd just hang out there tonight and then find something to do for tomorrow." Pate was engulfed in his phone with a shy grin on his face.

"Oh, God. Are you messaging with her?" I rolled my eyes.

"Yeah."

"You're already in love."

"No, I'm not!" He put his phone away.

"Don't treat this girl like you're losing your virginity the first time."

"Well, considering that I haven't had sex with anyone since transitioning, I guess as a man, I am a virgin."

We had arrived at the hotel, checked in and proceeded to our room when we ran into the girls. Maybelle immediately jumped into Pate's arms, nearly knocking him over. Kelly and I just averted our eyes patiently as they smooched on each other for an eternity.

"You guys go put your stuff down. We'll get a table," Kelly said as she yanked Maybelle by the arm, dragging her away from Pate.

The bar was large but empty. The girls had gotten a booth in the corner for extra privacy. I glanced at the clock, wondering how long I had to try to make awkward, causal conversation with Kelly while Pate and Maybelle fell in love. *Damn! We just got to Montana, and he's already going to be preoccupied with some girl.*

"Whatcha guys want to do tomorrow? We're going to shop for some clothes in the afternoon, so maybe we can do dinner and go out after?" Kelly suggested.

Damn! Now we don't even have anything to do all day tomorrow while we wait for some chicks to go shopping.

"We're not from here. We don't know what to do," Pate answered.

"Let's do something really crazy!" Maybelle squealed. She started searching her phone. "Oh! Let's do this!" She held up her phone to us.

"A drag show?" Kelly asked with a grimace.

"Come on! It will be fun! I've never seen one," Maybelle begged.

"Men dressing like women? Why would I want to see *that*?" Kelly argued. She pushed Maybelle's phone down.

"I don't know. But just think. It will be something crazy we can say we did, and we can tell everyone about it—"

"I don't want people to know that I went to *that*!" Kelly asserted. "That's gay!"

The girls continued to argue while Pate and I shot awkward glances at each other.

"What do you guys think?" Maybelle demanded.

"They don't want folks thinking they're gay, either!" Kelly insisted.

"Do you guys think it's gay?"

"No, it sounds cool," Pate said, putting his arm around Maybelle.

What the fuck! Not only am I stuck with a guy and his girlfriend and a girl with a boyfriend, but now I have to go to a drag show where I won't meet anyone and have to stare at ugly dudes with too much makeup and bad hair.

"It's done! We're going!" Maybelle planted a kiss on Pate's cheek.

* * * *

Later in our room, Pate lay on his bed, texting away with his new infatuation while I stared miserably at the ceiling.

"What's wrong, man?" Pate asked, setting his phone on the nightstand and sitting up on the edge of the bed.

"I don't wanna go to some stupid drag show." I groaned, covering my eyes with my arm.

"Why not?"

"Because it's lame."

"What makes it lame?" Pate snapped. He stood up and gently pulled my arm away from my eyes.

"I don't want to watch some guys dancing and singing in dresses. I'd rather go to a strip club."

Pate shrugged. "It's an entertainment show. It's not like the guys are trying to be sexual or something."

"You've been?" I sat up to face him.

"No. But that's what I know."

"It *is* gay," I claimed, slumping my body back down on the bed.

"No, it's not. And stop saying 'it's gay' like that's bad or something. Besides, it sounds like *you're* the one turning it into something gay or sexual. No one else is."

I shot him the evil eye.

"I know that you are...mostly cool," Pate assured me. "I know that you're trying."

"I didn't even know any trans people, and now my first love turned into a dude, and I'm watching him get it on with some chick while I watch men dancing in dresses—" The whole image already made me feel that Pate was abandoning me, and I worried that our new life in Cloverleaf would only entail me following Pate and his girlfriend around. But the tension in my gut suggested that maybe I was jealous...and a little bitter. I didn't expect Pate to find someone, especially so quickly. I just felt alone.

"I get it," Pate said.

We got ready for bed, and I was starting to relax a little. After all, I was already there, so I should make the most out of it. Maybe some pretty girls attended drag shows, who knew?

"Oakley?"

"Yep."

He sat up a little. "You do know that the problem is really *yours*, right?"

"What do you mean?"

"Everyone else is just being themselves. And if that bothers you, well, that's your problem. Not theirs."

I didn't answer.

* * * *

Pate

Things were going so well. Maybelle was already posting pictures of us on her Facebook page even though her relationship status still said "single." She seemed to be *into* me. My mind and my heart were intoxicated. Oakley and I passed time the next day by taking a short run around town, hitting the local coffee shop mid-morning, and seeing an early show at the theater that afternoon. It was a Ryan Reynolds film, so we watched him flirt and schmooze while also being a badass with six-pack abs. *I wonder if women see me like that.*

"I don't know what to wear," Oakley whined.

"I thought you weren't trying to impress anyone," I snarked.

He flicked me off. Oakley had been sour the whole day. Part of me wondered if he was jealous of me and envious of my new fling with Maybelle. I didn't want to make him feel like I'd abandoned him.

"Look, I'll go wherever you want next weekend. I'll go pick up chicks with you."

"Yeah, I'm sure that your new girlfriend will be fine with that," he muttered.

"I'll support you then."

"Just forget it." Oakley settled on wearing a tight-fitting black T-shirt with a demon on the front drinking a bottle of Jack Daniel's. "I just hope they have good beer there."

We met the girls in the lobby and got an Uber to take to the show so that we could drink freely. To my surprise, the place was packed. Kelly had called earlier to reserve a table for us since food was also served. The table was located close to the stage but at an angle.

"We're sitting right up front?" Oakley groaned.

"I thought if we were going to watch this shit, then we are going to *watch* this shit." Kelly smiled as she patted the seat next to her for Oakley. He collapsed into his chair.

"They got a lot of beers, man." I handed him the drink menu, which seemed to perk his spirits up.

Oakley and I ordered some high-volume dark porters while the girls ordered fancy fruit drinks. We decided to order a large veggie-lover's pizza with fresh pesto sauce and some baked garlic bread. The food was delicious. I could tell it was not something prepacked, frozen then reheated. With alcohol content in the fifteen-percent range, the porters were tasty, too.

We listened to Kelly tell the story about how she met Foster in her tenth-grade geometry class because he used to cheat off her during tests and that now, they planned to get married after college and move to Bozeman. Maybelle sat nestled against me with her hand on my thigh and I snuggled back with my chin resting on her head. The atmosphere was safe and comfortable.

About that time, the lights went dim and everyone started clapping and cheering. A tall and plump queen walked out on stage. She was wearing a snug white pencil dress that pushed her breasts — they looked real! — up firmly, drawing the eye directly to her cleavage. She wore a blonde wig that was teased up in front and carried down all the way past her thighs in the back. I thought she looked amazing.

"Oh God, here they come." Oakley rubbed his forehead.

"Shut up!" Maybelle laughed and put her arms around my shoulders. Her eyes lit up and her grin widened as she watched the speaker prepare us for the show. I wrapped my arm around her waist and pulled her closer to me, causing her to send me a large grin.

We watched, we laughed and we even sang along — except Oakley — as the performers sang and danced on stage. A few performers left the stage and approached the various tables, singing and embarrassing folks at the same time. They were so confident! They moved with elegance as if they were born with platform heels on their feet. I had never danced publicly as a man. I felt envious.

"Let's step outside and take a break," Maybelle suggested after a few shows. Oakley stared at me with annoyance, but I just shrugged my shoulders.

The evening was cool even though it was August, but that was how the weather rolled in Montana — heat one day and an icy snowstorm the next. But the night had just the right chill in the air, leaving the air feeling crisp and clean. Maybelle led us to a bench a little down the block, away from the loud music inside.

"Are you having fun?" she asked as she pulled her legs up to sit cross-legged on the bench. She held my hand on top of her thigh.

"Yeah. I think it's *awesome!*" I laughed. In fact, I couldn't wait to get back in. I was desperate to know the secret behind the dancers' empowering confidence.

"It's cool. I like it, too. Too bad Oakley is so pissed off about it," she mumbled.

"He's cool," I assured her, squeezing her thigh. "I guess it wasn't his idea of how we would spend our first weekend trip. But he's fine."

"He's just not as open-minded as you." She leaned forward to kiss me. "You're so laid back."

"Is that good?"

"Yes! Ugh, I get so tired of some of the guys around here. They are so serious all the time."

"You mean Bullet?" I asked.

"Yeah. He's a really nice guy underneath. But he's so possessive and controlling—of everything! Things always have to be his way."

"I guess when you're that big, you're used to everything going your way." I gently rubbed her back with my hand.

"I guess. But I just get tired of that macho behavior."

Wait, am I not macho? I wasn't sure if I should take that remark as a compliment or an insult. Was she indicating that she liked me because I wasn't masculine? Was that *bad?*

"I like you," she said, squeezing my hand.

"I like you, too."

"What do you like about me?" she said playfully as she nestled her head into my shoulder. I delighted in watching the way her curls fell along my chest.

Because you're into me! I thought. But that wasn't romantic.

"You're carefree. You don't hesitate," I replied.

"I don't hesitate? Like I'm easy?" She pulled away from me.

"Of course not!" I exclaimed, pulling her back to me. "I mean that you just talk to anybody or go anywhere. You just do whatever you want. You seem very confident in yourself."

"Oh, no!" Maybelle laughed. "I'm a total basket case. I'm fat, I'm stupid, I'm awkward—"

"You're *none* of those things." I widened my eyes to emphasize my point. I placed my hand under her chin to tilt her face toward me.

"Do you think I'm pretty, Pate?"

"I think you're gorgeous!" I grinned, placing my forehead against hers.

"No, I'm not." She shoved my hand playfully away.

"Yes, you really are. I can't even believe you don't think so."

"Well?" Maybelle asked with urgency in her voice. She started twirling a lock of hair in her fingers.

"Well, what?"

She took my hand again and turned toward me. "Are you going to ask me out again?"

"Oh! Yes, I was just going to do that. Where do you want to go?"

"You choose this time. You're the dude!" She giggled, tugging on my arm.

"I don't know anywhere."

"There's not many places to go. What about your house?"

Coming to my home felt personal and risky. What if she saw evidence that I used to be a woman? Of course, I had discarded all that evidence, but then again, what if she noticed that something was…strange?

"Oakley's grandmother is there," I told her.

"I don't care. I love grandmothers."

"Okay, then." I shrugged.

"I just want to be able to talk and get to know you. I don't think we need tagalongs this time." She jerked her head toward the club.

I nestled her chin in both my hands as I leaned forward to kiss her. I rested my forehead against hers, savoring the feeling of her breath against my cheeks and the feeling of her soft skin underneath my hands.

"Let's go back inside. We're missing the show!" she stated, holding out her hand to lead me back in.

As we walked back to the door, I stopped and pulled her toward me from behind, whispering in her ear, "Why don't you just be my girlfriend?"

* * * *

Oakley

I wanted to slap Pate for walking off and leaving me surrounded by drag queens who I feared sensed that Kelly wasn't my girlfriend and that I was prey waiting to be humiliated. They serenaded me, shook their breasts and one even sat in my lap. Kelly was laughing hysterically at my discomfort and snapping pictures with her phone.

"Can we fucking go now?" I demanded when Pate and Maybelle returned to the table.

"It's early," Pate argued.

I slumped back in my seat and waved my hand in the air for another round. All the mellow intoxication that I would have enjoyed from those high-density beers had worn off immediately as soon as I became the targeted straight guy to ridicule in the crowd.

"Yeah, another round!" Pate yelled across the room. He seemed different than he had been earlier. His body language was all over Maybelle and her giggling was making me crazy.

Kelly leaned forward and whispered, "Uh-oh," in my ear and gestured toward them. "He better watch out," she teased.

The lights dimmed again for the next show. The original speaker reappeared on stage, but this time, she was wearing a dark-blue sequined dress that shimmered dramatically in the stage lights.

"So next we have a brand-new performer, a virgin, if you will. Please give a round of applause to Sadie!"

We all clapped in support, and my beer arrived, so I felt prepared to face this next show. The stage turned black, and a dark figure strutted to the center. Suddenly a soft red glow fell onto the performer, and I leaned forward. She didn't look like a drag queen. She was wearing a polka-dot dress that ended above her knees and black pantyhose. The polka dots were bright rainbow colors and the red light made them shimmer and glow. The sleeves were oversized, causing them to fall elegantly when she lifted her arms, and the dress hugged her torso, highlighting her thin waist. Her hair was long and black with a small silver headband that pushed it down flat on her head, making her look like a hippie. Her makeup was simple. She wore black eyeliner forming cat eyes with soft pink blush and rose lipstick.

"That can't be a drag queen?" I gasped.

"It looks like a girl," Kelly agreed.

"Maybe she's trans?" I blurted. I immediately averted my eyes to Kelly when I saw Pate's face tense up.

"I don't know what one looks like," Kelly responded.

"Me either," I said.

Sadie sang the song *I'm So Excited* by the Pointer Sisters. When the chorus began, the stage lit up with multi-colored lights that moved across the room in circles, sending a shimmer fluttering along the polka dots of her dress. She spun around, swinging her long hair and shaking her hips. I laughed.

"Not so lame now?" Pate asked.

When Sadie approached the last verse of the song, her eyes met mine. Mortified, I immediately gazed downward. When my eyes rose again, she was still staring at me.

She sang, kicking her dress up a little, exposing more thigh.

"She's looking your way, man." Pate nudged me.

"Oh, they do that with everybody. It's part of the show," I insisted, and gulped down my beer only to find our eyes still locked on each other.

Sadie hit some high notes and twirled around, breaking our eye contact.

The crowd gave her a standing ovation. The announcer came out and lifted Sadie's hand in hers, urging the crowd on more. I stood up and whistled. Sadie smiled. They paraded off stage and chatter broke out into the room.

"That has to be a girl," Kelly asserted, pointing her finger up at the stage.

"Can girls be in drag shows?" Maybelle asked.

We all shrugged.

"Do they come out afterward? When the show is over?" I asked.

"I thought you wanted to leave?" Pate nudged me with his beer.

"I've never seen a girl like that. I'm just...curious."

"I think we're all curious to know if it's a girl or a boy. You can find out for us." Kelly laughed. "Oh look!" Kelly pointed across the room toward the bar. "That's *her*!"

I saw Sadie drinking a bottle of water by the bar while various people chatted with her.

"Go talk to her!" Kelly jerked on my shoulder.

"No! It's weird!" I hunched my shoulders up to hide myself.

"Go!" Pate joined in. "It'd be good for you." He winked.

"What do I say?"

"Just say you liked the show," he suggested, nudging me again with his beer.

"Just ask if he's a boy or a girl?" Kelly and Maybelle laughed.

"Go talk to her," Pate encouraged, ignoring the jokes.

"Okay." I set my beer down and got up. "I'll be right back."

As I walked across the room, my stomach tightened. *Damn that beer!*

Sadie was still talking to some people when I approached, almost causing me to retreat, but then her eyes met mine. She waved and mouthed, "Hi." Stopping in my tracks, I waved back. She said something to the people in front of her and walked over to me.

"Hi." She laughed. "How'd you like the show?"

Her teeth were glistening white and perfectly straight. The pink blush showered her delicate skin with a radiant glow—way too smooth to be a man's skin.

"I really liked it. I just wanted to come tell you that."

"Is that all?" She raised her eyebrows.

"Um…yeah."

She smiled bigger. "You want to have a drink with me?" She was fanning her face with her hands.

"Sure."

"Okay, but not here. It's too loud, and there's more singers coming out soon. I'll order some beers, and we can talk in one of the dressing rooms."

Dressing rooms? Mental images of naked men running panty hose over their hairy legs and over their groins filled my mind.

"Okay," I consented.

"Awesome! What do you want? I'll get one of the waitresses to bring it back for us."

I ordered another dark beer, a chocolate stout this time. Sadie went behind the bar and leaned over the bartender's shoulder. Then she returned and held out her hand. "Come on. I'll show you."

I froze way too long before accepting her hand. *I'm not going to be that guy. I'm not going to be a bigot who can't touch another guy's hand. If this is a guy…*

She led me through a corridor next to the stage and into the back. The hallway was so narrow that we basically had to push ourselves up against the walls to let performers pass as they raced frantically back and forth. She led me to the very last room, which was more like a small closet with a stool, a mirror and a lamp. She grabbed a stool from another room and closed the door, gesturing for me to sit.

One of the waitresses came in with our drinks. Sadie had ordered a cosmopolitan.

"I'm a cosmo girl tonight!" She took a sip.

"What was it like up there?" I asked, resting my elbows on my knees, struggling to hear through the music playing on stage.

"Oh my God! I've never experienced anything like that! I was so nervous that I thought I'd burp or fart or something. But once I started singing, it just came to me. I just felt free and sexy. Maybe I got even more sexy than I did in rehearsals!"

"I don't know what that feels like—I mean, performing. I know what it feels like to feel sexy." *Did I just say that?*

She laughed. Her voice was soft and light just like a woman's, and her mannerisms were ladylike—the way she crossed her legs and talked animatedly with her hands and arms. *She must be trans. Some drag queens are trans, right?*

I found my eyes wondering around her chest, studying the small lumps that rose underneath, but her dress wasn't low enough to show any real cleavage. She noticed, gazing down at her chest before shooting her eyes back up at me. My cheeks flushed.

"What's your name?" She smiled.

"Oakley."

"I'm Jody."

"Jody?"

"Yeah, Sadie is just a stage name. I'm not sure if it will be my official stage name. I'm still developing my stage persona."

Jody is a girl's name.

"Why'd you invite me back here?" I asked, taking a long drink of beer.

"Because you looked like you really enjoyed the show."

"I *did*?"

"Didn't you?" she asked as she sipped her drink, studying me with her eyes.

"Well…sure. You were really good out there. I didn't even know that I could like that song."

"Mister Metalhead, I can see." Jody laughed. "Your eyes were locked on me, and you were smiling, so I just used you as a focal point. It helps with stage fright. You can focus on one person and pretend that you are performing just for that person."

"So, I just helped you perform." I smiled.

"Were you not approaching me at the bar?"

I took another gulp of beer. "Yeah, I was."

"Well then."

"Well then what?"

"Well, it's clear that you think I'm hot, and I think you're hot, so I invited you back here." Jody took a long sip from her cosmopolitan. The pinkish red of the drink matched her long pink fingernails and rose lipstick.

I again averted her gaze.

"First drag show?" she asked.

"Yeah."

"Oh, you poor thang."

I laughed, mostly at my own pathetic embarrassment.

"What do you do, Oakman?"

"Oakman?"

"Yeah, Oakman. Strong and silent with some social rigidness to you, I see. Yet I'm sure there's some awfully sweet nectar underneath that exterior just waiting to be enjoyed."

"I'm a college student, mostly. I work at Walmart, too."

"Which school?" She leaned forward with interest.

"The one in Cloverleaf."

"Oh! I go there, too! I'm in my fourth year of graphic design." Her smile grew bigger, making her eyes sparkle.

"Wait, you don't live here? In Billings?" My posture got erect.

"No. I just came down for the show. I have a sister who lives here. I live in Cloverleaf. On campus, actually. What's your major?"

"Automotive. Freshman." I felt like a loser. Jody looked younger than me, but here she was, graduating in another year, and here I was, not having done anything with my life so far. She'd be out making big bucks before I even found an apartment.

"How'd you get into this drag stuff?" I inquired, attempting to change the subject to shy away from her discovering that she was better at adulting than me.

Jody said that she had always loved performing. When she was in elementary school, she joined every play or assembly that the school held, often securing the leading role. In high school, she lived with her uncle in Chicago where she took professional dance and singing lessons, performing at local clubs and events.

"My parents never understood me," she told me. "My dad left early anyway, and never took much interest in me like he did my sister. My mom and I just could never connect. But my uncle was a great singer and tap dancer, so I felt at home with him."

"My best friend is a dancer," I stated.

"One of the ones at the table?"

"Yeah, the dude. He danced a lot in school, too, but he's really insecure now."

"That's too bad. I can't imagine doing anything else with my life."

"You mean drag shows?" I asked.

"Drag shows — any kind of shows. There's going to be a new talent show on campus in December. I'm not sure what I want to do, but I definitely entering. My dream would be to star in a musical."

"Like on Broadway."

"Perhaps."

"You should. You're really good." I gently tapped her hand with my mine in encouragement.

I wasn't sure where time went, but soon, the sky outside grew dark, and the music stopped. Jody and I had enjoyed about three or four drinks together, leaving both of us a little tipsy. We talked about music, and I played some YouTube videos for her of one of my band's shows. Jody proceeded to give a brief demonstration of performing Abba's *Dancing Queen*.

"Pate always wanted to be Billy Elliot," I joked.

"Your friend?"

"Do you want to meet him? I'm sure he'd like to meet you."

Jody finished her drink and sat back, examining me with her emerald-green eyes. "Is that how you treat a lady?" she asked.

"You don't want to meet him?" I tensed in confusion.

"It seems like you want to jump the gun and introduce me to your people, and you haven't even asked me on an official date. We haven't even exchanged phone numbers."

I finished off my beer. *It's a girl. It's just a trans girl. I like girls, right?*

"I'd love to go out with you," I said, placing my bottle on the small makeup table that was now overflowing with bottles and martini glasses.

Jody sneered at me again. "That's not asking a lady out. How do you know I'll say yes?"

"Do you want to go out with me tomorrow?"

"I can't. I'm driving back early."

"Oh." I sat in silence.

"You sure do give up easily, Oakman. Geez, do you expect women to do all the work for you? Remember, you're talking to Sadie right now." She patted her chest.

"Do you want to go out with me?"

"Yes, I want to go out with you." She laughed, making me laugh, too.

"Stop teasing me!"

"Don't be such a victim then!" Jody held her hand out. "Give me your phone?"

"Why?"

"Not trusting, either! Give it to me, silly. I'm going to put my number in." She took my phone and added herself as a contact under the name "The Drag Queen."

"Why'd you'd do *that*?" I said in horror.

"Why does it bother you so much? Chill out!" Jody stood up. "I'll be busy with classes next week, but you can call me. Maybe we can do something on Friday?"

I was still staring at the words "The Drag Queen."

"So, are we going to meet your friends or not?" she asked as she stood up, rubbing the wrinkles from her dress.

The backstage area was crowded with other performers changing clothes. I was glad that Jody hadn't changed. Her dress was hypnotizing. The long, oversized sleeves danced along the breeze that blew by when she passed other people. Her hips shook from side to side when she walked. My eyes struggled to leave her tight, petite butt.

We found Pate, Maybelle and Kelly standing by the door. Pate had his arms wrapped around Maybelle as she laughed and joked with Kelly. They saw us and waved us over. Maybelle was the first one to run over and offer her hand to Jody.

"Oh my God! You were so amazing. Oh, I love your dress!" Maybelle squealed.

"Thanks. Jody." Jody shook her hand.

"Maybelle. This is Pate and Kelly."

Kelly waved at Jody from a distance. Pate walked over and offered his hand, and I noticed that Jody studied him intently. I crept closer to Jody.

"So, you're a dancer, too?" Jody inquired.

"You told her!" Pate snapped.

"Dancer? *You*?" Maybelle asked with wide eyes.

"Yeah, I dance," Pate answered defensively.

"I'd like to see you dance sometime," Jody said assuredly.

"We live all the way in Cloverleaf."

"So do I."

Pate shot me a surprised look, and I shrugged my shoulders. Jody saw me and grabbed my arm gently.

"Yeah, I do, and this little Oakman asked me on a date, so we should all go dancing sometime," Jody declared sweetly.

Pate's eyes grew wider.

"You're already assuming that there will be a second date?" I teased.

"Baby, with the way you're looking at me, I *know* there'll be a second date. And I want to dance." Jody shimmied.

"I listen to metal music. You don't dance to that," I insisted.

"Sure, you do," Jody contended. "You swing your head, your hair." She took her hand and flipped her hair up. "You jerk your body roughly but freely into other people. If you're moving, it's dancing."

"I don't dance to metal music," Pate responded.

"Who does, right?" Jody winked at him, making Pate smile. Jody's utter flirtatiousness drove me crazy. In the back room, I had thought I was special, but watching her with Pate, I wasn't sure.

"I want to see you dance!" Maybelle demanded, pulling on Pate's shirt.

"It's Broadway-style dancing. I throw a little funk into it, too," Pate told her.

"Yes, he does," I stated. Pate had an unusual style of dancing that blended the classical Broadway style that involved jumping, leaping, high-leg kicks, splits and theatrics with funk-style dancing that used classic eighties breakdance, popping robotics and locking. His theme songs ranged anywhere from Queen to George Clinton.

Jody, Maybelle and Pate went off on a tangent about moves, styles, music and increasing muscle and joint flexibility. I started feeling out of place.

"Don't worry, man. Headbanging is cool, too." Pate nudged me in the side.

"I don't just headbang! I play guitar. Do you know that metal guitar playing is one of the most underappreciated forms of playing guitar? You have to play fast and seamlessly."

"What about playing some metal guitar for a drag performance?" Jody asked.

"I didn't know metal music was used in drag shows."

"There's always a time to start, isn't there?" Jody smiled, taking my hand in hers. A rush of jitters ran up my spine, and I immediately looked at Pate, who was staring intently at me. But I took her hand and closed my fingers firmly over it.

"A metal drag show sounds cool," Maybelle interjected.

"I'd play for you. If you wanted me to," I told Jody.

Jody smiled. "Well, then. I guess I just have to create Metalhead Sadie!"

The image of Jody dressed in a tight leather miniskirt with a black-laced bustier, fishnet pantyhose and combat boots invaded my thoughts...as well as my genitals.

"It's getting late and we're driving back tomorrow," Kelly yelled from the door.

"We'll meet you outside," Pate told me, gently squeezing my shoulder and giving me a slight smile. He wrapped his arm around Maybelle's waist, and they followed Kelly out.

I looked down at our two hands, locked together. I could feel slight beads of sweat seeping from her soft, delicate palm.

"I guess this is goodbye for now, Oakman." She leaned forward to kiss me lightly on the cheek. "It was fun."

"It was fun. I'll call you."

"Sooner rather than later."

Release her hand and leave now, I chanted in my mind. *Wait...give her a friendly hug and leave. Yes, that's better.*

I started to lean forward but then stopped so awkwardly that I lost my balance and almost fell on her.

Wait...

I realized that I was standing there staring off into space at the door while Jody had never taken her eyes away from me.

"What's it going to be, my Oakman?"

I clenched my teeth and went for the safe side hug. "I'll call you when we get back."

"Good." She smiled.

I walked outside, feeling her standing there in her rainbow dress and watching my every stride. I turned as I opened the door and waved.

In the Uber on the way back to the hotel, Maybelle and Pate snuggled while Kelly sat up front, playing on her phone. I watched the city lights streaming by without really seeing anything at all.

Damn. I should have kissed her.

Chapter Seven

Pate

I was a nervous wreck about returning to school. Even though the local university was small, it still meant crowds and people. My fears around my transition had moved me away from the confident, social person I had been as a teenager into a place too far inside my own head. Fortunately, I had legally changed my name so I was spared the notion that a professor would call roll and say my dead name. Nevertheless, going to school meant using a public restroom daily, always praying that a stall would be open.

"I thought you wanted to get over your social anxiety?" Oakley asked.

Oakley and I were getting ready for our first day, but my body felt heavy. I slouched on the edge of my bed, staring down at my knees. I hadn't spoken the whole morning, and Oakley usually knew that silence meant anxiety.

Social anxiety was a bitch. The voices of people, especially laughter, ignited a pressure in my temples that tensed my whole body up like a pressure cooker. Mixed emotions inundated my brain. While a person talking to me might initially generate some relief, I spent hours afterwards replaying the encounter in my mind, searching for evidence that I was a social failure. Luckily, at Walmart, I mostly cleaned and stocked, so I wasn't required to talk to customers much.

"Things are going great. You got a girlfriend. We're making friends. You'll be fine," Oakley assured me as he constantly adjusted his pants and underwear.

"I told you that briefs would get caught on your new dick ring. You need to wear boxers," I reminded him.

"You're alive!" He sat beside me on the bed and placed his arm around my shoulders. "You'll feel fine after the first day."

"I'm not sure if this is what I want to do," I mumbled.

"That's okay because you're doing it for me and I need you."

I raised my eyebrow at him.

"I'm not a good student," he admitted. "I don't feel good doing it alone. I want you to help me."

"I can help you without taking classes," I hinted.

"I know. But...I don't want you sitting around alone. It's better to stay busy. That's what your therapist said."

Oakley enjoyed reminding me about my previous therapist's advice. He had never recovered from the trauma of my suicide attempt. I had been living with him and his father. I had been so confident in my decision to come out as trans and to pursue testosterone treatments and surgery. But when my parents didn't stand by me, my heart froze. I realized that I faced the real possibility of embarking on this journey alone, and if my own flesh and blood rejected me, what was society going to do with me? It wasn't so much the fear that disturbed me but rather my own fragility. I questioned being trans. I had lived my life to that point as a girl, so why not just continue and make life easier? The fact that I felt that I *could* continue to live my life as a woman seemed proof that I couldn't be trans. I imagined trans people experiencing intense psychological and physical distress, creating a depression that saturated their lives unless they transitioned. I couldn't say that I was that distraught, but at the same time, I was.

The ambivalence killed me. *Will it be worth it? Will I ever feel like a real man? Will people ever accept me as a man? What will I look like? Will I still be attractive, or will I look weird, like an "it?"* Nevertheless, ever since I had learned about medical transitioning, I spent hours on hours daydreaming about this man that existed in me, screaming to escape from under the female flesh that engulfed him. Yet my doubts made it feel like my dreams were slipping through my fingers.

Getting my first testosterone, or T shot, I thought all my worries would vanish. I was, after all, stepping through the door, and that first step was massive. I knew that the changes would take time, so I was eager to get things progressing. I had read all the posts on my transgender Facebook groups about how much T changed their lives and reduced their depression. I wrote off my depression as fear about coming out and believed that the T would alleviate that fear and let me focus my attention on my physical changes. After all, I had only heard positive stories.

My initial journey into weekly T shots in which I jabbed a needle deep into the muscles of my thighs was far from joyous. Within the first few weeks, the suicidal ideation began. Many people believe that suicidality means that people are consciously choosing to die. But after experiencing several bouts with suicidality, this was never the case for me. Instead, a stranger moved inside my head. I was me, but I now had this second person dwelling inside my thoughts. *You should kill yourself,* it would say to me. *Quit your job. You don't belong here.* One time I was driving home from work, and I saw a prostitute. *You can do that job. Quit your job. You don't belong. Just live on the streets.*

Then the suicidal daydreaming began. The daydreams started vague, but I became so obsessed with suicide that the daydreams developed more details daily. I was going to go into a pawn shop and purchase a handgun. I figured a pawn shop was inconspicuous and I would have the gun within a few days. Oakley's house had a garage in back where his dad kept his Mustang that he mostly drove on weekends. I would move the car out of the garage and shut the door. However, there would still be splatter, so I decided that I would put several large, garbage bags, preferably Hefty, over my head to help catch the mess. I was too proud to choose any method that might not be one-hundred-percent effective, and I didn't want to leave a horrific mess behind for Oakley and his dad to clean. Nope, it had to be right, and it had to be neat.

Every time I drove past a pawn shop, the voice spoke to me. *Go in there. You can just look around...maybe even hold the gun...*

I daydreamed about suicide the same way I daydreamed about being a man, about being a rock star, about meeting Santa as a kid. It devoured my consciousness. Then the anxiety came. I had always had elevated anxiety, but my dancing and running kept most of it at bay. This anxiety was a menacing monster that hijacked my body. I woke up in the mornings feeling that pressure circulating in my temples. By the time I showered and left for work, the shakes came. I found myself constantly moving to hide them from people. But the worst part was the agitation. My body felt like it was on fire with prickly nerves and the unrelenting urge to constantly move even though I was exhausted at the same time. I just wanted to find an escape from my body, but there was none. That was when I understood that people with anxiety could kill themselves.

The endocrinologist had warned me that I could experience some mood fluctuations, and when I told her what I was feeling, she just shrugged.

"Yeah, that's normal," she informed me. "And we're about to increase your dose, so you'll have another dip again."

Assuming that this was going to be a waiting game, I poured my heart out to my therapist, hoping that he could be the lifesaver for me to cling to in this black hole. His response wasn't helpful. He just stared at me with this puzzled, tense look, and I pondered that either a) I was freaking him out with my suicide talk, or b) he felt like he had made a mistake giving me his letter of support to the endocrinologist. He didn't proceed to ask me any details about my suicidal thoughts, which I took as a sign to shut up about it. The last thing I wanted was to have what I had started stolen away.

The voice was strong that day and the agitation was unbearable. I stood up. I sat down. I fidgeted. I even went to the bathroom and tried mindfulness. I felt defeated. I didn't want to go back, but I couldn't handle this anymore.

I went directly to the garage when I got home. There had to be something around that would kill me. I saw a jug of antifreeze. I remembered a famous murder in Georgia where a woman had murdered her husbands with antifreeze. Plus, I had heard that antifreeze had to be kept away from cats because they would eat it since it tasted sweet. If that was true, then I figured I could swallow it down easy. I just hoped it happened quickly.

I stared at the jug for an eternity. The jug was a dark but bright blue. *Is it blue? What's blue taste like?*

I thought I could drink it and go to bed. No mess. Just peace. The voice in my head constantly urged me on. At that moment, I realized how much the voice had taken over.

I lifted the jug up quickly and took a sip. That was when Oakley entered the garage.

We made up a phony story at the hospital about Oakley pouring some in a glass as a joke, and I accidently took a sip — he had yanked the bottle so hard from my hands that only that sip reached my stomach. The nurses and doctor were skeptical, but we both insisted. They gave me Antizol and kept me overnight.

Oakley and I never talked about it, but he never left me alone after that day. He always made sure that either he or his dad were there, even though I don't think he ever told his dad. Seeing the sadness in his brown eyes that still contained that trauma, I knew that he really wanted me to physically go to school with him. I scared him.

I put my hand on his knee and gave it a little shake. "The social anxiety is getting better. It's a new place. It's gonna take some time for me to feel secure."

"Good." He gave me a little peck on my lips.

* * * *

We had writing class that morning. The room was about the same size as a high school class, but instead of desks, there were square tables with chairs. Oakley and I sat toward the left side of the room.

A tall, bulky guy walked in and sat beside me. He was wearing a gray vest—which was an unusual fashion choice to me—with fitted jeans and a beanie. He looked pretty ranchy. Two other guys walked in, laughing and rambunctious. They both paused to stare at Oakley and me before sitting at the table in front of us. They kept laughing, but more secretive now as if they knew some inside joke. Laughing was the worst for me. I *loathed* it. My thoughts convinced me that the laughter was directed at us, or at least, at me.

"Who's in the house!"

Startled, I looked up to see Bullet entering the classroom. He carried his writing textbook, but he didn't have anything else. The two other guys laughed more as Bullet approached them, and he peered at us from the corners of his black eyes with a sly grin.

"What's up, Stormy?" Bullet said to the guy next to me, offering a fist bump.

"Not much." Stormy didn't offer his fist back.

Bullet sat down with the other guys as if Oakley and I were invisible. He whispered back and forth with the other two.

"Football players," Stormy whispered to me.

One of the guys turned around. "So, do you go out with Maybelle?" His tone of voice was like a little kid teasing me on the playground.

"Yeah," I murmured.

"Oh, shit!" The three started laughing again. "I'm sorry," he said, turning back around to me. "We just thought you two were gay." The three laughed more.

"What's wrong with that?" Oakley intervened.

"Nothing," Bullet answered. "Unless you like being a fag. Oh, but you're *not*."

"I thought we were cool? We hung out the other week," Oakley inquired, throwing up his hands, more as a confrontation.

"Sure, we're *cool*," Bullet sneered.

"Then what's the problem?" Oakley confronted him, never letting his eyes leave Bullet.

"There isn't one. You're the ones being sensitive."

"*We're* the ones who are being sensitive? Pate hasn't even said shit, and you're calling us gay," Oakley claimed.

"Yeah..." Bullet peered at me. "Why hasn't Pate said shit? Can he talk?"

"Why don't you guys just cool it?" Stormy intervened. "It's not fucking high school anymore."

"No one asked you, motherfucker," Bullet snapped.

Stormy started picking up his things. "You guys should probably move. You don't want to sit with these dudes."

"Well fuck you, Stormy. Little pussy ass!" Bullet scolded him, slapping his hand on the table, causing several classmates to jump in their seats.

Even though his language was hostile, Bullet didn't seem as aggressive with Stormy. When Stormy stood up, he looked even taller than Bullet, which possibly explained why Bullet was being so tame with him.

"Let's move," Oakley said, grabbing up his stuff.

"Oh, I guess no one wants to sit near us." One of the guys laughed.

"All the pussies can sit on *that* side of the room!" Bullet joked, pointing his finger toward the back of the classroom.

We grabbed our stuff and walked over to a back table where Stormy had moved.

"Ignore those guys," Stormy said to me as I sat down. "They're fucking assholes."

"Thanks." We introduced ourselves to Stormy, commenting on his unusual name. He told us that he was born during a massive thunderstorm that produced golf-ball-sized hail that had wreaked havoc on the town's homes, businesses and cars. In the hospital while thunder roared and hail crashed, his mother underwent twenty hours of labor, pushing out an eleven-pound, two-foot-tall kid.

"So, I was born in a storm and I caused a storm, or at least, that's what my grandma says," he joked as he got out his materials for class from his backpack.

He said he was a diesel major in his second semester and wasn't looking forward to completing his general education classes, especially writing.

"I don't even know how to use a computer much. I'm not that keen on reading this shit, either." He held up a large biology text.

"Pate's a good writer," Oakley told him, gesturing at me. "He's definitely going to be helping me!"

"Good, he can help me, too."

* * * *

Oakley

Awkwardness and intimidation fueled any experience that involved having classes with Bullet. Ever since we had first met Bullet, I had suspected that he still saw Maybelle as his property, and knowing him, he would likely fixate on Pate. On the one hand, I was proud of Pate for potentially ending his celibacy and entering his first relationship as a man. On the other hand, I truly wished that his new love interest was anyone but Maybelle. Bullet's possessiveness was certainly a concern, but there was also this frivolity that radiated from Maybelle. I wanted to support Pate, but the relationship seemed doomed to me.

Being on a college campus was alien to me. All the other students were younger and seemed smart. I opened my writing book and didn't even know where to begin. *How do I learn this stuff?* I was starting to realize that my years of stagnation were more about my fear of pursuing something that might result in failure. My gut just wanted to quit, but I didn't really have anything better to do.

The afternoon biology class was large, and the professor stopped us when we walked in the door.

"What's your names?" he asked. He was a young professor who sported jeans with a blue buttoned-up shirt and bow tie.

We told him our names, and he pointed to certain lab tables for us to sit. "I'm seating you with your pre-assigned lab partners," he explained.

Pate and I sighed as we walked over to our tables that were across the room from each other. Our partners were not present yet.

Maybelle and Kelly walked into the room, throwing their book bags on their lab station before frolicking over to Pate. Hopefully, just having their presence along with mine would ease Pate's tension about us being separated.

I saw Stormy from our writing class enter and walk over to Pate's table. *Good. Stormy seems cool,* I thought. More and more students crowded into the room as time for class drew near, and still, no one sat beside me. *Great. I'm stuck with the slacker.* The professor stood at the front of the classroom, asking everyone to sit down and get quiet. It was then that Bullet stomped into the room, and my stomach dropped as the professor waved him over to my lab table.

Bullet's face twisted in a scowl as he reluctantly plopped down beside me, sliding his seat as far away from mine as possible. Every now and then as the professor discussed the course syllabus, we'd trade disgusted glances. *I'm learning biology with Bullet.* I pouted.

After class, I found a quiet bench under some trees to call Jody. Her voice, her hair and her sassy walk had surged through my brain ever since the weekend. I had never considered dating a trans girl, but it couldn't be *that* different than dating a regular girl, right? The body parts were all the same, and Jody looked and acted just like a girl. Part of me was even more intrigued. *I'm cooler with this stuff than Pate thinks I am. I can do this. It's just like dating a girl.*

Jody answered after a few rings. "I was wondering when you'd get around to calling me. Just leave me waiting."

We made some small talk about my first classes, and Jody talked about some exciting projects for her senior year.

"One of my friend's dads wants me to help him with his store's website. It's pretty cool! I'm *that* close to almost working professionally! Just one more year!" she exclaimed with a slight giggle.

With Jody in her last year, we didn't have any classes together and she seemed committed to school.

"Sorry, I prefer to focus on my classes during the week," she insisted. "I don't want anything distracting me from school. But that leaves my weekends open."

"What do you want to do?" I asked her.

"Well, there's not a ton to do here, but the weather is still nice. We could meet after classes on Friday and take a walk."

"A walk?"

"I'm a walker." She chuckled. "It keeps this body slim and healthy. I can show you around town, too. If we get hungry, we can always grab something simple. Besides, isn't the point to talk on a first date anyway?"

First date. I was going on a date with a trans girl. What if she's like Pate, though? What if she still has a penis? Her performance dress had been clingy and short, making it difficult to believe that there could be a bulge resting between her thighs. However, her frame was so small that if she still had a phallus, it was probably also rather small...I hoped.

I agreed to meet her Friday after my biology class. It dawned on me that it had been well over a year since I had dated anyone. Having my first love morph into a dude and my last girlfriend fucking my drummer didn't leave me very receptive to dating again. But with Jody, I was, after all, trying something new. I doubted trans girls had many dating options, so the possibility for infidelity seemed less likely, and she certainly wasn't going to transform into a man! *But can I be with a girl if she has a penis? How do I even find this out?*

* * * *

"Don't ask trans people about their genitals," Pate told me the next night while we were studying in our room.

"So...will they just tell you what's down there?" I asked, dumbfounded.

Pate stared at me.

"I'm not trying to be rude," I promised. "But don't I have the right to *know*?"

"Do you think you can handle it?" Pate asked.

I didn't know. I was obsessing about whether Jody still had a penis, but at the same time, I didn't even know what I would do with this information if I had it. *What if she tells me on the first date that she's still partially a dude? Do I leave? Do I finish the date to be nice? What if staying sends the wrong message? Will I hurt her feelings if I leave?*

"Well, no offense," I asserted, "but you can't blame people if they're not gay. I like girls. I'm not a bad guy because I don't want to have sex with a dick. It doesn't make me prejudiced."

"Why does a woman have to be defined by whether or not she has a vagina?" Pate leaned back in his chair, crossing his arms. "You saw her. She's a woman, right?"

"Yes."

"You're harping too much on a body part, which is just one detail. Think about how you feel about the *person* inside."

I sighed. "But I *can't* touch a penis."

"How do you know that?" Pate grilled me, rolling his eyes. "Have you ever tried? You touch your own penis, don't you?"

"*That's* not the same!"

Pate smirked. "Sure, it is. And when you watch porn, do you *not* see other men's penises?"

"Well, *yeah*, but—"

"And does seeing these other men's penises turn you off? Does it stop you from masturbating?"

"It's not the same thing, Pate!"

"You can touch your own dick and be aroused, and you can watch pornographic scenes with not only dicks, but dicks so big that you can't *not* focus on them, and you're still aroused. If you're able to navigate those situations, I think you can you move through this, too." He studied me with his eyes the way he always did when he felt like he'd won a debate with me. Just a long, intense stare as he waited to see what my comeback would be.

"I like girls, though," I insisted, throwing up my hands in exasperation. "I like vaginas! I like going down on girls. I like...you know, feeling my dick inside of girls. How am I supposed to have sex with a dude?"

"Well—" Pate started.

"Ugh, don't answer that! I don't want to visualize it!" I stammered, covering my eyes with my hands.

Pate leaned forward, placing his elbows on the little study table in front of him. He gave me an endearing smile. "I think you need to expand your imagination. To me, it sounds like you take sex too literally."

"What's that supposed to mean?" I asked, puzzled.

"You're too literal!" He laughed. "You focus too much on what you literally see in front of you. I think if you explored your emotions more and the connection you have with the person, you might find that more things can become sexual or arousing for you. You're too rigid. You're shutting doors before they even open. Trust me."

"That's not fair."

"Maybe not." He shrugged.

"I'm not gay like you. Why do you think we stopped having sex—" I slammed my lips shut before anything else escaped. I immediately averted my eyes to the biology textbook opened in front of me, but I could feel Pate's eyes on me.

Pate was quiet for a moment. "Okay. But explain this to me?" he inquired.

"What?" I asked, looking back up at him with caution.

"I still have a vagina. If that defines a woman, how come you *can't* have sex with me?"

My throat tightened, and no words emerged. I grabbed my bottle of water and took a long sip.

"Maybe we should just get back to studying," I suggested, turning the page in my book.

"Okay," Pate agreed.

My emotions and thoughts were a never-ending roller coaster for the rest of the week. Several times, I caught myself staring at "The Drag Queen" on my phone, tempted several times to hit "call" and cancel our date. *What am I doing?* In my gut, I felt nearly certain that if Jody still had a penis, there was no way that I could accept it, so what was the point? I thought about the way that Jody danced along the stage, slinging her long hair. Most of the girls that I had dated were dependent and insecure. Either they constantly begged for my reassurance, or they fucked around on me for their own external validation. I had never seen a girl with confidence that radiated off her like a golden sunbeam until I saw Jody. Also, she seemed smart — way smarter than me! For a girl who might have a penis, she seemed out of my league.

I was excitedly nervous when biology class was over on Friday. Fortunately, we hadn't started any labs that would require Bullet and I to interact with each other. *What if he knows that Jody is trans? It's a small town. Will he give me shit?*

I walked outside with Pate and Maybelle. He was taking her back to Granny's house where he planned to cook Southern-style chunky meat loaf and homemade, creamy mashed potatoes, one of his culinary specialties.

"Oh, you're meeting Jody. That's so cute!" Maybelle squealed, softly slapping me on the shoulder

"Just be nice," Pate told me with a nod of the head.

I walked over to the designated date bench. It was empty. I read through my Facebook feed, not focusing on any posts. *What if I really like her?*

Hearing a noise behind me, I eagerly turned around, but it was just a nerdy-looking dude with fiery red hair.

"Hello there, Oakman."

I turned around again. It was the same dude.

"Uh, hi," I stuttered.

The guy walked around to the front of the bench. "Geez, you're not very friendly on a first date, are you?" He grinned. His smile showed off his white teeth and dimples.

My esophagus tightened and my temples throbbed. I surveyed the guy again. He was Jody's height, and the voice sounded like Jody. He had Jody's bright, emerald-green eyes that shone out from beneath a mop of curly bright red hair that resembled a loose afro. His build was petite. He must have been only five feet six and one-hundred-twenty-ish pounds.

"How'd you know my name?" I asked in disbelief.

"It's *me*, stupid!" Jody laughed.

"Jody?" I gasped.

"Yes!" Jody spread his arms wide and gave a little twirl. "It's me in the flesh!"

I just stared with my mouth open so long that drool started leaking from the corners. Jody sat down beside me.

"You were expecting Sadie?" he inquired with a slight smile.

"I...ugh..." I rubbed my palms together to wipe some of the sweat off of them.

"It's okay. You can tell me," he told me, tilting his head to the side as he watched me.

"Well...yeah." I flushed.

"My female persona is pretty good, isn't it?" Jody beamed.

"You're no—"

"Not a girl?"

Thoughts ricocheted off the corners of my brain, searching for any words that didn't sound bigoted, but nothing came. My brain went tense but blank.

"You must not attend many drag shows," Jody concluded, leaning back with one arm propped up along the top part of the bench. "Lots of the performers are not girls, as someone like you may classically define them, anyway."

"What are they then?" I asked, turning my body to face him more. I feared that passersby might notice that we were sitting too close to each other.

Jody snorted. "Well, foremost, they're *people*. But some guys like crossdressing. And others like crossdressing *and* performing. There's a few trans girls there, too."

My face was getting hot and my hands couldn't stop fidgeting. I could feel his eyes on me, but I refused to look him in the eyes.

"So..." I started carefully, "you're a guy?"

"Yes," he answered proudly.

"You...dress like a guy?"

"Most of the time," he affirmed.

We sat in silence. I picked at my belt buckle while I saw him peer out at the campus.

"This really bothers you, doesn't it?" Jody asked apprehensively after a few moments. "I didn't mean to deceive you or give you the wrong impression. I assumed you knew.'"

"I know. I'm not angry. I don't know..." I rubbed my forehead with my right hand. I would have done anything to have Pate come along and rescue me. He would know what to say.

"We can talk about it?" Jody offered.

"Talk about what?"

"*This*." Jody waved her hands toward her face and body. "Come on, let's take that walk, and I'll tell you about it."

Does a walk mean that we're on the date? I wondered. *Is this still a date?*

I wanted to get the hell out of there! But he was being so calm and polite that I couldn't bring myself to hurt his feelings. Better to let him down on the phone or via text. Besides, what harm could a walk do? Guys walked around and talked, didn't they?

We walked a little way off campus and into the surrounding neighborhoods where it was quiet. Jody told me that he had always known that he was different. He was enamored with dancing, singing and performing even when he was still in diapers. He would have to sneak behind his father's back to play dolls with his sister. Jody said that he loved playing with the dolls and spent hours doing their hair and clothes to perfect the flawless look. One Christmas, his father gave his sister a Barbie that was a large head, and they could do its hair and put real makeup on it. Jody was fascinated with this doll. His sister would secretly collect lists for eyeliners, eye shadows and lipstick and get his dad to buy this stuff for her doll, but really, it was for Jody. Jody started to create wild mixtures of colors and designs. One day, when he was about twelve years old, he'd asked his sister if she'd try some of his designs on him. The afternoon turned into trying on his sister's dresses and Jody was hooked.

"I just fell in love with the art form," he continued, swaying his arms back and forth gracefully as he walked. "I loved how I could take these layers of makeup along with girdles and bustiers and transform myself into this other person—this stage person who could do anything. Plus, it just felt good to feel the long hair tickling my shoulders and back and twirling around in long dresses and skirts. I felt pretty."

While Jody and his sister tried to keep his behavior secret, his father sometimes found traces of evidence. Jody would get his sister to sneak him women's underwear and bras that his father discovered in his room. His father was an old-fashioned, conversative man who did not approve of this behavior. If he found bras, he threw them in the trash or burned them in the fire pit so that Jody could not retrieve them. If he found makeup, he flushed it down the toilet. His father rarely confronted Jody about it, but he would confront his sister.

"He'd tell her not to buy those things for me and that she was messing me up in the head," Jody explained. "I think he knew that the message would get back to me, but he didn't have the guts to tell me himself. Mostly, he just avoided me and focused on my sister, who was his little princess. But when I started high school and still wasn't dating girls, he got more hostile toward me."

"You're gay?" I confirmed.

"Yes, I'm gay," Jody admitted. He nudged me in the arm to lead us down a little road that led to a small cemetery. "I've always known that I was gay. I just knew that I needed to keep it to myself, though. At least until I moved out and stayed with my uncle in Chicago."

"He was cool with it?" Jody walked a tad in front of me, and I couldn't help but notice the way his jeans hugged the same petite butt that I'd savored in the club. I immediately looked away when he turned his head back to look at me.

"Yes, mostly because he's gay, too." Jody laughed. "But he taught me that it was okay to be myself. He was a singer—he sang opera, and he loved tap dancing. He also took me to clubs—not adult clubs—but LGBTQ support kind of clubs, and it felt so refreshing to be in a place where we could just *be*. I missed my sister terribly, but my uncle, in many ways, was the best thing that ever happened to me."

He turned his head back around, and I found my eyes again focused on his ass. *Wait, what am I doing?*

I quickened my pace so that we were side by side. "Why didn't you stay in Chicago then? If it was so nice."

"My uncle died," Jody replied. He stared down at his feet, kicking a rock on the road.

"Oh. I'm sorry. How?"

Jody slowed his pace, and his arm brushed up against me, sending shivers through me. "He got cancer. Pancreatic. He found out that he had it and two months later, he was dead. That's when I returned to Montana to stay with my sister. She had just gotten married after high school and needed someone to help her with my nephew, who was a baby at that time. So, I came back and finished high school in Billings."

His arm brushed up against mine again, bringing with it more tingling sensations.

"So why Cloverleaf to go to school?" I inquired, moving a little closer to him so that our shoulders slightly touched. "I would think Billings is a more LGB—you know, open place for that stuff."

Jody smirked. "Good question!" His fingers touched my hand as if he were attempting to hold it, but I quickly moved it away. I pretended to scratch my nose so that the rejection wasn't obvious.

"I just wanted to be on my own," Jody continued, not seeming to take any notice of my aversion. "My uncle had lived for years on his own. He inspired me. I wanted to prove that I could make it being myself no matter where I am. That's the level of confidence that I wanted. In a way, standing up for who I am in a place like this is like standing up to my dad."

"But still close enough to your sister. That must be important." My hand was now in my pocket, but our shoulders still touched as we walked together.

"Right. It was my sister who encouraged me to consider doing drag shows, but it's taken me years to work up the courage to perform in drag. I'm kind of a perfectionist. I've been working on Sadie for forever. I wanted it to be just right. Plus, college keeps me busy, too. But now that I'm into it, I can't get enough of it! The rush! I can't wait for the next show!" Jody jumped up and down a few times like an excited child. I laughed at his excitement.

Jody was animated when he talked. His arms moved so frenetically that he often hit me in the arms, yet his voice was so sweet and...happy. He seemed so vital and carefree. His frame was so small and...feminine. His lips were full and feminine. His skin was smooth, delicate and feminine. Even his voice was light, soft, and feminine.

"Do you dress up in your home?" I inquired. We had made a lap around the small cemetery and were now walking back down the road toward campus again.

"Yes! All the time." Jody jumped again. "How do you think I design my makeup and outfits? In fact, I even sew my own clothes. I made that dress you saw."

"You made that dress yourself?" I asked in amazement. Boy or girl, I loved that dress on him.

"I sure did." Jody beamed.

"Do people here know that you do drag? Like people at school? In Cloverleaf?" I asked. I was dying to know about the local climate on campus regarding queer identities. Not just for Jody but mostly for Pate.

"I don't know." He shrugged. "Frankly, I don't care."

"They know you're gay, right?"

He shrugged again. "I don't know and I don't care. You seem pretty preoccupied with other people."

"I'm just looking out for Pat—never mind," I stopped myself. "So, do you date?"

"Not much, sweetie. I'm demisexual. I must get to know people, or at least, get a sense of their character before I feel like pursuing them. I despise dating, honestly." He nudged me with his shoulder again to indicate that we were making a right turn. "It feels like a long job interview where you're putting yourself out there just waiting to have the other person evaluate you as a potential partner. Or they realize that you're really a man." He giggled and nudged harder this time.

I blushed. "I hate dating, too," I said, which was my awkward attempt at avoiding Jody's last comment.

"I've had a few boyfriends but nothing lengthy and nothing local." Jody playfully poked me in the side. My ticklishness caused me to squirm.

"So why did you want to go out with me?" I poked him back, and he laughed, throwing up his hands to protect himself.

"Are we going out, Oakman? Are we having the date right now?" He got closer and placed his hand on my shoulder.

Clinching my teeth, I stared ahead.

"Sorry, sweetie." Jody smiled. "I didn't mean to make you nervous. Um, I guess it was the way you looked at me when I was performing. I don't usually have guys look at me like that."

"Like what?"

"Like they're enamored with me." He squeezed my shoulder. "You just looked so fascinated...so engaged. I felt like it was just us and that I was singing to only you. When I saw you approaching me at the bar, I swear, I thought I was going to throw up! I was a nervous wreck!"

"With *me*?" My eyes widened in disbelief.

"Yes, with you! I noticed you looking at me, but I thought maybe I was reading too much into it until you wanted to talk to me. No one's ever approached me first...let alone a straight guy!" Jody pinched my shoulder teasingly, but I squirmed away.

"You know" — I placed my hand on his shoulder this time — "I didn't mean to hurt your feelings back there on the bench," I apologized.

"I know. You didn't." Jody gazed at me with those beautiful, intoxicating green eyes. I noticed the way his freckles dotted the skin around them.

"You're very different than anyone I've ever met. *Really* different," I told him, still maintaining eye contact.

"It sounds like you need something different in your life." Jody stopped walking and turned to face me. "Oakman, give me your hand."

"I don't know." I searched the area around us, but no one was around.

"Come on, just give it to me. Trust me."

I slowly extended it with my thumb up as if to shake his hand. Cradling my hand, Jody placed his other palm over mine and overlapped our fingers.

"That's not so bad," he said, piercing me with his green eyes.

"What's not so bad?" I was too focused on feeling our palms touching that I hardly deciphered his words.

"You haven't pulled away." He smiled.

I stared down at our hands. My stomach twisted and tensed, and my heart raced. But Jody was right. I didn't want to pull away. Something — I didn't know what — felt good...felt thrilling...

"I'm not sure what's going on here," I whispered.

"It's okay. I don't know what's going on, either." Jody lowered his eyes. "I have this feeling about you. I thought about you all week."

"Me, too," I answered instinctively, also avoiding eye contact.

"What about now?" Jody's eyes met mine again. "Are you thinking about me right now? In the same way?"

"I'm…" I choked from all the various sensations running through me in that moment. "I feel really confused."

"Confused isn't no," Jody noted, squeezing my hand. "Confused I can work with."

There were so many random but complex thoughts rushing around my head that I didn't know what to say or do. Suddenly, a car turned onto the road, and I yanked my hand from Jody's, pulling my body away from him. The car passed, and we were alone again.

"I guess I'm afraid to leave now," Jody admitted.

"Why?" I tried to play off the fact that I had just pushed away from him.

"Because I'm afraid that you won't want to see me again." Jody pointed at me as if highlighting my recoil.

I exhaled loudly. "I'm okay with seeing you again."

"I mean take me out on a second date," Jody clarified, placing his hands on his hips.

"Was this a date?" *Did I just have a date with a dude? Unintentionally?*

"Yes." He nodded. "You asked me on a date. That doesn't change when I show up as a man, does it? And you didn't run away. You spent the last few hours with me. When did we decide to change it from a date to two guys hanging out? And besides, we held hands."

Running my hands through my hair, I couldn't make my eyes leave the pavement. I wished Pate was there. Damn! He had been smart enough to bring me on his first date with Maybelle.

"Do you agree?" Jody pressed.

"Yeah, I guess so," I muttered under my breath.

"So, you and me just had our first date?"

"Okay," I agreed halfheartedly.

"So do you want to go out again?" Jody asked, moving closer to me with his hands still on his hips.

Say no, say no, say no. No words came to me.

Jody stepped up even closer to me. I could feel his breath on my cheeks. "Close your eyes."

"I don't want to," I blurted out, shaking my head.

He raised his eyebrows. "And I didn't want to accidently go out with a straight guy, but I did. Just because we don't want to do something doesn't automatically make it bad. Close them!"

I shut my eyes. Jody lightly cradled my cheeks in his palms and gently pulled my face against his. His soft, warm lips pressed on mine for a second then pulled away.

"You have my number," Jody purred as he started walking back toward campus.

"Wait!" I called after him.

"No." Jody turned and held up his hands as if they were stop signs. "You know how I feel about you. You figure out how you feel. You've got my number."

Jody sauntered away with a slight shake of his hips. I must have stood on that street for an eternity gaping after his silhouette that still shook and shimmied like a woman. When his body was no longer in range, my phone beeped. There was a text from him.

You know for a straight guy, you sure are gay.

Chapter Eight

Pate

Granny was tired and said that she planned on relaxing in her room but wanted me to bring her a plate when I finished cooking my famed meatloaf. She looked tired and weak, but part of me wondered if she were avoiding me or avoiding me with Maybelle. It was my first evening without Oakley around, making things a little awkward. However, when I carried in a steaming plate of spicy meatloaf and creamy mashed potatoes, Granny's eyes lit up ravenously.

"Not many people make dinner for *me*," she said softly.

"I'll come back later to get the plates," I told her, setting her glass of tea down on the bedside table.

"Don't worry. I'll bring them out later. I may be sleeping."

I closed her door gently. Seeing her enjoying my food eased some of my apprehensions concerning the way she felt about me. When I returned to the kitchen, Maybelle was hungrily stuffing her face.

"I guess you don't wait for anyone, do you?" I snickered.

"Sorry, I'm starving! And it smells so good. I don't get many homecooked meals."

I poured us some wine. Maybelle wasn't old enough to drink legally, but like my hometown in the South, underaged drinking wasn't a big deal. It was more important to learn how to drink early in life and hold your alcohol. Unfortunately, Maybelle had wanted white wine, which was mostly tasteless to me, but I humored her.

"I never had a guy cook for me." Maybelle grinned, making the slight amber in her eyes shimmer. "It's nice. The food at the restaurants here isn't any good anyway, and I am getting way too fat to be eating pizzas and hamburgers all the time. How do you stay so skinny?"

"Dancing. And running." I shoved a huge forkful of mashed potatoes in my mouth.

"You should show me some dance moves," she joked, waving her fork at me.

"How would you like to dance?"

She chewed her food for a few moments and flushed it down with some wine. "Waltz?"

I nodded. "That's a classic."

"It's one of the only dance names I know!" She giggled. "Isn't that what those people in big ballgowns do?"

"How about salsa?" I suggested. "It's more fun."

"Salsa? That's a dance? I thought it was something you eat!" She chuckled.

"I think you'd like it. Better than the waltz." Really, I just knew that salsa was more socially and romantically engaging than the waltz—at least to my fancy. I fantasized about Maybelle in a skirt, letting me swing her around. It also gave me a safe way to be somewhat physical with her without it intensifying into sex.

"We can go to the barn after dinner," I offered. "That's where my stage and speaker system is set up."

"Speaker system?" Her eyes widened. "Wow, you're *that* serious!"

"Watch me dance, and you'll see how serious I am." I beamed.

* * * *

After dinner, I took Maybelle to the barn. Oakley was helping me make it a safe place by hanging up Christmas lights all around the roof and walls, creating a mystical atmosphere that allowed me to block out the real world easier. I selected some Marc Anthony from my playlist and turned up the speakers. The music caused Maybelle to jump.

"Wow! That's loud!" she yelped.

I took off the flannel shirt that I was wearing, keeping on the tight-fitting T-shirt underneath.

"Take off your shoes," I instructed her as I was undoing mine. "It'll make the footing easier for you."

"But my feet will get all dirty," Maybelle complained as she gazed at her sandals.

"I'll wash them for you."

She slipped off her sandals reluctantly. She was wearing a loose white miniskirt and tight-fitting gold tank-top, which were ideal for dancing.

"Let your hair down, too," I told her, gesturing with my hands.

"Why? It's hot!" she protested, grabbing her ponytail.

"It'll create more of a mood," I assured her.

She groaned and removed her hair-tie, letting her dark brown hair flow over her shoulders in a wild mess. She started finger-brushing it, but I took her hand.

"Leave it. It's beautiful like that. All wild!" I admired her with awe.

"God, why do guys always want girls to look like shit?" She rolled her eyes. "You do your hair, and they can't wait to take it down. You do your makeup, and they can't wait to slobber it all off. You put together a cute outfit, and they just want you naked."

"Come on," I said, pulling her to the center of the barn.

We started with the mambo. Maybelle seemed tense and awkward, often stepping on my toes or not transitioning moves smoothly.

"I can't do this!" she whined, frustrated.

"It's fine. Everyone has to learn. But once you get it, you'll love it. It's fun!" I encouraged her. "Don't take yourself so seriously when you dance. Just let loose."

"I feel *stupid*," she moaned.

We proceeded with a routine in which Maybelle would seriously try one minute and grumble in frustration the next. It was a behavior that most of us dancers experienced with non-dancers. We'd hope that they would give it time and just let their bodies loose, which was the real secret behind any dancing. But too often, people were too much inside their own heads so they couldn't let loose, and thus, never truly danced. Ironically, dancing was the one experience where I was completely out of my head.

"Why don't you just place your hands in mine and try focusing on just moving your body to the music?" I recommended.

"I feel stupid. Let's do something else." She jiggled her body in defiance like a little girl demanding to get her way.

"Just watch me. Watch my hips." I placed my hands on my hips to focus her attention.

Salsa was one of my favorite dances to do for fun. It was great when Oakley occasionally joined me, though he was even more awkward than Maybelle. Salsa was a way for me to move my body with confidence. Dancing, in general, was the one activity where I integrated my feminine and my masculine sides, making me feel whole. I only wished that I could be a dancer in all areas of my life.

"I think you're too good. You're intimidating me," Maybelle complained, pulling away. "Can we just go talk?"

"Sure." I turned the music off and grabbed some towels that we stored in the barn for my dancing sessions. I tossed one to Maybelle.

"Thanks. Ugh. I feel so gross now!" she grumbled as she patted her face with it.

I turned on the light at the back of the barn. Oakley and I had moved Granny's old porch swing into the barn to give us a nice place to relax and smoke weed. I moved the wine bottle and glasses that we had brought over with us to a table near the swing and grabbed a blanket. I motioned for her to join.

"This is better," she said as she sat down. "This is really nice, actually. You've got a good place in here."

"It gives us a private place to hang out. And gives me a space to dance." I handed her a glass of wine.

"You're *really* good. Sorry I suck so bad!" She covered her face in embarrassment.

"You can't suck at anything." I kissed her.

We talked for a few hours, finishing our bottle of wine and rubbing our toes into the dirt below our feet. I chatted about dancing and how I got into it as a young child, always strutting, jumping and twisting to any music that played. But my parents were never too supportive even though they'd attended my dance shows in high school. If I could be a professional dancer, I would, but the industry wasn't a realistic career path, which had left me clueless about my future. I also informed her about starting college with the hopes of teaching literature.

"Teaching! English?" she asked with disgust. "I didn't know people wanted to do that! I hate writing! Why'd you stop college before then if you want to be a teacher?"

I swallowed hard. "It just wasn't a good fit for me at the time. You're right. Only weird people want to do that anyway. Maybe I should do something else."

"You sound so cool!" Maybelle said as she snuggled her head into my shoulder. "My life is so boring. Nothing to do in Cloverleaf but just drink and hang out camping or on the ranch, which is actually pretty cool at night. I like listening to the cows. I like the stars, too."

"You're the most interesting thing to me in a long time," I whispered in her ear, pulling her close to me.

We kissed again, and our torsos pressed firmly against each other. Her soft, squishy breasts brushed up against my still-numb post-surgery chest. Her hands began exploring my body up and down my back, then lower toward my butt. My hands followed the same dance, moving slowly, carefully to her bottom, and she moaned.

"You can touch me, if you want," she breathed in my ear.

I kissed her again, and she took my right hand and guided it to her breast. It was the first breast that I had touched as a man, and I wasn't sure what to do with it. I softly squeezed and released, and she reacted with more moans and heavy breathing. *I guess it's working*, I thought to myself. Then I moved my thumb back and forth along her nipple until I could feel it harden. She moved her hand softly down my side causing me to shake a little from the tickling sensations along my skin. Her hand moved to my hip, landing on my thigh. Suddenly, her fingers crept toward my crotch.

Grabbing her hand away, I stood up.

"What's wrong?" She leaned backward on the swing, staring at me with hurt and confusion.

"Sorry," I stuttered, but I remained standing. I saw her look down as if ashamed. "I'm sorry. It's not you," I pleaded, sitting back down beside her and taking her hand.

"Are you not attracted to me?" Her voice was shaky.

"Yes! Very much. I just..." I saw a white screen in my mind with a blinking cursor. "I'm...I'm not ready to have sex."

"Um...we didn't have to have *sex*. I thought we were just fooling around," she stated, embarrassed.

"I know. But...I'm not ready for all that. It's nothing with you, I promise." I squeezed her hand in mine.

"I don't get those kinds of reactions from guys normally. You're not really gay or something, are you?" She peered at me, waiting for me to answer.

"No. I'm not gay." It was mostly the truth. "I don't like to...I don't want to jump into things...sexually."

"Oooookay..." Maybelle's crinkled her face up, puzzled.

Fuck! I wasn't explaining this well at all! *She'll never want to see me again.*

I inhaled a deep breath. "Sex is really intimate to me. It's not something that I do with a lot of people."

"But we weren't having sex—"

I stopped her. "I know."

"So, we can't do *anything*? Usually you do stuff before working up to sex." She stared away from me. Her toes kept digging into the dirt beneath her.

"We can. I want to." I touched her chin with my hand, pulling her face toward me.

"I'm confused. Maybe I should go home." Maybelle stood up, brushing the dirt off her skirt.

"No, please," I begged. "I just want to take our time. We can do lots of stuff! I promise. Just...nothing under the waist."

Maybelle grimaced. "Seriously?"

"Haven't you ever wanted to get to know someone first? Some romance?" The turmoil was brewing up inside of me. *Don't leave!*

"I'm sorry, Pate, but this is all too weird. I feel like an idiot. Or I guess I'm a slut to you."

"No!" I grabbed for her hand again, but she pulled it away.

"Just take me home. I'm too embarrassed." She put her sandals on her dirty feet and stomped outside with her arms crossed.

I didn't know what to do. Everything had been progressing so wonderfully, but now the moment that I had dreaded emerged like a monster from the swamp, sucking it all away from me. *Should I tell her the truth? Either way, she thinks I'm a freak. No, if she can't even handle waiting for sex, how would she understand this?*

When I went outside, Maybelle was standing by my car, peering away from me a little. My throat was so tight and dry that I could hardly swallow. Tears swelled up in my eyes that I immediately, desperately wiped away, frantically breathing to prevent any more from sneaking up on me. *Be a man. Be a man.*

"Um, I need to go grab the keys from inside," I told her. She didn't respond.

My heart continued to tighten and suffocate me, and the anxiety started burning in my temples. I knew by the time that I returned to the car, the shakes would begin. Tears bled through my eyes once more. *Get it together. Drive her home, and then you can go to your room and fall apart.*

When I returned outside, Oakley was pulling up. He examined Maybelle, who waved but didn't offer her typical cheery smile or giggles. As he approached me, his face was also strained.

"Early date?" I asked.

His head turned back and forth between Maybelle and me. "Early for you, too?" he whispered as he moved close to me.

I leaned forward so that Maybelle wouldn't hear. "Things got...physical."

"Oh. Is it bad?" Oakley mouthed.

"I don't know. I have to drive her home now. I'll be back. What happened to yours?"

"She's a dude."

* * * *

Oakley

I made myself a white Russian and went out to our swing in the barn so I could roll us a massive joint to smoke the whole evening away. Jody's eyes — and his lips — would not leave my thoughts. I was baffled about why I hadn't pulled away from him in disgust. Any time I ever thought about touching or kissing a guy, my brain defensively pushed that image away from my consciousness immediately. After all, I had grown up in a climate that conditioned me that any contact with a dude was gay and something to be completely avoided. Even snuggling with Pate was more acceptable because, in many ways, I still saw him as a girl. He wasn't a *pure* guy, so it didn't count. Of course, I had never told him this.

I realized that I had never permitted myself the luxury of even considering dating a man. I was too busy trying to avoid it. The gut instinct in me now told me to suppress, to joke and most of all, to run. At the same time, my consciousness communicated a different message. *What is it about men that repulses me? Does it repulse me?*

Okay, so women had soft, flabbier bodies that offered warmth and cushioning. They usually smelled good even without perfume. Their hair was usually longer, and I loved running my fingers through it and seeing it fall all around my face while we made love. Girls seemed caring and calm. They offered support when I was down and were good listeners. Girls let me feel okay with expressing my thoughts and feelings. When Pate presented as a girl, I was able to be more vulnerable and open with him than I could ever be with other guys. More importantly, I wouldn't be accused of being gay.

Then there were men. *What do I think about men?*

Men were rough. They had rough skin and cracked knuckles even if they worked indoors. They weren't as neat and moved awkwardly. While women's bodies were wonderlands of soft, smooth curves producing a proportioned physique, men's bodies were straight with their genitals dangling ungracefully between their legs. While I didn't mind my own parts so much, the idea of seeing a man's genitals as erotic made me squeamish. The wrinkles, the smooth, wormy head and the veins! On the other hand, an erect penis did have a smooth, soft feel to it. What would I do with a penis? It was one thing to imagine dating Jody as a girl with penis—it was quite another to imagine dating a dude.

Pate joined me on the swing as I handed him a beer and the joint. We took a few hits without talking or looking at each other. I guessed we both were frozen in perplexity. For once, we were both having genital issues.

"Do you want to tell me about it?" Pate asked.

"Do *you?*"

"You first."

I told him about the "date." Nervous, I informed him about the hand holding, the brief kiss and the ambiguity over whether it was a date. Pate listened, stroking his chin.

"Does this make me gay?" I asked

"Only you can answer that," Pate insisted. "No one else can define your sexuality for you. Why didn't you tell him that you changed your mind?"

"Like just blow him off?" My eyes almost bulged out. Pate was telling me to blow him off? I thought he was Mr. Compassionate. "That would be rude."

"So, you care about him? Most straight guys probably would have either left, yelled at him or at least verbalized clearly that the date was no longer a date. You did none of those things." He gave me that stare again, the one when he knew that I had nothing to respond with.

Pate's statement puzzled me. I considered myself a polite person, so how would not breaking a date with a dude in order to spare his feelings suggest that I had feelings? Was there more to my politeness?

"How many straight guys do you think would proceed with the date?" Pate noted.

"I didn't proceed with—"

"You didn't clarify that it *wasn't* a date, and you proceeded to hang out with him." Pate interrupted me.

"But..."

Pate held up his hand to stop me. "You didn't pull away when he held your hand. Even *he* noticed that. You didn't pull away from his kiss. You think he's never hit on straight guys before? I think he'd know by now that straight guys pull away—"

"And gay guys don't?" I asked.

"They don't if they are interested. Oakley, sexuality is not either/or. Maybe you have some attraction to him. Maybe not toward just any man, but toward him."

I had been so busy trying to analyze my repulsion toward guys that it had never dawned on me to consider what made Jody attractive to me. His emerald-green eyes alone were enough to mesmerize anyone. His skin was silky and soft like a woman. His frame was small and delicate. But thinking on it, it wasn't so much those physical traits as it was his confidence and free spirit. I had never seen a girl perform and light up a room as if she owned it the way Jody had dominated the club in Billings. When he realized that I thought he was a girl when I made the date, his response was calm. He didn't get offended or even embarrassed. Jody was going to keep being Jody. I hadn't found that certainty for myself yet.

"What if I told you that I like him because he's like a girl?" I asked, inhaling a deep hit from the joint.

"It wouldn't mean anything different than me preferring to stay a feminine guy," Pate replied, shrugging his shoulder. "It's not about girl or boy. It's about the feminine and the masculine that's in all of us. Some of us connect to or are attracted more to one side over another. It doesn't make you a bad person. Wait." He stared at me with wide eyes. "Did you just say that you *like* him?"

Did I?

"I don't know," was my reply.

"If you're thinking on him this much, I think you like him. Otherwise, you wouldn't entertain the conversation." Pate wagged his finger at me.

"Is this the right place to explore a gay relationship? Cloverleaf? I don't know what I'm doing. I don't know how to handle what other people may think about it...about me." My throat tightened as I tried to envision the possible stress that would come with dating a guy in such a small rural town.

"Is there ever a good place? A good time? You'll never find one. What are you afraid that other people will think?" Pate inquired.

I hesitated. Pate picked up on it.

"You think they are going to think something bad? That you're a bad person? Who knows...maybe a pervert?" Pate argued.

"I didn't say those things," I protested.

"Are you thinking them, though?"

"You know that I accept gay people. I accept you...your bisexuality, don't I?" I snapped.

Pate smirked. "Seems like it changes when you begin applying it to yourself. Suddenly, if it's you, then it's bad."

I used my silence this time to protest Pate's typical self-righteous arguments that always seemed to want to paint me as a homophobic or transphobic asshole.

After a few minutes, Pate asked, "Do you want to see him again?"

"Should I?" I asked, still waiting for Pate to tell me if I was gay or not.

"I can't answer that for you. But it sounds like he was pretty understanding with you, so he may really like you," Pate stated, slapping his hand on my thigh. "At the same time, a person like Jody isn't going to wait around for anyone either. I think this is your chance. If you want it, of course."

Wrapping my mind around dating a dude was overwhelming enough, but viewing the opportunity as something slipping through my fingers was even more baffling. *I should be fighting for this?*

"I'll think about it some more," I replied. "So, what's your story? Maybelle didn't look happy."

"I wouldn't have sex with her."

I jerked, widening my eyes. "What? You guys were going to fuck in Granny's barn?"

"And how do you suggest that I fuck a girl with a vagina?" Pate sneered, rolling his eyes. "No! We were just making out."

"How was it?" I pried. I just had my feelings about Maybelle. Something wasn't right, and I was dying to know if my concerns were valid.

"It was fucking awesome!" he started with a large grin. "The way she makes me feel alive from head to toe... I even got a woody."

Pate had informed me within the first month of hormones that testosterone increased the clit size, almost producing a small penis. Like any sexual image involving a man, my brain swiftly brushed that image away.

"What happened?" I put the joint out and gently swung, moving my feet gently up and down.

"She went for my pants."

"What'd you do?"

He told me that he immediately stood up, an instinctual reaction that he now regretted, one that he didn't know how to make up for.

"How many girls have a dude jump away from them when she tries to grab his jock? Do you know what that shit does to a girl? Her self-esteem?" Pate contended. "I'm fucked!"

"You actually told her that you didn't want to be touched below the waist?" I gasped.

"Yes."

I put my head in my hands. "Yeah, man, that sounds pretty weird. You can do things below the waist without having intercourse. She probably thinks you have a small dick or some physical disability."

"No, I'm sure that she feels rejected. I hurt her." Pate groaned.

I snorted. "I don't think you're going to hurt that girl."

"What do I do?" Pate's voice was squeaky as if he were about to sob.

"You really like her, don't you?" I asked, putting out the joint.

Suddenly, Pate took out his phone and started scrolling.

"What are you doing?" I asked.

"I want to see if she changed her Facebook status to single," he said with a strong tone of desperation in his voice.

"You're in love with her," I sneered, shaking my head in disapproval.

"So what?" he snapped.

This time, I held up my hand in self-righteousness. "I don't think it's a good idea to get so close when she doesn't know the truth. I'm just trying to look out for you."

Pate rolled his eyes. "You act like I'm a liar or something."

"Isn't it lying?" I demanded.

"Why do I have to announce my genitals to the world? Do you disclose the size of your penis to all your potential dating partners?" Pate argued. He leaned back and pouted.

"It's the world we live in, Pate!" I asserted. "It would be great if no one cared about trans people. But people *do* care. I don't want you to get hurt."

"It's not fair." Pate threw his phone down.

"Did she change it?" I asked.

He didn't answer. I picked up the phone that was still open to Maybelle's Facebook page. The relationship status read "single."

"She's immature, man," I assured him. "She probably jumped the gun and changed her status because she didn't want to look stupid. I'm sure she'll change it back when you talk to her. Girls do that shit all the time."

Pate refused to look at me, and I could hear him sniffling. *Is this what Jody goes through, too?*

"Okay." I placed my arm around him and leaned him into me. "Let's come up with a logical explanation to tell her. You can call her tomorrow and explain. It'll make sense."

"Like what? I already tried explaining that I don't sleep around and want to take it slow. Why isn't that enough? Why is everyone so fucking sex crazy!" Pate whined, rubbing his temples.

"Yeah, but your genitals are off-limits. There's got to be some explanation for that." I rubbed my chin as I brainstormed. "Otherwise, you could still mess around without having full-on sex."

Pate shook his head in agreement. "What can I say?"

"I have no fucking idea!" I took my phone out and entered, "People who can't have sexual intercourse," in the search bar.

"You're googling it?"

"I'm yahoo-ing it," I corrected him. The top results were about women with sexual problems or going through menopause. I scrolled down and found one about sexual problems in men and clicked on it.

"What does it say?" Pate asked, leaning over with curiosity.

I skimmed the website. "It's talking about men who struggle to find sexual partners and are afraid of being labeled losers."

"Well, that's not helpful," Pate said.

I typed, "penis problems that need surgery," in the search engine, but the results were mostly about penis enlargement surgery.

"You can tell her that you recently had penis enlargement surgery?" I suggested.

"That's stretching the truth quite a bit," Pate admitted.

I typed "penis health problems," and the list included penis conditions, including penile cancer and penile skin conditions.

"No!" Pate yelled in horror. "I don't want her to think something gross is wrong with it!"

I threw the phone down in surrender and leaned back. *What can be a reason...?*

"Okay, I got it." I said, slamming my hands back down on my thighs. "Before we moved here, you were dancing, and you fell onto a...a..." —I saw a gardening hoe— "...a gardening hoe!"

"What? That would chop it off!" Pate gasped in horror.

"Okay, not a gardening hoe." I rubbed my chin some more. "What's something that you could fall on?"

We both thought deeply in silence.

"What if a baseball hit me?" Pate suggested

"No one's gonna believe that you or I play sports," I argued.

We pondered some more.

"I got it! You fell on a cactus! It got infected, and you have to avoid sex for a while." I stood up and did a small victory dance.

"But then she's going to imagine my penis all swelled up with pus. That's not attractive!" Pate shook his head in disgust.

"Then you name something!" I sighed.

"I was showing you some dance moves, and you accidently kneed me in the groin," he suggested.

"Yeah, dancing…with me, another dude. That will just prove everyone's assumptions that we're gay." I moaned, running my hand through my hair.

"Okay, we were wrestling around. Guys do that, don't they?" Pate claimed.

"Guys who are accused of being gay do that," I muttered.

Pate groaned.

"Okay, we were wrestling," I agreed. "I kneed you in the groin, and the doctor said that you have to refrain from any sexual activity down there for three months."

"Six months," Pate insisted.

"Okay, six months," I agreed.

Pate rubbed his chin. "So, when did it happen?"

"It's not important," I insisted.

"She'll count down the months. When?" Pate begged like a spoiled child.

"Two months ago," I recommended.

"But I would only have four months left!" Pate whined.

"If the injury was *that* bad, it would take time for you to move around, run and dance. There has to be some time passed," I pointed out to him.

"Okay," he murmured begrudgingly. "Do you think it will work?"

"She'll probably ask you why you didn't just tell her, but yes, I think it can work," I assured him.

"I can tell her that I'm embarrassed. What guy wants to admit to injuring his penis?" Pate grinned at his own plan. "What if she asks me a lot of details like what the doctor said?"

"Tell her that it's embarrassing to talk about," I replied. "Plus, I don't think she'll ask much about it. She's a little young and naïve."

Pate smiled. "Thanks. I think it may work. I'll call her tomorrow."

"What do you think might work for me with Jody?" I asked him.

"Just being yourself," Pate said as he patted me on the back.

Chapter Nine

Pate

I must have stared at my phone for hours, using any excuse to avoid dialing Maybelle's number. Calling people these days seemed so obsolete, but sending a text was out of the question. Who knew who might see it?

At around two p.m., I decided to put myself out of my genital-insecure misery and just call her. She picked up quickly.

"I wanted to explain last night," I told her as I felt the shakes emerging in my hands and the tension building in my temples.

"Why didn't you explain last night?" Maybelle snapped. "You just drove me home in silence. How do you think that made me feel?"

Fuck. Last night, I was sitting beside her in the car, terrified to speak while she was sitting there, feeling that I was just another asshole to her. *Ugh, social anxiety definitely sucks your thoughts into this black vacuum, leaving you oblivious to others' feelings.*

"I..." I inhaled a deep breath. "I was embarrassed."

"*You* were embarrassed?" I heard her smirk. "I'm the one who goes to touch you and you flip out and get as far away from me as possible."

"I know. I'm sorry," I pleaded, trying to control the shakiness in my voice. "I had an accident a few months ago."

"Accident?" she asked in a more concerned tone.

"Oakley and I were playing around, like rough-housing, and he accidently kneed me in the groin," I told her, holding my breath as I hoped that it sounded reasonable.

"So, because you got hit in the balls, you can't have sex? Like ever?" she asked, surprised.

I sighed. "It was a bad injury, and the doctor said that I should refrain from any sexual activity for at least six months to let it fully heal." *Please let her believe it.*

"You broke your dick? Is that possible?" I could sense the bewilderment in her voice.

"No, not exactly. I mean, it is possible, but I didn't break it." I was trying to avoid confirmation of statements that included "penis" or "dick." If I just navigated this conversation carefully, she couldn't accuse me later of lying to her.

"When you went to touch me," I continued, "it freaked me out. No one's touched me since it happened, and it was a painful injury, so it startled me."

After a pause, she asked, "That's why you want to wait?"

"Yes," I confirmed. My throat was so dry, and I wanted to vomit. But her tone seemed to have changed, giving me hope.

"Why didn't you just tell me?" she asked, as if telling her was the most obvious choice.

"Because what dude wants to talk about something like that?" I informed her. I didn't need to pretend to be embarrassed. This whole predicament was embarrassing. "I would appreciate it if you didn't tell anyone, either."

Maybelle giggled. "I don't foresee it arising in any immediate conversations."

"I'm really sorry that I hurt you." I grew serious, still unsure if she would take me back. "I didn't mean to make you think it was you. I'm a little insecure, I guess. Can we work it out?"

"It's a little strange for me," she admitted.

"I understand." I sighed deeply.

"How long can't we do anything, Pate?"

"About another four months. Just below the waist stuff. Below my waist, anyway." *Shit, should I say that?*

"Who says it's easy to get below my waist?" she teased.

"I just want to work this out, Maybelle," I told her. "Please don't hold this against me." I felt like I was groveling, and that I sounded too desperate.

"You're probably the weirdest dude I've met. Dancing and broken dicks." She laughed.

"You're the most beautiful girl that I've dated," I replied.

"Really?" she asked. "You really think so?"

"Are you still my girlfriend?" I closed my eyes when I asked even though I knew she couldn't see me. It just felt safer.

She sighed before giving a little chuckle. "Okay."

A huge weight melted off my shoulders. However, reality also kicked in—I would have to tell or show her who I was. The real question was how long would I put that off?

* * * *

Going to writing class the next week, I hadn't even thought about any assignments, nor had I opened any books. I was too distracted by this potential romance that I longed for more than my own manhood. Stormy sat down beside me.

"I don't know what I'm going to do," he said, obviously frustrated.

"What's wrong?" I asked him, doodling on my notebook.

"I don't know how to write a paper, and we've got one due this week." He groaned, holding the syllabus in his hand but not really reading it.

"Did you take writing in high school? It's not that different," I tried to console him.

"Yeah, and I made decent grades, but I've been avoiding classes like this. I'm a hands-on guy. I don't do this academic stuff." He twirled the small writing book around in his hands as he referred to "academic stuff." I couldn't help but notice the inch of dirt on his boots. No, I couldn't envision Stormy working at a desk in an office.

"Do you want some help?" I offered.

"I don't know." Stormy rested his head in his right hand, staring blankly at his writing book.

"I'm pretty good at writing," I told him.

"Have you started this paper?" He held up the assignment sheet.

"No, but papers are easy for me." I shrugged.

Stormy sat quiet for a few minutes. "I don't know. I feel stupid." He groaned again.

"I feel stupid in biology class," I admitted. "I don't know jack about these labs we have to do. I never liked science."

He laughed. "Me, too!"

"Let me know. I've got to work on it, too, so we can work on it together," I suggested. For some reason, his hardened exterior didn't intimidate me. Stormy was like a teddy bear in an enormous body.

"Okay," he agreed. "Do you have anything after this class?"

"No. Do you want to go to the library and work?" I asked, pointing toward the direction of the library with my finger.

"Yeah," he replied.

Stormy and I found a study room area where we could use our laptops and had adequate table space for our other materials. The paper topic was to write an informative essay with at least four sources. The professor said he was starting us off small, and the assignments would slowly increase in rigor.

"It's an informative paper, so choose a topic that you already know well, but also, choose something that is easy," I recommended as we were arranging our computers and books.

"I need to choose something that I can write about fast?" Stormy asked, taking out a soda from his bag.

"You don't want to make the assignment take longer than it should," I told him. "You need to get it done and get it in. So, what's something that you know a lot about?"

Stormy tugged on his beanie while he thought about it. "What's your hair look like?" I asked.

He looked puzzled, but he took the beanie off, revealing a thick but short mane of brown hair. "Why you wanna know?" he asked as he put his beanie back on.

Guys don't ask other guys what their hair looks like. I'm a weirdo!

"Just curious. I like hair." *I like hair? What a spaz!*

"I know a lot about engine repair?" Stormy suggested.

"Okay. Can you research that topic?" I asked, pointing at my computer.

We both browsed the internet together searching for academic-worthy sources, but we didn't find any fancy articles about engine repair.

"What about engine design or engineering?" We searched that topic, and we instantly got an article on diesel engine engineering design.

"Yes! I like this one!" Stormy exclaimed. He hit the button to print out the article.

"You have to read it, too," I informed him since he seemed so ecstatic from just locating an article.

"That's okay. I love diesel!" He grinned. "Just because I don't like academic stuff doesn't mean I don't read. I read diesel and mechanic magazines and websites all the time!"

I smiled. "Not my taste, but good for you." His excitement over engines fascinated me, but then again, other people found my passion for dancing odd.

"What are you going to write on?" he inquired after collecting the article from the local printer.

My mind went blank and I shrugged my shoulders.

"What's something that you know a lot about? We found my articles really easy." His newfound excitement over research was quite amusing.

"Dance," I answered automatically.

"*Dance*?" He looked as if I spoke in another language. "Like what?"

"Any dance. But I don't think writing a paper describing dance is very interesting," I conceded.

"You said to make it easy, not interesting," he corrected me. "Why do you dance?"

"It makes me feel good. I always feel best when I'm in motion," I told him, gesticulating with my arms as I said "motion." Even when I spoke, I always liked moving.

"In motion. Like, hands-on, like me?" He smiled.

"Sure."

Stormy typed "dance" into the search engine. "Looks like we got dance therapy?"

Was my dancing therapeutic? Yes. But I was too afraid that even a small research paper on anything related to therapy would conjure up too many issues in me. "How about dance as exercise?" I suggested instead.

"Yes, it looks like we have articles there. You want me to print these for you?" he offered.

"I thought I was helping you!" I teased. "You don't seem so clueless about this stuff."

"Maybe I'm not, but I feel better doing it with someone else. Plus, you make it sound easy," he admitted, winking at me.

Stormy chatted about his long history of ranching, car mechanics and hunting. His father had worked many years at a GM factory in Kansas City until the plant shut down. They had moved to Montana where his grandparents owed a ranch, and his father had opened a repair shop in Bozeman.

"I love Montana. I love it! I was born to be here," he stated with awe. "I loved visiting my grandparents and staying with them all summer. I don't feel normal if I'm indoors or in cities. I need space, fresh air, animals, tractors…"

"So, you're saying you don't dance," I joked.

"No." He snorted. "I don't dance. You wouldn't want to see me dance! But maybe like you, I prefer being able to move versus being glued to a desk."

I smiled, listening to him talk about the love of movement. "How'd you end up here? Why not go to school in Bozeman?" I asked him.

Stormy leaned back and took a long sip of his soda. "It's more rural here. I have some friends here that I share an apartment with. They're from Bozeman, too. We grew up ranching together at my grandparents. We mostly go hiking and hunting. I go to the gun range sometimes. Oh, and the Badlands. Have you been there?" His eyes widened in excitement.

"What's that?" I asked him.

"It's really dry land where you can find fossils and other stuff. I think they found most of the good stuff, but it's still cool to walk around over there—when the weather's good. It feels really…historic. Like you are stepping on something ancient. Do you want to go sometime? You're new here. I can show you." The eagerness burning in his gaze took me aback.

Another outdoor excursion. What's up with people always wanting to go outside with the bugs and lack of bathrooms?

I didn't want to be rude, and he seemed elated, so I agreed.

"Are you free this weekend? It'd be good to go now. When the weather changes, it sucks," he informed me, checking the weather forecast on his phone.

"I'm not sure what my plans are yet." I certainly didn't want to lose a date with Maybelle to rummage around some desert with this six-foot diesel dude in a vest.

"What's your phone number? I'll message you, and you can let me know," he asked, waiting for me to give him the digits to enter into his phone.

I gave him my number, even though the situation felt weird. I had spent so much of my postsecondary years with just Oakley. *Is this how people make friends? Why does this boot-wearing, diesel-loving, gun-shooting titan want to hang out with me? Is it even safe?* Examining his fitted jeans over his gargantuan, dirt-covered boots as he entered my number into his phone, I could only imagine the reaction I would get if he discovered that I was trans. I was nervous about possibly being alone with him because we seemed so different, and trans people always needed to consider safety with strangers. With his large built and my petite frame, I would be defenseless if he wanted to hurt me.

We got back to work on our papers. I helped him create an outline up to where he just needed to use his own prior knowledge and research to fill in the blanks. He seemed more confident as we left the library.

"Do you mind working together the whole semester?" he asked, lighting a cigarette.

Gross, a smoker. "Um, no, I guess not," I muttered, waving the smoke away with my hand.

"Thanks." He grinned appreciatively. "I don't have a lot of money. Neither do my parents. I can't afford to fail. No one in my family has ever gone to college."

"Okay," I agreed.

"You sure you don't mind?" he checked again, blowing out another huge wave of smoke.

"Not at all," I assured him with a smile.

"Awesome! I'll see you in biology, man!" He galloped across the campus toward the student center.

"Faggot!"

I turned around and didn't see anyone. Suddenly, I got a glimpse of Bullet ducking behind the library building, laughing hysterically.

A few weeks here, and I'm already a weirdo.

* * * *

Oakley

I knew that Jody focused on his schoolwork during the week, but I didn't want to wait until next weekend to contact him. I needed to message him that weekend. My ambivalence tormented me. On the one hand, I wanted to call him and see him again. There was this eagerness burning inside me every time I thought about him, and I could still feel the lingering butterflies in my gut that arose when I was near him. On the other hand, I wasn't sure what I wanted to happen, and I worried about hurting Jody. Watching Pate struggle and worry about his feelings for Maybelle... I didn't want to open the door for Jody only to realize that I couldn't walk through it.

But Jody's image consumed my thoughts. His sweet, light voice and curly red hair with freckles sparkling around his cheeks. He was still pretty. He was also smart and altogether unlike me. *What do I even have to offer?*

It was ten p.m. Saturday night. I smoked a few joints and ingested probably four or five beers. Pate went to sleep early, and I was lonely. In my stoned and buzzed haste, I texted Jody.

Me: *This is Oak. Oakman. What are you doing?*

It sounded so dumb, but I had no idea what else to say.

A few minutes passed, confirming my status as a pathetic, lonely loser. I started rolling another joint to cloud out my failure, and the phone beeped.

Jody: *Hello there.*

I waited, but the phone didn't indicate that he was typing. *You fucking idiot. I messaged him. I am supposed to talk.*

Me: *I was thinking about you. Is it too late to talk?*

I felt relief that he answered, but also nervous. Now that I have him on text, what do I want to say?

Jody: *No, I'm up. What's up?*

Me: *I enjoyed hanging out with you.*

Okay, that's a good way to start. I stared at my phone, impatient. Every second that it took him to respond felt like an eternity.

Jody: *At the club?*

Me: *Yesterday.*

Jody: *On our date?*

Me: *Yes.*

I called it a date! I am actually telling him that I enjoyed our date. Am I really doing this? I knew that something in me wanted to talk to and be near Jody. Yet I still doubted my ability to date a guy and to deal with all the challenges involved. This whole conversation scared me.

Jody: *So, what do you want, Oakman?*

Butterflies twirled all around my stomach again, hitting the sides and trying to escape into my esophagus, making my throat tighten.

Me: *You're really making me say it, aren't you?*

Jody: *Why, say what?*

I still worried that I would lead Jody on then not be able to follow through with it all. I was also nervous that if I shared with him my doubts about dating a guy that he would get discouraged and not want to date me. I didn't want to get rejected.

Me: *I need to ask you an honest question first. Do you really want to go out with a straight guy?*

Jody: *I want to go out with you. I accept the heterosexual lifestyle. I'm not prejudiced.*

I laughed. Jody's wit truly enamored me and definitely drove my attraction to him.

Me: *But what if I find out that I can't do it?*

Being honest sent a shiver of fear through my core. *Please don't get discouraged.* But was it fair to expect someone like Jody to put up with someone like me? Someone who was questioning?

Jody: *I guess you'll never know if you don't try.*

Me: *But what if I hurt your feelings?*

I didn't want to sound like I was talking him out of it, but I knew it was better to keep being upfront with him. After all, it would save me from getting accused of being an asshole if things didn't work out.

Jody: *If I was worried about that, I wouldn't have finished the date with you. Sexuality is a fluid, gray area. I think you just haven't discovered that, yet.*

Me: *What if I'm nervous?*

I was scared but intrigued. I wasn't sure if my curiosity would overpower my fear. At the same time, I really wanted to pursue this. *Am I trying to talk myself out of this? Why do I keep arguing?*

Jody: *I'm nervous, too. It's been a long time since I dated.*

Me: *I don't want to lead you into something that I can't finish.*

Jody: *Do I come across as so fragile?*

Jody was far from fragile. Underneath that petite, elegant physique was a fiery, assertive soul that no one was going to push around. And he had the scorching red hair to match.

Me: *No.*

Me: *Are you okay with being patient with me? I can't do this really fast.*

I was demanding too much. But I also knew that if Jody wasn't patient with me, then this would likely fail. So I needed to be honest.

Jody: *I don't make anyone engage in anything that they don't want to. I'm not a rapist.*

Me: *I know that. I just don't want to hurt your feelings if I struggle with things.*

Jody: *How was the kiss?*

I gulped. At the time, the kiss had terrified me. But afterwards, I couldn't get it out of my mind. Jody's soft lips pressed against mine only conjured fantasies of what his body would feel like squeezed up against mine. But there was still discomfort in admitting that I liked it.

Me: *The kiss felt good. But I don't know if I'm ready for tongue.*

Jody: *Or blowjobs?*

My face flushed, and the butterflies exploded.

Jody: *Sorry, I just had to.*

Me: *No, I'm not ready for that.*

The thought of giving a guy a blowjob stuck in my mind. I could daydream about kissing Jody and grabbing his seductive little butt, but placing his penis inside my mouth... *What if I can't get there?*

Jody: *So?*

Me: *Would you like to go out with me? Again?*

I proceeded even though everything felt uncertain. In a way, the unknown was exciting.

Jody: *Yes, on one condition.*

Me: *Yes?*

Jody: *You take me to dinner. And you treat it like a date, just like you would date a girl. I don't expect the world, but some degree of chivalry that is usually bestowed upon girls you date would be appreciated.*

Chivalry? I didn't know what that meant. I had just kind of fallen into my other relationships. There was none of this courting or romance in any of them. But Jody was different. I had to up my game.

Me: *You want me to bring you flowers or something?*

Jody: *I wouldn't reject flowers! But I expect you to treat it like a date and not two guys hanging out. You asked me on a date, and if you are genuinely going to try this, I expect full effort. Otherwise, Oakman, don't waste my time. We can just be friends.*

Jody was right. I would probably easily just fall into a friend role to avoid my own discomfort going on a date with a guy. *Okay, I need to learn how to be romantic…and how to romance a dude.*

Me: *I'll try.*

Jody: *You will. I don't want to be played around with by some bicurious guy. I respect people exploring their sexuality, but I am not someone's experiment. If you want to be friends, we can just be friends. Just choose now. Do you just want to be friends?*

Me: *No. I'll do my best.*

Jody: *And if your best isn't good enough, I'm gone.*

Reading that text, my heart sunk. I didn't know how much Jody would tolerate before giving up on me.

Me: *Do you think I'm bisexual?*

Jody: *I think you are whatever your heart tells you. Only you can listen to your own heart.*

We agreed that I would pick him up on Saturday and take him to The Spare Tire, one of the only restaurants in town, but it was nationally famous for its cuisine. Relief flooded through me when we finally stopped texting at midnight. Then I realized—I didn't know how to date a guy.

* * * *

The next morning, I decided to pick Pate's brain at breakfast. He had made strawberry cornmeal pancakes with homemade strawberry syrup. Granny was feeling well enough to join us, so we took our plates and sat outside on the back porch to enjoy the warm, clear morning.

Pate had a long history of dating guys, so he had to possess some wisdom about how to woo a dude.

"Why you want to know about dating a man?" Granny asked as she sugared her coffee. I didn't have the heart to lie to Granny.

"I'm dating one," I told her, shoving a mouthful of pancake into my mouth to avoid saying more.

"He's *trying* to date one," Pate corrected me.

"I'm going on dates with him, so doesn't that make us dating?" I snapped in annoyance. "So, what do I do?"

Pate and Granny looked at each other, waiting to see who wanted to tackle the question first.

"I'll take a shot," Pate started. "Honestly, I never treated dating a man much different than dating a girl. It's more about how addicted you are to gender roles. I always held doors open for guys, bought them flowers and gifts—I don't care. Romance is romance. Plus, I don't think Jody is your stereotypical masculine dude who would be averse to those things."

"I guess you mostly dated feminine guys, too, so that makes sense. But are there differences between dating men and women?" I inquired.

Pate thought hard while he savored his pancakes and coffee. "I think it's as different as you want to make it. It's more about the person, not the gender. What do you think Jody wants? What makes him happy?"

"Probably just love. Respect. Acceptance," I responded.

"I think so, too. So why make it a gender thing?" Pate asked. "Just think about the way people want to be treated, and once you get to know him more, you can do things for him that you know will make him happy based on what he likes."

"Girly man or not," Granny interrupted, "men love to eat." Granny waved her fork with a mouthful of syrup-soaked pancake on it. "Bring him here for some soul food, and he'll never leave. They always say the way to a man's heart—"

"Is through his stomach," Pate and I both agreed simultaneously.

"Yes! Also, wash his clothes," Granny continued.

"Wash his clothes?" Pate and I both asked, looking up from our food in bewilderment.

"Men love being taken care of. Feed him and wash his clothes. Oh, and iron his underwear. They like that." Granny smiled, satisfied with the wisdom she was bestowing on us.

"Granny, do you iron our underwear?" I cringed.

"I sure do! Isn't it nice?" She chuckled.

Not worrying about my laundry was definitely a perk with living with Granny. Both Pate and I tried to insist that she not trouble herself with that extra workload, but Granny had ignored us and continued doing it anyway. However, it wasn't until now that I realized that even my boxer briefs were nurtured with love.

"Are you suggesting that I invite Jody over to feed him soul food and offer to wash and iron his underwear?" I asked.

Granny and Pate snickered.

"I need help. What am I supposed to do?" I pleaded.

"Cooking him a meal isn't a bad idea. It's pretty romantic. Maybelle seemed to really like it," Pate suggested after hearing the seriousness in my tone.

"He wants me to take him to the The Spare Tire," I informed them.

"What else did he say?" Pate asked.

"That he wants it to be a date. He emphasized that a lot," I told him.

"It sounds to me that he expects everything you just listed. Love, respect and acceptance," Pate asserted. "He expects you to pursue him just like a girl, which would entail not acting ashamed or embarrassed with him. I think I get it. If you are with him, you act like you are *with* him."

"What does that mean?" I asked. "He'll expect me to hold his hand? In public?"

"Maybe. Would you hold hands with a girl?" Pate asked, holding his palm up as he made his point.

"Yes," I admitted, nodding.

"Well then," Pate stated, returning his attention to his pancakes.

"I don't know if I can do *that*." I groaned, averting my eyes to avoid Pate's potential judgment.

"What's stopping you?" Pate asked.

"I...I don't know what other people will think...or do," I shared. It was true. I had never dealt with discrimination or prejudice. After all, I was a straight—relatively speaking—white male. I had it easy. So I wasn't sure that I wanted this new complexity in my life.

"Then what do you think love, respect and acceptance mean?" Pate pried, leaning back and crossing his arms. "It's not just accepting him. It's accepting you and him together. He wants you to validate the relationship. Doing that publicly is a clear statement to make there."

"Relationship?" I gulped. "I don't think we've gotten that far."

Pate leaned forward, placing his elbows on the table. "You went that far when you asked him out again. Besides, what's the point if you aren't going to legitimately give it a try? Do you not want to see if it becomes a relationship? You're not just fooling around, are you?"

"You're right, but...it's a public place," I pointed out to him. "I'm new to this. Like why does everything have to cater toward him—or you? You guys know what it's like to be gay, trans, whatever. You didn't get used to it overnight. You had years to get comfortable with who you are. So why am I expected to just change like that?"

Pate's face grew serious. "Because you're choosing to ignite someone's feelings. It isn't a sexual experiment to Jody. It's real. Besides, if you don't give it one hundred percent, you'll never know if it will work or not. Are you being asked to change? Is anyone forcing you? Because if you think you are being forced to *change* your sexuality or change who you are, I don't think you should go any further."

"I don't understand," I replied.

Pate finished his coffee in a big gulp. "Sexuality grows. It doesn't *change* by force. If it did, don't you think that all gay people would just change their sexuality to heterosexuality to avoid all the shit they put up with? But we can always learn more about our sexuality that we may not currently be aware of if we expose ourselves to new experiences. So, it isn't *changing* you. You're learning about yourself. If you clicked with Jody, it's because there was already something inside of you that is attracted to either men or perhaps just Jody. You may not be *gay*, but you're not one-hundred-percent *not* gay. It isn't either/or. There's a huge gray area there."

"I just never thought of myself as a little gay," I admitted with a shrug.

"But you met a person who exposed that part of you to yourself. And you keep saying that you want your life to change. You're searching for something different. Well, maybe this is a side of you that needs to be released," Pate argued.

"Well, this is different!" Granny interjected. "My boy, follow your heart. If your heart tells you that you care for this boy, if this boy makes you happy, that's all that matters. Trust me, I know more than *anybody* right now that life is too short."

"I'm..." I mumbled.

"It's scary," Pate said. "I know. Trust me, Oak, I know."

I didn't want to use that word, but Pate was right. It *was* scary. I was worried about what other people would say or do. I wasn't the most confident guy anyway, and then to add this on top of the pathetic mess that was me was overwhelming.

Pate must have sensed my anxiety. He put his hand on top of mine. "It's okay if you feel scared. It's been scary for me, too. But you can get past it. Things might be good. *Really good.*"

"You can do it," Granny concurred, giving me a side hug from her seat. "I may worry about you—both of you. But never let fear hold you back. Be true to yourself. Again, I know that now more than anyone. *You* make it okay. You show other people you're okay with it. Then other people don't have any power over you, my boys."

We finished breakfast, and Pate and I collected the dishes. As we were walking back inside, Granny hollered, "By the way, son, I thought you said you *weren't* gay." Her chuckle echoed in my ears as we left the patio.

Chapter Ten

Pate

Maybelle already had plans with her parents on Friday. They were driving out to Missoula for a weekend of hiking and camping before the school year got too hectic and, of course, before Montana blistered the earth with rivers of white snow. We had hung out casually during the week, eating lunch together and hanging out between classes when I didn't have to work. We talked on the phone each night, but Maybelle wasn't much of a talker. Her surroundings easily distracted her. Holding a conversation on the phone proved futile. But I still liked feeling her presence through the phone, even if we didn't talk. However, there was still a lot about her that I didn't know, which made me nervous.

On the other hand, I had no interest in rummaging around some hilly wasteland with Stormy. He hadn't said anything else about it during class, so when the professor dismissed us, I flew to the bathroom in hopes of dodging him. Much to my surprise, he was waiting for me outside.

"Hey, man." He grinned, slapping me on the back. "Did you want to track over to the Badlands? It's a good day for it. The sky is clear. It makes it easier to see things. Plus, it rained hard a few days ago, so maybe it loosened things up."

"Are you a paleontologist or something?" I asked.

"No. I'm just outdoorsy. Come on, I'll bring beer." The giant dude was already walking away from me but waving his lanky arm behind him to entice me to follow. In reality, I didn't have anything else more exciting to do. Oakley was working the evening shift.

"Do you have a car?" I asked as we went outside, and he immediately lit a cigarette. "I don't have one. Oakley has the car tonight."

"I've got something better than a car." He gave a big grin and pranced over to the parking lot. With me following a few steps behind, we walked toward the far corner. I noticed a large, beat-up, ancient and ugly-as-hell Chevy truck with a full inch of dirt caked over it.

"Look at that nasty thing!" I shouted, pointing at it.

"That's my ride," Stormy declared proudly.

"Oh…" I flushed.

"I guess you city boys ride in those fancy sports cars, right? Tiny cars you can't fit anything into, but they look good and go vroom, vroom!" Stormy snickered.

"Why do you say I'm a city boy? I grew up in the suburbs," I corrected him. The suburbs in Georgia were not equivalent to growing up within city limits. I had always felt like I had a small-town mindset.

"The suburbs *are* the city," he argued with a laugh. "Remember, you're in rural America now."

We got into the truck. I squeezed my elbows tight into my torso to avoid all the dirt that had leaked in from outside in addition to the bags and papers all over the floor. This was the messiest dude I'd ever seen. Stormy glanced down at my arms. *Damn! Don't act prissy. Don't act prissy. Act like a man.* I relaxed my elbows, placing one on the door frames, and I spread my legs wider. *Yes, men take up space.*

"Don't you stay on a ranch?" Stormy asked as we took off.

"Yeah, right now," I told him, holding onto the arm rest tightly as he turned sharply. "I don't know if we'll stay there or get our own place at some point. Oakley is helping his grandmother. He takes her to chemo every other Tuesday. She's a little weak afterwards, so we help out and cook and clean."

"Who does the ranch work?" he asked.

"She doesn't have many cows. Oakley's uncle comes by to tend to that part. Oakley helps with a few daily things with them," I informed him.

Stormy giggled.

"What?" I asked.

"With two young, in-shape dudes, your grandma has to have her son come over to help?" he asked sarcastically.

Uncomfortable, I stared down.

"Sorry, I didn't mean anything by it," he apologized. "I'm just so used to jumping in here and jumping in there. I've never been one to let others do things for me. So, Pate, what do you do?"

"I don't think you'd be interested," I dismissed him, shaking my head.

"Try me," he offered.

"I'm a dancer, mostly," I said.

"Yeah, you mentioned that. Is it something that you do all the time?"

I shrugged. "I dance every night. And every Saturday and Sunday morning. And any time I feel like it. It's like breathing. It's just something I have to do."

"I guess I thought it was just some random hobby," he commented, tilting his head toward me as he also watched the road. "Do you dance in shows or something?"

I sighed. "I did in high school."

"Isn't there a talent show or something coming up? I saw a flier. You should do something in it," he suggested.

I sighed again. "I don't know about *that*."

"What else do you do for fun?" he asked.

As I tried to think of a response, it dawned on me that I was just a big, boring loser. Aside from dancing and taking a three-mile run, I didn't do anything. I wasn't behind on my schoolwork, yet, but I hadn't done much, either. I was still hoping that Oakley would change his mind about the college thing, even though I enjoyed seeing Maybelle all the time. Other than that, I smoked weed and sat around pondering what to do with my life but not finding any answers. Now with Maybelle, I mostly sat around thinking about her.

"I've got a girlfriend," I said after a few moments passed. It was all I had.

"Yeah. That Maybelle girl, right?" Stormy remarked with a nod. "Do you know about her?"

We hit a gravel road heading to the Badlands, and the vibrations triggered my anxiety as I tried to carry on the conversation. Stormy tilted his head at me when I didn't answer.

"I don't want to discourage you," he continued, "but…she kind of hangs out with bad people."

"Like Bullet?" I asked.

"Yes, he's bad enough," Stormy concurred.

"How do you guys know each other? You and Bullet."

Stormy pulled the car over to the side in front of a public area of the Badlands. There were no other cars, and the houses were few and far between. The Badlands were composed of sandy white dunes. I could see cattle silhouettes on top of some hills in the distance.

Stormy rolled down his window and lit another cigarette. "I've met him around here and there over the years. Seen him at a few rodeos. Even did some branding with him before."

"Are you friends?" I asked, even though I sensed from their interaction in class that there was hostility there.

"Do I *act* like I'm his friend?" Stormy asked with wide eyes. "Hell no! Let me tell you about Bullet. My little sister Pammy was fifteen when I took her to a rodeo with my dad. It was her first time, and she was helping out. My dad likes to ride bulls. He was pretty good when he was younger. He won some competitions. Anyway, Bullet was there, just drinking and hanging around. I think he came along with people to help, but I never saw him helping. It's a shame, too. With his build, he could be a lot of use. But at the end of the day, he's useless, you know what I mean?"

"I'm sure you're a big help with your build," I commented, eyeballing his biceps as they rested on the steering wheel. He noticed, and I immediately switched my gaze to examining the Badlands around us.

Stormy shot me a huge grin. "So, I was busy with my dad, and Pammy went off. I think she was going to get some snacks, but she didn't come back. We were too busy to chase after her, so it was probably a few hours later that my dad sent me to find her. I walked all over the grounds but couldn't find her anywhere. Finally, I go to the parking lot, and I come along Bullet's truck. From the corner of my eye, I see a flash of pink. She was wearing a pink ball cap. So, I crept up closer and peered in. There's my sister, my fifteen-year-old sister, sucking his dick!"

I gasped. "How old was he?"

"Oh, he was already eighteen," he told me. "I yanked open that door and pulled my sister so hard by her arm that it left a bruise there. Bullet was all angry, yelling and threatening to kick my ass. But hell, look at me! Not many folks in this town can stand up against that Goliath, but I can!"

"Did you guys fight?" I asked, turning my body to face him with intrigue. It would make quite a scene to see those two big guys in a brawl. A real clash of the titans!

Stormy snickered. "He got all in my face, threatening to beat me down, so I finally just punched him. It wasn't even a hard punch. It wasn't the fullest force I could use, but it was enough to leave a black eye. He had some explaining to do with people!"

"Was this when he was with Maybelle?" I asked.

"Pretty sure," he replied, throwing out his cigarette butt.

"Did she know?" I asked. Certainly, Maybelle wouldn't tolerate this kind of treatment.

"I would only guess, but it's not like I talk to her. She's got issues, too." He looked over at me. "Oh, but I probably shouldn't be telling you all this."

"It's cool. I want to know," I assured him.

"I can't confirm," he reluctantly continued, "but a lot of people say she's been known to suck a lot of dick, too. Even when she was with Bullet. In fact, I think she did it just to make him mad. She seems to really like that tough guy stuff. You know, making the guy all jealous and worked up where he fights another dude for her."

"She likes making him jealous?" I thought back to our first date at the camping site. I had wondered why he was there.

"I think so." Stormy nodded. "Look, I'm not trying to ruin your relationship. It's been a while since those two have officially dated. So, who knows, right? I would just be careful if I were you. That group brings lots of drama with them."

We ventured into the Badlands. The ground was mushy and sank a little when we stepped on it. The white hills were covered with large cracks. It looked like land that used to be ocean floor. Stormy led the way and would randomly pick up items that he thought could be bones or fossils only to discard them when he realized they were merely rock. He chatted about the dinosaurs that had been around the area and other fossil-rich lands around Montana. I just listened and nodded. We walked around for about an hour until he found a grassy spot to sit down and again, smoke.

"This probably doesn't interest you much," he commented "Sorry, I thought with you being new and all that you may like to see what's around."

"It's cool," I assured him. "I just don't know anything about this stuff to contribute much to the conversation. But it's nice out here. It's peaceful."

"I love it out here. I could sit out here for hours." Stormy grinned, spreading his arms and inhaling a deep breath of fresh air.

"And smoke," I teased.

He giggled, winking at me.

"Granny's ranch is pretty nice," I told him. "If you want a break from your house and want to hang out in the country, you're welcome."

"I would love that actually!" He nearly squealed in excitement. "I sure do miss nature. And good ranches. Sometimes it feels like my soul only comes alive when I am in nature. It's like you. Nature moves like a dance. You never know how it will turn or lead you. In my heart and my brain, I dance along with it."

"That's pretty philosophical of you. I wish I felt the same about it. But I don't know if I belong here," I mumbled.

"You do. You *definitely* do," he promised me. "You and Oakley are a breath of fresh air around here. I kind of need some new people in my life. So many around here are all the same. It's hard to just let loose with folks here. Too much drama. Too much gossip."

"Says the most trucky, ranchy dude in school!" I laughed.

"I'm *that* ranchy?" He chuckled back.

"It's cool. You're cool for a country dude," I said as I slapped him on the shoulder.

Stormy stood, brushing his pants off. He stretched his back and waved his arms about before resting his hands on his hips. "I haven't had many outside experiences myself. Outside this kind of life anyway.

You and Oakley seem so much more experienced with the world."

"Us!" I covered my head in my hands. "We haven't experienced shit. In fact, we're here because Granny knew that Oakley wasn't doing anything with his life. Neither was I, so he asked me to come with him. We're just a bunch of nobodies."

"But you have all these tattoos and piercings." He pointed to my arms and gauges.

"Yeah. Poke yourself with a bunch of needles! That's living!" I joked. "I'm just a loser. Aside from Oakley, Maybelle's the only other person that I've ever seriously dated —" My stomach sank into a hard, heavy rock as I realized the words escaped my mouth. *Fuck! I'm not used to talking to other people aside from Oakley. Other people who don't know.*

Stormy turned to face me and walked a little closer. "You dated? Each other?"

Damn, damn, damn! Leave it up to the stupid trans, bisexual person to out himself. I inhaled a gulp of fresh air and looked Stormy dead in the eyes. "Yes." My shoulders cringed up as I waited for him to yell, to cuss, to punch me or to just run away from me to his truck, abandoning me in the middle of the Badlands.

"What's that like?" he asked. His hazel eyes sparkled in the late evening sun with what appeared to be intrigue.

Wait, huh? I had already mentally prepared myself for name-calling or even a physical assault. Now this dude wanted to talk about it?

"It was good," was all that I could get out.

"But you date girls, too?" he clarified.

"Yes."

Stormy stared blankly with a confused crinkle appearing on his forehead. "So…did you used to be gay or something?"

"We don't have to talk about this." I started walking back to the truck to run away from my own mortification. Stormy jogged to catch up to me.

"It's fine, man," he claimed. "I just never met anyone gay — bisexual. I'm curious."

"I'm bisexual, and can you please, please not tell anyone? Please, Stormy." Tears were welling up in the corners of my eyes. I brushed them away with my sleeve, quickly turning my head so that he didn't see.

"I'm not going to tell anyone. I'm not a homophobe," he comforted me after catching up with my stride. "I think it's very…interesting. It's pretty cool actually."

Oh my God, I'm like the new small-town entertainment for the town!

Stormy gently grabbed my shoulder to stop me from walking, causing me to flinch. He immediately removed it.

"Sorry," he said. "I just want to let you know that it's cool with me. Don't feel embarrassed. I'm sorry if I bothered you with all the questions."

"Your questions don't bother me. I'm not used to questions, that's all," I explained.

"Did you guys have sex — sorry, it's my country coming out. I don't know how not to be blunt." His tone conveyed a caring curiosity.

"Yes, we did. He was my first. I was his first," I informed him.

"*Really?* Both of you had sex with a guy on your first time?" His eyes grew wide. "Is he gay or is he bisexual?"

My initial, automatic response was usually no. But now, I thought about Jody. *If I tell Stormy that Oakley isn't gay, what will he think if he sees Oakley dating Jody? Would he think that I lied?* On the other hand, it wasn't my place to out Oakley. *How did things get so complicated?*

"I don't know," I answered. "I think he's still figuring himself out."

"You don't know?" Stormy asked, confused. "Is he bi…bise…"

"Bisexual," I finished for him.

"Yeah. What does that mean exactly?" he asked.

"It means you date both girls and guys. You could still have a preference for one over the other, but you date both," I told him. "I don't know if he is bisexual. Maybe."

Stormy squinted his eyes in deep thought. "So…you don't know if he's gay, and you don't know if he's bsexual—"

"Bisexual," I corrected him.

"Bisexual. But you guys had sex." I could hear that he was puzzled. "Was it more than once?"

"Yes," I admitted.

"I'm confused, I guess."

"So am I." I laughed nervously.

"Hmm…does Maybelle know about you guys?" he asked.

"No!" I snapped, and desperation consumed me. "Please don't tell her. Don't tell anybody!"

"Course not," he promised, holding up his hands.

"Please don't say anything about Oakley either," I begged him.

"Of course not," he agreed. "I kind of felt that you guys were a little closer than other guys, though."

My eyes widened! *What! I've been giving off gaydar! Is that why Bullet keeps calling us fags?*

"I don't mean that you come off gay," Stormy stated after seeing my expression. "You just seem very close. You're always together."

Stormy's observations only proved to me that my dependency on Oakley was getting a little out of hand. At the same time, so was Oakley's dependence on me.

"Do you guys, ever...you know?" he pried.

"Do we ever what?" I asked.

He cleared his throat. "Do things now?"

"Not really," I answered. "Nothing sexual anyway. It's been years. We cuddle. We're still more affectionate than other guy friends, I suppose."

"Why'd it stop?" he asked.

Because I turned into a dude. "It just did."

Stormy drove me home to the ranch. The sun was just beginning to set, and the waves of various oranges, reds and even purples danced along the big Montana sky.

"Have you fallen in love with these sunsets yet?" Stormy asked.

"Definitely." I smiled. Montana was a beautiful place. The sunrises and sunsets could easily mesmerize me enough to forget about my problems for a little while.

"This is nice," Stormy commented as he pulled up Granny's driveway. "Out here alone. I could definitely hang here. Oh shit! I forgot that I promised you some beer today."

I got out of the truck and leaned over the window. "Maybe next time."

"I'm sorry if I made you uncomfortable with all my questions. Thanks for answering them. I had fun hanging out with you, Pate." He grinned. His smile turned his rugged face into an almost boyish and charming expression.

"Me, too. Maybe you can come by here tomorrow or Sunday. If you want," I offered.

"I got a few jobs this weekend, but I'll hit you up next week for sure. I'll still see you Monday to work on the papers," he told me, still grinning.

"Of course." I nodded.

I watched his ozone-killing truck kick up a cloud of dirt as it drove down the driveway, and it dawned on me that I had just spent the evening with a fossil-loving redneck who now knew I was bisexual. Fear burrowed into my stomach lining. *I can trust him, right? I just met the dude. What am I thinking?* Waiting until Monday was going to be agonizing.

Chapter Eleven

Oakley

I stared at the long mirror hanging from our closet door. I was examining the dark, worn blue jeans with skull patches and holes in the knees and my bare, hairless chest.

"I think they require shirts at The Spare Tire," Pate suggested.

"I know. I'm going to put on a shirt. Are these jeans too risky?"

"No," he replied, shaking his head. "You don't change who you are for girls, so don't change for boys, either. Be you."

I found a white T-shirt and pulled a black button-up shirt over it to dress myself up a little more. Jody was so stylish. I didn't want to embarrass him.

Pate put his book down and sat up on the bed. "I've been dreading this, but I have to tell you something."

"Can't we talk later?" I asked, dismissing him with my hand. "I'm trying to get ready. I'm nervous enough as it is."

"I accidently told Stormy that we dated," he told me, squinting his eyes closed as if he could hide while he said it.

"That who dated?" I was moussing my hair into a small mohawk.

"You and me."

"What!" My mouth dropped in horror.

"He knows we had sex, too." Pate's eyes were still closed.

I hit Pate upside the head with my bundle of socks. "Are you fucking nuts!"

"It just came out. It was an accident. He seemed cool with it." Pate had opened his eyes now but was avoiding eye contact.

"So, he knows you're trans now?" Part of me was relieved that he outed himself as trans so that we could put that worry behind us.

"No," he responded. He laid back down on the bed. "Just that we dated and used to have sex."

"And you thought he needed to know that information?" I stared at him with my eyes wide. I wanted to slap him. "Does he think we're gay now?"

"Well, I didn't know what to tell him, Oakley." He sat up again. "I mean, you're going out with a guy tonight. I didn't want to confuse him."

I walked over to him. "You told him that I'm gay?"

He held up his hand. "Not exactly. I just told him that I didn't know if you were bi or gay or what. And I told him not to tell anyone."

"I'm pretty sure heterosexuals don't just have random sex with dudes," I argued, rolling my eyes.

"Are you saying that you're not a heterosexual?" Pate inquired.

Ignoring the question, I stammered, "Damn it, Pate! What a fuckup!" I punched him in the side.

"I'm sorry!" he yelled, twisting his body away from me. "And maybe I do trust him. He didn't yell or beat me up."

"What'd he do?" I asked.

"He was very curious about it," he told me with a puzzled look. "It was a little weird. He didn't seem grossed out, though."

I sank down into a desk chair to put on my shoes. "Curious?"

Pate shrugged. "He wanted to know what it was like and if we had sex."

"Why the fuck would he want to know *that*?" I asked, throwing my arms up in the air. "You mean he wanted to know the details? Does he have some guy fetish? Is *he* gay?"

"I have no clue. I guess it was different to him. He seems very fascinated by us. It's kind of weird." He leaned back again, and I lay down beside him.

I closed my eyes momentarily to try to picture the six-foot-four cowboy who always wore vests and dirty, rugged boots, displaying naïve curiosity and visualizing Pate and I having sex.

"Is he gay?" I asked again when the image never appeared.

"I don't think so," Pate replied. "I think he would have said so. You meet some other gay or bisexual person, you'd share that you're also gay, right? Plus, he said he had never met any gay or bisexual people. He would have met himself, right?"

"I don't know, Pate." I groaned, rubbing my temples. "It seems fishy. What if he was just baiting you?"

"Baiting me?" Pate raised his eyebrow.

"Yeah. Like to get information out of you about you or me or us so that he can make our lives hell."

Pate snorted. "I think you're dramatizing too much. I'm supposed to be the paranoid freak, remember?"

I gave him a serious glare that quickly ended his smirk. "You don't know people here. They gossip. They make up drama. We could be just some amusement for them."

"That's a little harsh." Pate lay on his side to face me. "I don't think everyone here is bad."

I sighed. "It's true. You've got to be careful in small towns. Everyone knows everybody, and don't forget that you and me are the outsiders. That makes us prime targets. Plus, how many other punk dudes do you see walking around town?"

"Well, if outsiders look down on them the way you do, no wonder." He looked frustrated.

I returned to the mirror, straightening my jeans. "How do I look?"

Pate walked up behind me, placing his hands and head on my shoulders. "Are you sure that you're open-minded enough for this?"

"Give me a break." Annoyed, I shrugged off his hands. "Why are you always giving me a hard time?"

"You just seem too...in your own head. You don't bend easily."

"I'm very open-minded!" I shouted. "Who stays with his trans ex-girlfriend? Get off my back!"

Pate stepped back and peered at me with his arms crossed. "But you didn't stay with your trans ex, did you? In fact, we stopped having sex —"

"I'm not going into all that, Pate!" I shouted, turning around to scold him. "You should be supporting me. I'm pushing myself, aren't I? Fuck, it's like damned if I do, damned if I don't with you."

"Okay, sorry." Pate bellyflopped on his bed, burying his face in his arms. "I just don't want Jody to get hurt."

"What about *my* feelings?" I asked, walking back over to him. "Why does everyone assume that I'm this jerk who's going to purposely leave Jody high and dry? At least let me *try*."

"Okay, okay." He rolled over. "Go try."

* * * *

I drove over to campus to pick Jody up outside his dorm. I had spent the morning cleaning my car so that it was date ready. Jody was already standing outside when I pulled up. His red curls made him easy to spot, and he was wearing skinny girl jeans and a clingy, black V-necked T-shirt with a bright red sequined belt. When he climbed into my car, I noticed that he was wearing light brown eyeliner and eyeshadow with pale lipstick. I immediately flinched.

"What's wrong?" he asked as he pulled the door closed. "You expected me to gussy up for our date, right? Besides, I thought the makeup would make me more a girl for you." He laughed.

"Sometimes I think you just get off on my discomfort," I told him.

"Oh, darling, but it's so easy to make you uncomfortable!" He leaned over to squeeze my chin.

"Have you always been this...forward?" I asked as I started driving to the restaurant.

"No, I wasn't born with innate confidence, my dear," he told me with a smile. "I just learned my plight early, and I had to decide if I was going to let myself be silenced and invisible for the sake of others or if I was going to fight for my right to live my life openly just like anyone else. I chose the latter. Besides, whether I was open or hidden, I still got bullied and beat up, so why not just be me?"

"It's a little intimidating," I stated.

"Most confident people are. Not many people know what to do with us." He winked at me.

We got to the restaurant, and I turned the car off. My hands rested on the wheel.

"What's the deal?" Jody inquired.

"I don't know what you expect me to do," I mumbled anxiously.

"Huh?"

"Am I supposed to open your car door? Hold your hand when we walk in?" I turned to him. "I don't want to do something rude."

Jody giggled. "What did I make you promise before you took me out, Oak?"

"That I'd treat this like a date. So that's what I'm trying to do."

"Have you never been on a date?" Jody asked sarcastically.

"Well, yeah." I snorted.

He held up his palm. "Then do whatever you normally do on a date. Stop pretending like it's different just because I'm a guy."

"I'm just afraid to disappoint you."

Jody beamed. "Okay, Mr. Gentleman. Yes, it would be lovely if you would open the door for me. In terms of hand holding, I think we can see how the date goes first. Usually, physical contact comes after people feel some chemistry."

"You don't feel chemistry?" I asked, surprised and worried.

Jody grinned bigger, taking my hand. "I wouldn't be here if I didn't."

I walked around the car and opened his door. I also opened the door for him at the restaurant entrance and proceeded to pull his chair out for him, too. *What am I doing? I'm never this nice to girls.*

The waitress came over with some waters and asked for our drink order.

"Well, it's definitely a night for drinking!" Jody teased. "I think I'll let my date order for us, though."

The sides of my face felt like a ton of tiny ants were crawling and biting my cheeks. I saw the waitress turn to me from my peripheral vision, but my eyes stayed glued to the drink menu. *Maybe she didn't hear that part. Maybe it didn't register.*

The waitress's pen tapping on her small black pad forced me to respond.

"So what will it be for you and your date, sir?"

Fuck! Jody looked down, but I could see a huge grin on his face and hear his smirking.

"Um, I'll have this Moose Drool beer. Get him a glass of this white wine."

"I'm a red wine gal!" Jody interrupted.

"This house cabernet is fine." I pointed to it on the menu.

"Bottle or glass?" the waitress asked.

"What do you think, dear?" Jody inquired. "Do you think the date will last long enough to consume a whole bottle?"

My teeth clenched together so firmly that I thought I was going to break a tooth. "How about a bottle. You can cancel the beer. I'll have the wine, too."

The waitress walked off, and my eyes danced all over the room to avoid Jody's gaze.

"What are you thinking?" Jody grilled.

"What was the reason for that? She didn't need to know that."

Jody searched me with his eyes. "If you're going to date a man, you need to get used to being with a man. I don't live my life stealth, Oak. Would it have been different if I was a woman?"

"Do we have to tell the whole world *now*? Give me some time. This is all so new for me. I don't even know if I can do…" I stopped myself.

He grew serious. "Do what? Date a man? I thought we already went over this."

"I'm sorry," I apologized. "Forget it. It's fine. You're my date."

"Why did you want to go out with me, Oakman?"

"I'm not sure."

"Well, that's flattering!" He chuckled sarcastically.

I'm a dating idiot! "No, that's not what I meant. What do you want to know?" I sat up and forced myself to make eye contact with him. Yet every time I looked into those green eyes, my stomach became all jittery.

"Do you like me?" Jody asked.

I nodded. "Yes. You seem cool."

"Do you like me in *that* way?"

"I don't think I'd be here if I didn't."

The wine came, and we waited patiently as the waitress opened the bottle and poured two glasses. Jody ordered a chicken burger, and I ordered some wings. When the waitress left, Jody leaned forward intently.

"Okay, Oak. You have got to learn to speak directly with me. Stop with all this *I wouldn't this* or *I don't know that*. Just tell me. Why do you like me in that way?"

I leaned back and thought. It felt so unnatural to speak about a man the same as a woman. Or maybe it was a battle between two voices inside me. One said that I had never felt such a strong inclination toward another person, and another said, "Yuck, run away!"

The situation reminded me of the last time Pate had tried to be sexual with me. When Pate had started hormones, the process was slower than I had expected. I had assumed that within a week, he'd have facial hair, a man's voice and a large jaw. But he had stayed very soft and feminine with only a slight change in his voice. So, we had continued to have sex here and there. It was only one year after starting hormones that Pate had gotten a mustache and goatee. His smell had changed, too. His body odor had become stronger, like a man, and his skin texture had changed. Then when he had gotten his breasts removed and opted not to have his nipples reattached, I was done. I could bend my imagination enough as long as female body parts were still present and if I could still touch someone who felt like a woman. But when Pate had sat on top of me with a flat, scarred chest, manly body odor and face fuzz, my penis had fallen forever flaccid. We had never tried again.

My eyes met Jody's emerald-green ones that were so incredibly rare and feminine. To me, I was looking at a woman. So much about Jody made me feel like I was with a woman even though he was obviously a man.

"I'm scared to tell you," I responded after a few minutes of silence.

"It's okay. You can tell me. Be honest. The more honest you are, the more this may work." He placed his palm over mine across the table.

I stared down at his hand over mine. I worried about other people seeing it, yet I also didn't want him to remove it. I took a deep breath. "Because I don't see a man when I look at you." I tensed up in fear that I just admitted that I liked his femininity. *He'll probably say that this is proof that I am incapable of dating a man.* I didn't want him to feel that way.

"You see a woman?" Jody asked, confused.

I shook my head. "I don't see that, either. I see a woman, but I see a man, too. In a strange way, it's like you don't have a gender or you're the perfect combination of both genders, and that's what attracts me."

Jody placed his hand over his heart. "That's beautiful, Oak."

"It is?" I asked, shocked.

"Yes," he choked with tears in his eyes. "I often think of myself as someone with two souls. I love being Sadie! I love her! But most of the time, I'm Jody, and I love him, too. I don't want to have to choose. I just want to be. Not many people can handle it. Not even gay men."

Now I couldn't take my eyes off his. The jitters were turning into urges. I wished that I was sitting beside him...maybe even kissing him. "I was scared that you'd be upset if I said that I liked your feminine features."

"No!" He dismissed me with his hand. "Those make me who I am! I've always been girly, or shall I say, I have always embraced the ladylike qualities in me. We are all feminine, my dear. Unfortunately, if you are a man, society teaches you to hate that part. To hide it. To suppress it. I prefer to be a full human."

I smiled, caressing the top of his hand with my finger. "Maybe that's what I'm trying to do. Be a full human."

"How so?"

I sighed nervously. "I'm sorry that I don't have the words. This is all new to me. I haven't had time to process everything. I only know that I was drawn to you at the club. Not just because you were a woman, but your presence. Your spirit. When I saw you as a guy, I thought I'd be repulsed. But I was still drawn to you. However, I was drawn to you in a way that I can't explain right now. What I'm trying to say is that I worry that I may miss something in life if I don't try this with you. Perhaps I'm not used to being fully human or maybe I am impacted a lot by what you said about society. This anti-gay society that molds people, especially men, to fear anything gay. I worry that I may be blocking something inside myself. I guess that's the only way to explain these feelings I am having for you. I don't want some fucked-up society bullshit to make me deny these feelings. I think Pate taught me a lot about that, too."

"What did he teach you?"

Considering that Pate had confessed to telling some Sasquatch about us, giving the impression that I was gay, I figured he couldn't get upset with me about telling Jody, especially given the situation.

"Please don't tell anyone," I whispered, leaning closer to him. "It's not my place to talk about it, but I feel that it's important for you to understand me."

"I won't tell, sweetie."

"Pate's trans."

Jody smiled slightly and nodded.

"You knew, didn't you?" I asked.

"I suspected. Please don't tell him that. I have a few trans friends, and I know how sensitive the issue of passing is. I don't want to make him self-conscious. His girlfriend seems oblivious, though," he replied.

"She is," I concurred.

"Tell me about Pate."

I told Jody about Pate and I dating in high school and losing our virginities together. I told him about Pate coming out to me, and my father and I taking him in when his parents kicked him out. I brought him up to date, leaving out the part about not being able to maintain an erection with Pate anymore.

"I'm telling you this because I was stupid about all this before," I told him. "I didn't know jack shit about being trans or even that girls could be trans, especially someone that I was in love with."

"When did you stop loving him?"

"I never did." I paused. "I don't want you to get the wrong impression of us. But I can't imagine life without Pate, which is why it really scared me when he tried to kill himself. I don't think I could go on by myself. Sure, he's annoyingly shy and super insecure, and he overreacts to everything. But..." —I suppressed the tears boiling up in me—"he's this amazing person inside. He's so much braver than I am."

Jody placed his hand to his heart again and smiled. "You two have a beautiful relationship."

"Yes, we do." I wiped my eyes with my napkin. "But I wasn't romantically in love with him anymore. Not after his surgery."

"It changed when he changed, didn't it?"

My eyes looked down in shame.

"Be honest, Oak." Jody squeezed my hand.

"Yes, it did."

Jody removed his hand from mine and sat back. "So how will it be different with me? You know I have a penis, and I have zero plans to extinguish it."

"Well...I touch my own penis." I was desperately trying to use Pate's rationalizations but felt like a total goofball.

Jody laughed. "I like your attitude! That's a start, I guess!"

Our food arrived, and the subject changed to more benign matters, such as Jody's work in graphic design and my hopes to be a mechanic who restored old cars. He showed me some of his work, which was very good. He also showed me some graphic artwork that he had made and displayed in art shows.

"Nothing big," he said as he held up his phone for me to see the images. "Just things around the school or town, but I just love showing my work! I sell it cheap, too. Probably not the smartest thing, but I just love the thought of my artwork hanging in someone's home or my designs decorating someone's webpage. It's like I'm part of people, and they don't even know it."

We finished our food and our bottle of wine. I felt relaxed and energized. I reached over and held Jody's hand.

"So, I have a question for you," I stated with my newfound alcohol-induced courage. "What do you like about me?"

"Oh, the male ego. You just can't help yourself!" Jody taunted. "What do I like about Oakman? Geez, I guess I must get pass your social awkwardness and the fact that you're convinced you're not gay. I like how much you seemed to enjoy my show. I liked that you sat in the back room and talked to me—like really talked. Real topics, not superficial small talk. When you didn't run away from me or ditch me on our first date, it impressed me."

"Impressed *you*?" I grinned, eager to hear more. "Is it possible to impress you?"

"Most men would have left. Hell, others would have called me a fag or even beat me up because they arranged a date with a man and somehow, it's all my fault. But you didn't. You froze, but you didn't flee. You finished the date. It showed me that you are willing to push your boundaries, and that is the kind of person that I need and want. Someone who is willing to grow."

"It makes me feel really good to hear you say that. I get so tired of all the shit from Pate about how closeminded I am and how anti-gay I am." I playfully placed my foot against his beneath the table.

"You are a little bit," Jody corrected me.

"I am?"

"Just a little bit." Jody grinned as he pinched his thumb and index finger together. "But life is a work in progress. As beautiful beings, we are constantly in creation. That's the best part of life. We can always change and grow. We never have to stop moving. At least you're willing to move."

"You sound like Pate," I acknowledged.

"Oh no! You're chasing after your first love!" he joked.

"No, I'm not." I grew serious, rubbing my foot on his leg. "You're different. He doesn't compare to you."

Jody smiled. "For a non-gay guy, you sure are good at wooing me."

We left the restaurant near closing time, mostly because of pressure from the staff to get the hell out. The night was cool, and considering the parking lot was nearly empty, I wrapped my arm around Jody's shoulder.

"Physical contact. In public! I guess the date did go well," Jody remarked, leaning his body into my side.

My eyes danced around, searching for anyone nearby. The restaurant was right beside the road and cars were driving by. I was nervous that a driver might honk or yell some profanity out of the window, but nothing happened.

I let Jody inside the car and circled back around to my side. It had turned dark, so the car offered a great deal of shelter. I reached over and took Jody's hand.

"Jody?"

"Yes."

I took a deep breath to calm my nerves. "I'm sorry that this is so awkward, but I would like to try to kiss you."

"You either kiss or you don't, honey. There's no try."

I chuckled before resuming my serious tone. "It may be strange for me is what I mean. I don't want you to be offended."

He smiled endearingly. "Oak, you know another thing that I like about you?"

"What?"

"You sure are sensitive about my feelings. I can't say that I've had that before."

Still holding his hand, I leaned over and pressed my lips to his. We held our lips closed but together for a minute before I pulled away slowly.

"How was it?" Jody asked.

"It was a warm-up."

I closed my eyes and let the alcohol guide me. Jody's lips were soft, so it felt more like kissing a girl than a boy. I slightly opened my mouth allowing the tips of our tongues to slightly touch. My hands rested gently on his thighs.

"How was that?" Jody asked.

"It's a little weird, Jody. But it wasn't bad. It wasn't gross."

"Oh thanks! Another one of your wonderful compliments! Kissing me isn't gross!" Jody covered his eyes with his palms.

I leaned forward again, and this time we let our tongues touch a little more, but we never went into a full French kiss.

I drove him back to the dorm, pulled into a parking spot then turned the engine off. Even though we had kissed, I wasn't sure how to end the date. I wanted things to go further, yet I was still scared of what I was feeling for him. I picked at my steering wheel.

"What do you think?" Jody asked, twirling his curls with his pink nail-polished fingers.

"About what?" Inside, I knew what he meant. Why couldn't he just let it be? He was too much like Pate, always demanding an explanation. Always needing to know how I felt. I hated having to verbalize it, especially when I didn't know what any of this was.

"About everything," Jody continued. "The date? The kiss? What do you want to do next?"

"I liked the date. I think I liked the kiss, too." *I think? Why did I say that? I'd liked it very much. In fact, I wanted to do it again. Why do I need to actually say it?*

"You *think*?" Jody asked as if reading my thoughts.

"I've never kissed a guy before," I told him.

"You kissed Pate," he argued.

"Yeah, but that was different. He wasn't a guy then." Or was he? I knew Pate hated it when I referred to it as "when he wasn't a guy" as if he was ever a girl. Yet I had mentally separated the feminine Pate from the masculine Pate.

"Yes, he was. You just didn't know it," Jody stated.

"But that's different," I remarked, poking at my steering wheel.

"Why?"

"Because he didn't *look* like a man," I argued. I felt my stomach drop. *Now Jody's going to think I am not attracted to him. I'm blowing it.*

"You're too literal," Jody commented as he caressed my cheek with his soft hand. "You know how you were saying that it was my spirit on that stage that caught your attention?"

"Yeah."

"It's the same spirit now," he told me with a slight smile. "Bodies are just bodies. Gender is just an expression. It's our spirits that count. It's the spirit that you fall in love with. Besides, have you ever considered that maybe it was Pate that rejected you?"

"Huh?" I turned to him, surprised. "But I told you that we messed around until he became a guy. How could he reject me?"

Jody shrugged. "It didn't sound to me that he was as romantically in love with you as you were with him. It sounds like you used him transitioning as an excuse to finally let your own feelings for him go."

"That doesn't make sense," I disagreed. I ran my fingers through my hair as I tried to conceptualize that concept.

"Yes, it does," Jody continued. "You knew that there was no romantic future there, yet you still had sex with him to hold on to your own dream. Once he transitioned, I think you finally had to accept it. You stopped having sex with him because his physical transformation was a form of him moving on with his life, something that you had failed to do."

I stared straight ahead, dumbfounded. Pate had rejected me? "How do you guys come up with all this deep stuff?"

"It's true, isn't it?"

"You're getting way personal. Plus, you don't know me well enough or Pate well enough to make such a judgment," I said defensively.

Jody moved away from me. "Sorry," he said in a low voice. "I am only trying to help you think about this stuff differently. Perhaps if you realized that it wasn't Pate's masculinity that ended things, you might approach our situation differently."

"I want to see you again, Jody," I whispered after a few silent moments.

"Do you want to kiss me again?"

"Yes, very much," I told him, reaching over and placing my hand on his thigh.

"Yet, you don't know how you feel about it?" he stated more than asked.

"No."

"Fair enough for now." He nodded. "Do you want to walk me to the door?"

"Like high school?" I laughed.

"Sure, I didn't date much in high school. I need to create memories."

I opened his car door again, and we held hands to the door. There weren't any people around.

"So, this is goodnight," Jody whispered, snuggling into my shoulder.

"Did I do a good job? Was it like a date?"

Jody rubbed his hands along my cheeks. "You did good, Oakman."

He leaned in to kiss me, lifting his arms to wrap around my neck, but I gently stopped them from wrapping around me.

"Um, maybe we can wait on the…the…" I stuttered.

"Pressing our manly bodies up against each other? Scared you're going to feel my hard-on?"

I blushed. He leaned forward again, keeping his body at a distance this time. I didn't open my mouth. There were too many noises around, cars in the distance, people in the dorms.

"Give me a call. Oh, and I'm doing another drag show. Do you guys want to come?"

"Yeah. Who do you want to come?" I asked.

"Bring Pate and his girlfriend. Does she know?"

"About us? I don't think so." If Pate hadn't told Maybelle that he was trans, I didn't think he had mentioned that I was dating Jody or that Jody was a man, either. But then again, his big mouth had told Stormy.

"Do you think she's cool?" Jody asked.

"I have no idea. I don't know her. He doesn't really know her either," I admitted.

"I guess if you're cool, she'll be cool, Oak. It all depends on how okay *you* are." He poked me in my chest, teasing.

"I'll invite them." *What am I saying? I'm going to tell other people that I'm dating a guy?*

"Do what you want. But you'll come?"

"I'll definitely be there."

Chapter Twelve

Pate

A few weeks went by, and the weather was already beginning to shift. The summer days in Montana were some of the longest I could imagine, but once September reared its head, the nights emerged quicker and quicker. But I loved it. There was something I had always hated about hot weather. I couldn't hide in hot weather. I had to wear as few clothes as possible to endure the one-hundred-degree, one-hundred-percent-humidity heat in Georgia. Then the long daylight hours left me feeling exposed everywhere I went.

It was my favorite time of year when I stepped outside in September to feel the warm air and sunlight but also a fleeting brush of autumn crispness in the air. I could only sense it if I was actively searching for it. It was enough to fill my whole body with nostalgia of all the memories of autumns and holidays past. It was the signal that I could be hidden again.

"You know, you guys got that big barn," Maybelle was saying one day during lunch. "We should have a Halloween party."

We were having lunch at a little picnic table on campus. It was our usual lunch place, at least until it would get too cold. Even though it had some relieving shade from a nearby tree, it was pretty out in the open, leaving me feeling slightly self-conscious. However, I also got to sit next to Maybelle, holding her hand, kissing her and informing the whole world that she was mine. I felt like a middle-schooler with my first girlfriend again.

"What do you think? Would you guys want to do that?" she asked again, squeezing my arm.

"I think it'd be a blast!" Kelly agreed from across the table. She and her boyfriend Foster usually joined us.

"I don't know," I said hesitantly. "Oakley's grandma is sick, you know? I worry that too many people or too much noise would bother her." The truth was that too many people bothered me. Also, I wasn't keen on having a bunch of people around my dance sanctuary. It all felt too exposing.

"Well, it's not a lot of people. Just us group of friends," Maybelle assured me as she ate her peanut butter and jelly sandwich. "Smaller, intimate parties are more fun."

"Like, who all are you thinking?" I asked.

"Hmmm…" Maybelle rubbed her chin in thought.

"I hope we're invited!" Kelly interrupted with a smirk.

"Of course!" Maybelle agreed, her eyes widening with excitement. "And Bubba and Jimbo. And Oakley."

"He lives there. I hope he's invited to his own house," I blurted out.

They all laughed.

"I know! Silly," Maybelle said as she squeezed my thigh with her hand. "You're friends with Stormy, too, right?"

"I don't think he's a partier," I remarked, taking a large bite out of my apple.

"No kidding!" both Maybelle and Kelly chorused.

"So, you two," I said, pointing at Kelly and Foster, "Oak, Bubba, Jimbo and maybe Stormy? Is that all?"

"Seems a little small to me," Foster stated.

"Well, maybe a few more people," Maybelle suggested.

"Like who?" I insisted. *Please don't say Bullet.*

"We'll figure it out! God! Why do you have to know all the names right now? Is it an exclusive party?" Maybelle pestered me.

"I just don't want things to get out of hand. I told you. Granny's sick. And she's old."

"You have a whole stereo system set up in there. You blast music all the time. So, what's the difference if some people are in there with you? Come on," Maybelle urged, making puppy-dog eyes at me.

"I have to talk to Oakley," I told her.

"Well…it might be better if he didn't come. I'm sure he can find other plans," Foster remarked with a smirk

"What?" I snapped. "It's *his* house. I live with *him*. He's my best friend. You honestly think I'm *not* going to invite him?"

Kelly nudged Foster in his side and placed her finger to her lips. Maybelle stared down, and the table grew quiet.

"What is it?" I demanded.

"I heard something about your friend," Foster responded.

"It's just a rumor," Kelly insisted. "People make up shit around here all the time."

"They don't make up shit like this unless it's true," Foster said matter-of-factly.

Confused, I turned to Maybelle. "What are they talking about?"

She sighed. "I didn't want to tell you. But someone told me that Oakley is dating a guy. Like a guy who goes to this school who is gay."

My heart sank in my gut. Oakley had brought up the possibility of all of us going back to Billings for Jody's next drag show, and I knew that the odds that no one would notice that he was dating a guy at the college were slim. Yet I hadn't had the guts to tell Maybelle. I was worried that if her reaction was bad, it would prove ominous for our own relationship. Plus, I just didn't feel right having this conversation without my friend present.

"Yes, he's dating a guy. It's Sadie. From the drag show." I tried to say it as confidently and nonchalantly as possible. *You got to own it.*

"He's dating her—him? I thought that was a girl!" Kelly exclaimed with wide eyes.

"His name's Jody. He's a senior in graphic design," I informed her.

"I know that guy," Foster mumbled.

"Wait," Maybelle turned to face me. "Oakley's gay? You never told me that."

"Because I don't think it's anyone's business." I said this very slowly and quietly to avoid sounding defensive.

"Look," I said, raising my head up to stay firm but friendly, "he's my childhood friend. I don't know if he's gay, but he's dating a guy right now. It's *his* business if that's what he wants to do. I would appreciate it if you guys didn't help spread the rumors. Just let him be."

"Rumors? It's only a rumor if it isn't true, isn't it?" Maybelle declared, motioning for Kelly and Foster to agree.

"Do you have a problem with it?" I asked her.

"I *guess* not..." she stammered. "But I don't really want to hang around him and his boyfriend, you know? Like I wouldn't want to be seen with them."

"Why not? We went to the drag show where they met, and it was fine," I argued.

"That was different," Maybelle said to me even though she was looking at Foster and Kelly. "We were just watching a show. Plus, I thought he was a girl. I don't want to hang out with two gay dudes."

"See them kiss," Foster joked with a sneer on his face.

"Yuck!" Maybelle squealed.

"See their manly bodies all rubbing on each other," Foster continued.

"Eww!" Maybelle grimaced. "That's what I mean. I don't want to *see* it. They can do that stuff in private."

"They better do it in private around here. Bullet already thinks you're fags. Wait until he hears this," Foster said.

"Then maybe don't tell him," I ordered.

"He'll probably find out anyway." Foster shrugged.

"Bullet's just an ass because we're going out," Maybelle explained. "He's looking for anything to torment you guys with. Just ignore him. He'll get bored."

"Not when it comes to his true love," Kelly teased, kicking Maybelle from under the table.

Maybelle threw a potato chip at her. "Hush."

"How do you live with him, man?" Foster inquired. "Don't you share a room? Does he watch you undress and shit?"

"He's not gay!" I insisted.

"But he's dating a guy. Sounds pretty fucking fag to me," Foster retorted.

"I don't know any guys that fuck guys and aren't gay," Kelly agreed.

"I didn't say they were having sex." I tried to reason with them. "It's none of our business. He's my friend, okay?" I looked to Maybelle for support, but she sat eating her chips and listening as if it were any other conversation.

"If a dude is hanging around *me,* and he's a fag, I want to know—I think I'm entitled to know," Foster asserted with a serious frown on his face.

"Why's that?" Kelly asked.

"Because I have the right to protect myself, you know what I mean?" he responded, making a fist. "I don't want to be alone with a fag or like you're doing, changing clothes around a fag."

"He's not a fag!" My anxiety was growing, and I could feel my hands trembling. Liquid was forming in my eyes. *Don't cry. Don't cry.*

I stood up. "Look, he's my friend. I don't like you talking about him this way."

"Chill out, man." Foster waved his hand at me, rolling his eyes.

"You were all cool with him before. This shouldn't change anything. He's got the right to do what he wants."

"Yeah, and I have the right to not have to be around fags." Foster laughed.

I looked at Maybelle again, who was still eating silently as if avoiding my glare. I picked up my stuff and tossed in the nearby trashcan.

"Forget the party," I said, walking away.

"Wait, come on, man," I heard them saying behind me, but I kept walking, wiping tears from my eyes and walking fast so that the movement disguised the shakes. Maybelle ran up behind me, placing her arms around me from behind.

"Where are you running off to?" She squeezed harder until I stopped trying to escape. She moved in front of me, seeing remnants of my tears.

"God, you sure are taking this seriously," she noted, as she wiped them from my face.

I stared down in humiliation "I'm not good at arguments."

"We weren't arguing! That's just how we talk. They didn't mean anything by it. Oakley's fine." She wrapped her arms around my neck.

"They were calling my friend a fag," I stated, still trying to avoid her gaze in case more tears emerged.

"Well, don't gay guys sometimes call themselves fags? It's not always a bad word." She remarked, pulling me close to her.

"Oakley's not a fag. And fag is a slur."

She pulled away from me. "Okay, he's not. What is he then?" She stood before me with her hands on her hips.

I shrugged. "He's just a dude. He's never even dated or kissed a guy before."

"So why is he dating a guy then?"

Ugh, one of the worst things about being sexually fluid is trying to explain what that means to people who don't get it because they are married to these binary constructions of sexuality. To them, people must be straight or gay. There are no gray areas. Worst, will she think it's weird that I know so much about it?

"He met Jody, and he liked her—him," I explained to her.

"*Him*." She waved her finger at me.

"He thought he was a woman. Then he found out he was a man. I guess he still likes him. It's complicated."

"So, he doesn't like girls anymore," she concluded.

"Sure, he does. He was obviously attracted to Jody because he thought he was a girl. Jody looks a lot like a girl."

"But don't a lot of gay guys look and act like girls? Just because you date someone who acts like a girl doesn't make you less gay," she claimed.

My stomach became tight, and my mouth went dry. "Oakley would never date a guy unless it was someone *very* different."

"But...he *is* dating a guy."

I groaned. "Sometimes if you meet the right person, you can move beyond that."

"What does that mean?" Maybelle crinkled her forehead in confusion.

"It means that you are attracted to the person, so you can look beyond gender. You can kind of bend your sexuality." I bent my fingers downward to make the point.

"Yuck! I don't care how special a girl is, I am *never* touching another girl's junk." She snickered, clearly expecting me to laugh with her.

"Okay, think of it this way," I continued. "What if we dated for a few years, and things were great? You were the happiest person with me. Then I get into a car accident and lose my legs. Now I would guess that normally you go for guys with legs, but would the absence of my legs end all attraction for me?"

"That's different, though. You'd still have the same parts. I can't touch another girl's vagina. That's gross," she whined.

"But it's not *that* different. Haven't you ever been in love?" I tried to hide the desperation in my voice. *I have a vagina. Can she touch me?*

"Yes." She nodded. "I dated Bullet for a long time."

"Was it love?"

"I just said it was," she snapped.

"So, what if Bullet had been in a car accident that…shattered his penis?" I felt really awkward using her love for Bullet in the argument.

"Well, that wouldn't be his fault."

"Being born a man or a woman isn't anyone's fault, either."

"Yeah" — she spoke in a little-girl tone — "but Bullet would not have gotten a vagina if his stuff was injured. It's still different. There is no woman out there that's wonderful enough to make me want to, you know, do *that*."

I could tell I wasn't getting anywhere and should just let it go.

"Don't you have to agree that if Oakley dates a man and does things with him that he has to be gay?" she demanded, holding her palm up.

I walked closer to her and placed my hands on her waist. "It's not either/or, though. Yes, he would need to expand his understanding of sexuality enough to incorporate a man into his sexual attraction. So, I guess he may be a little gay. But it doesn't mean that he still doesn't prefer girls."

"It totally makes him gay! That's the point!" She snorted.

I shook my head and stared down in defeat.

"Why are you taking this so personally?" Maybelle questioned, wrapping her arms around my waist. "Are you a little gay, baby?" she teased as she brushed her lips lightly against mine and rubbed her nose on me.

I didn't have the balls to tell her. Coming out as bisexual just seemed like it would confuse her more, and worse, make me too much of a weirdo for her.

"No, I'm not," I replied.

"Good." She kissed me. "So, what about the party then? Puh-lease!"

"I don't think it's a good idea. I mean, with the way they're talking about Oakley. I don't want any drama." I leaned my forehead against hers.

"They won't say that stuff to his face, silly!" She giggled. "Don't worry. He can bring his little boyfriend around as long as they don't like touch each other and stuff."

"I don't feel comfortable asking them not to do that," I informed her.

"Why not? They should be used to it, anyway. People don't do that in public. At least not in a place like Cloverleaf."

"Maybe we can try something else first?" I recommended, taking her hands in mine.

"What's that?"

"Jody is doing another drag show. He invited us to come."

"Invited who?" Maybelle asked.

"Oakley, of course, but also, you and me."

"Oh God, like a double date?" She rolled her eyes.

"Yeah. Why not?" I shook her hands playfully.

Maybelle pouted. "Will they be doing stuff? In front of us? Are we sharing rooms?"

Fuck. It hadn't dawned on me that if we took another trip to Billings, Maybelle might be up for sharing rooms.

"I don't know what they'll be doing. Would we share rooms?" I asked cautiously.

"How about they get a room, and *we* get a room?"

Aren't dudes supposed to be ecstatic when girls want to share a room with them? The whole idea consumed me with both anxiety and fear. What if I couldn't keep her hands off me? What if she insisted on seeing…it? Wait, I didn't even have an "it" to see — that was the problem.

"Okay, we can do that." *What am I saying?*

"Okay, then. I'll go with you. As long as they promise not to be too gay. I've got to get ready for class now."

"Maybelle, can you promise me one thing?"

"Yes, baby?" she answered, wrapping her arms around me again.

"Please don't spread it around about Oakley — or Jody. Please ask your friends not to."

She groaned. "Ooooookay. But if someone else is talking about it, hey, that's not my problem," she said, throwing her hands up in the air.

"Please don't tell Bullet. He's Oakley's lab partner."

"Well, I'm sure he already knows. He knows everything." She shrugged.

"How often do you talk to him?" I asked, disguising any tone of jealousy.

"Every day. We're still friends."

"What does every day mean?"

"I've got to go to class, Pate. I'll see you tonight. Make sure you get us a good hotel room. Something romantic to make it up to me."

"Make what up?"

"Forcing me to hang out with gay guys." She giggled and kissed me before waltzing back to the table where I could see Foster and Kelly laughing as if nothing had happened.

The discussion festered with me all day. I was scared to tell Oakley. He was already tormenting himself daily with this new relationship. If he knew everyone had discovered that he was dating Jody, he'd freak out and maybe end things. I liked Jody. I thought he was just what Oakley needed.

Oakley had gone to take Granny to another chemo appointment, so I had Stormy give me a ride home from school. It felt nice to have the whole house to myself to smoke a joint and ponder this crazy, dramatic world that I was creating. I should have kept my mouth shut. At the same time, other people must have been talking about Oakley, and at least I got to set Maybelle and her friends straight. *Did I set them straight?* Frankly, I didn't think I helped anything.

She said that she can't do vaginas. The fact haunted me. I had been savoring the hours of daydreaming about kissing her, holding her and even making love to her. Now, I felt guilty when I thought about it.

There was a letter on my bed when I went upstairs. It was in a dark-purple envelope with my name and address but no return address. I opened it, pulling out a piece of paper with typed letters.

The raging, roaring winds of East Montana blister the skin

The Herculean, frigid winters freeze the toes
But when you enter the room, summer breathes into me
again
Through the radiant warmth of your splendored spirit
that blows.

There was no name on it. *Who wrote this? To me?* I examined the envelope again, but there was no name. The address was written in a very neat, generic handwriting. Maybelle? Girls could often produce that pristine kind of script, but she didn't seem like the romantic, love-letter type. Then again, what if she was? It wasn't like we had known each other that long. Did she send it after hearing about Oakley? Did she feel bad?

I spent the evening sitting on the porch, nursing a beer and smoking joints while twirling the paper over and over in my hands.

Is it all a joke?

Chapter Thirteen

Oakley

So many various emotions flooded my brain and my gut. I had never seen myself as anything but an average straight guy. The thought of dating a dude had never entered my brain until Pate came out as a guy. However, I was still mystified about what Jody had said regarding my reasons for losing my physical attraction to Pate.

I studied Pate's body one day as he was changing clothes after showering. He was a tiny guy. He only stood five foot seven and probably weighed one hundred and thirty pounds. His body was as thin as I had ever seen it, but it was lean with curvy, muscular tone. His skin seemed to hang off his body instead of hugging it. His chest tattoo of black and gray skulls and gravestones camouflaged his lack of nipples.

His face had changed. His jawline looked less round and more square, and his cheeks sunk inward more, showing his elegant cheekbones. However, his lips were still plump, and his skin was still smooth and milky. *Why am I not attracted to him?*

I was puzzled about why I could not see the feminine in Pate but always seemed to see the feminine in Jody, even though I had known them both in female form first. Jody was also tiny in his frame like Pate, but he was more feminine. He shook his hips from side to side when he walked and used colorful gestures with his hands and arms. In fact, Jody utilized his whole body when he communicated, which made it difficult to take my eyes off him. Maybe Jody embraced his femininity and that was what drew me to him whereas Pate subdued his femininity. Perhaps I needed someone who was feminine and expressed it. Pate's rejection of his feminine side didn't connect with me.

"Why are you staring at me?" Pate asked. He had turned around from the mirror, still shirtless, with a raised eyebrow.

"Nothing," I muttered and went back to typing a paper for class.

Pate walked over and sat on the bottom of my bed. "You haven't watched me like that in a long time."

"What are you talking about?" I didn't look up.

"Like…checking me out?"

"I was not!" I snapped.

"You were, too!" Pate rubbed his hands along his bare chest. "What does Jody look like?"

"I wouldn't know."

Pate kept studying his chest with his hands. "Is this attractive? A man's chest?"

"You look good," I mumbled dismissively.

"That's not what I asked," Pate replied as he took my hand and placed it on his bare, muscular chest. It startled me because he was adamant about no one touching his chest. "What do you think?" he asked.

In a way, it felt like touching a really skinny girl, just without the breasts. His petite frame also made it feel very feminine. My hand slowly caressed his chest from his pecs to his scars. It was soft and thankfully, hairless.

"It's nice, actually," I admitted. I placed both of my hands on his sides. "You're so tiny!"

"You're a pretty small guy, too."

I removed my hands.

"I've been afraid to tell you," Pate began with a more serious expression, "but Maybelle and her friends somehow found out about you and Jody."

I closed my laptop. "What? How would they know?"

"I don't know. Have people seen you two together?"

Considering that Jody had focused on school for most of the week, we had only had a few dates. I had been careful not to touch him or kiss him with anyone around. *What if it was that waitress at The Spare Tire?*

"I've been careful. No one's been around when we kiss or touch," I told him.

"It's a small town. He lives in the dorms. People could easily see you. Or…do you think he told people?" Pate asked.

"I don't think he'd do that without talking to me first. What did they say to you?"

Pate sighed. "It wasn't good. They kept calling you a fag. I tried to make them promise not to tell anyone."

"You just let them call us fags?" I scolded.

"No! I defended you. I tried to explain things. It just wasn't any…use. I'm sorry."

"Yeah, I'm sure that they won't tell *anybody*. Fuck!" I pulled my knees up and rested my arms on top of them.

"Are you scared?" Pate inquired, moving to sit beside me.

"I don't know." I groaned, burrowing my head in my arms. "It just feels like too much. I'm trying to figure out this thing with Jody. I'm not ready to figure out being openly gay."

"Do you like guys??" Pate asked me, placing his hand on my leg.

Still not lifting my head, I said, "I'm in a gay relationship. Whether I like guys or not, other people are going to see us as gay. We're presenting as gay. I don't know how to live my life like that."

"Oak, are you sure that the problem is feeling attracted to Jody or is it more about what other people think?"

I rubbed my temples pondering the question. "What do you think it is?" I mumbled.

"I can't answer a question about your sexuality for you. But you seem very concerned about what others think or will do. I just wonder how much of that part is getting in the way. You're not the most secure person."

"Neither are you!" I declared, and we both laughed.

"You remember what people thought about us? Even back home?" Pate asked, moving behind me and rubbing my back.

"They thought we were gay. Hell, we move to a new town, and they still do!"

Pate chuckled. "I don't think there's much we can do to not have people think we're gay or weird or whatever. Maybe that's just the way it is. I can't say that you are the most masculine guy, either. We're just different from other people. Are you afraid of getting hurt?"

"Like beat up or something?" I asked, lifting my head up. "A little. Mostly just harassed. I don't want to be tormented when I go out in public. I guess I am really insecure. Jody acts like it doesn't even bother him."

Pate gave a small smile. "It bothers him," he assured me. "He just doesn't let it stop him from being himself. He fights back by owning who he is. I wish I could be like that."

"Me, too!" I agreed.

Pate leaned forward and rested his chin on my shoulder. "I had to learn a few things when I transitioned. I was so afraid to go out in public and have people think I was off or not know if I was a boy or girl. I was really scared to use the restroom. There may be assholes out there, but there's also a lot of times where nothing will happen. Besides, don't let society dictate your life. You're covered in tattoos and piercings. They'll probably be afraid of you."

"But you've been through this. You know how to handle it," I claimed as I leaned back against him with my head in his lap.

"I do?"

"Well, more than me."

"There is no 'more than you'," Pate stated. "It's hard for *everyone*. Being confident in who you are is hard for everyone. It's just that the people who are confident do not let their fears hold them back. But it's an ongoing battle. It's not like you just reach some point where you are secure in who you are and everything is easy. You have to keep fighting for yourself."

"I'm not confident."

"Join the club."

* * * *

I went over to Jody's that Friday evening. His dorm room was small but at least it was private. We both sat on the floor beside the bed with our shoes off, listening to eighties New Wave and drinking red wine, Jody's favorite. I wasn't used to seeing him so casual in standard blue jeans and a blue T-shirt with no makeup. Aside from constantly waving his feet back and forth, he seemed more masculine.

"Jody, did you tell anyone about us?"

"No. Is there an 'us' to tell? I don't think we've discussed Facebook official status yet," he teased as he took my hand.

"People know," I informed him.

"Who knows?"

"Pate said Maybelle and her friends were talking about it. Calling me a fag and stuff."

"Sound like a bunch of assholes," Jody remarked.

"How do you think people found out?"

"I don't know. Maybe it was the waitress. Does it bother you, sweetie?" He nudged me in the side.

I sat in silence, unable to locate any words or explanations that wouldn't make *me* sound like an asshole. Instead, I just picked at my fingernails. Noticing that I was silent, Jody shifted to face me, sitting cross-legged with his hand still holding mine between his legs.

"Oakman, you have to talk to me if this is going to work. What's wrong?"

"It bothers me," I muttered.

"Tell me about it." Jody gently rubbed his other hand along my arm.

"I don't want to be gay — like I don't want to have other people treat me like I'm gay." Worse, I was an imposter in a way. I hadn't identified as gay all these years. Living my life as a person in a same-sex relationship now was so new.

"Join the club," Jody said. "You think that I want to get called names or get harassed? No one does, sweetie."

"You've done this your whole life. How did you do it?"

Jody told me about the relentless bullying in elementary school that had started early and intensified each year. He said people always knew he was different and exploited it as a weakness. Words like "fag," "queer," and "pussy" followed him wherever he went, and he was often attacked in the boy's restroom when the teachers were not present.

"They'd pull down my pants," he told me. "They'd flush my head in the toilet. It wasn't until middle school that I got punched and slapped. I took gym, and we had to shower. Somehow, no matter what direction I looked, I was accused of checking out guys' junk. One time they held me down and beat me with wet towels. It left marks on my back."

"What'd you do?" I asked as I took his hands in mine.

"I didn't do anything." Jody smirked. "I was too afraid. Besides, I couldn't go home and tell my dad that I was being beaten for being a fag. When I got to high school, I just kept to myself, aside from singing at some school assemblies. People still called me names in the hallway, but the physical assaults went away." His expression grew sad. "Are you afraid that's what will happen to you?"

I had never worried about getting assaulted, and the image of someone hurting Jody filled me with emotions. "I don't want to say that I'm *not* worried about stuff like that because that would be naïve. But I worry about...I guess being treated differently? Will people not talk to me anymore? Will my parents not talk to me anymore? Pate's parents disowned him."

"No one asks for this plight," he said, wrapping his arm around me. "It's the way society is. You have to make a choice."

"What choice is that?"

"Do you want happiness, or do you just want to make everyone else happy? Either way, you're going to struggle. I'd rather struggle for my own happiness."

"You make it look so easy."

He grinned. "But it's not. I still hear the occasional 'faggot' here and there. Family members won't talk to me for doing drag because it embarrasses them. I get some hate on my social media accounts for sure. It hurts. I'm human, after all. But I just write them off as miserable people who are jealous to see someone live his life authentically and with no apologies. It's not enough to stop me from being me."

"I never figured I was such a weak person until I talked to you and Pate. You both seem so much stronger than me."

"You're lost, Oakman. It's okay. Lots of people in their twenties are lost, trying to figure out who they are and where they want to go. But you won't figure it out if you don't be yourself."

Jody was right. Despite playing in a metal band, covering myself in tattoos and shoving needles in my nose and penis, I had always been a sideline kind of guy. I was always in the background, never speaking up for anything, including myself. I had known my ex-girlfriend Carly was cheating on me with the drummer, but I didn't have the guts to confront her. It wasn't until I literally caught them fucking that I had to deal with it. Even then, I worried that I was making a mistake by leaving her. Maybe that was part of what broke my physical attraction to Pate. He had moved from the background to the foreground. He was taking charge of his life without anyone's permission or blessing. I was afraid that I would be left behind in the side show.

I put my arms around Jody and kissed him. "I know what you're saying," I told him.

"Can we try something?" Jody asked with a slight smile. I nodded.

Jody told me to get on the bed and lie face down without my shirt. I reluctantly followed directions. Jody took off his shirt and lay on top of me, pressing his chest against my back. He rested his head on my shoulders and caressed my arms. His red curls tickled my neck, sending shivers up and down my spine and creating jerks in my penis as blood flowed down there.

"What are we doing?" I whispered.

"Don't worry," he said. "I'm not going to try to have sex with you or touch you. I just want you to feel me — to feel us. Just relax and enjoy it. No sexual pressure."

I closed my eyes and tried to focus on the weight of his body on mine that proved soothing. It had been a long time since I had held anyone other than Pate or had anyone hold me. Jody's tiny body placed just the right amount of pressure on me to feel really good. Nevertheless, Jody kept moving his head, causing his curls to keep tickling me and his eyelashes to flutter across my shoulders. Each tickle created a corresponding jerk in my groin. I shifted underneath him, adjusting my pants.

"Everything okay? Am I squishing you?"

"You couldn't squash me if you tried!" I laughed.

"Ha ha, maybe we can try sometime. I like it a little rough."

We laid silently for a long time. Sometimes he caressed me and sometimes he just laid still. I could hear the patterns of his breathing and the prickles of air on my back. I pulled up.

"You ready for me to get off?" Jody asked, sitting up on his knees. "No pun intended, of course!"

I rolled over and lifted my arms up, motioning for him to crawl inside the cubby my arms created. Jody grinned and started turning so that his back would be against my chest. I placed my hand on his shoulder to stop him so that he lay down under my arms, facing me. I pulled him close, keeping my groin area distant but the rest of me close. Jody rested his head on my cheek.

"Well, isn't this a big step? We're half naked, too!" Jody teased me.

He was so small that holding him felt very much like holding a woman, only one with a flat chest. I had never seen Jody's chest before. Like his face, it was smooth and hairless. He didn't have the muscle tone that Pate had, so his body felt thinner and more delicate. His smooth skin and perfumed scent were not only feminine but erotic to me. As my little guy from down under kept trying to poke his head out, I fantasized about Jody sexually.

I could only picture him in the more passive, submissive position, letting me, or any lover, take charge of him. I pictured pulling his red curls between my fingers as I kissed his neck, or pulling him up to me from behind, grabbing and clawing his chest and maybe eventually trickling my fingers down along his narrow hip bones. I imagined the sounds of his moans. There was something so intensely sexual behind the mysterious. I had never seen a man, outside of porn, get aroused, excited or come. It was a side of men that I had never known. That unknown hardened my erection even more.

It was then that it dawned on me. I had always been with strong, assertive women. Even Pate was strong and assertive before he transitioned. I was used to playing the docile, subservient role, even in bed. I would never try anything without having the woman's permission first and even then, I was usually too scared to ask for what I really wanted. After so many years, I felt suppressed sexually. But now here was Jody. I didn't feel like I needed any permission with him. Since he was a guy, I imagined a lover with a similar sexual drive that would allow me to express the erotic man that was inside of me burning to get out. Perhaps sex with a man would be more free, more passionate and more sensual. Perhaps with a man, I could actually be myself in bed.

"Can I ask you something?" Jody whispered in my ear.

"Yes."

"Are we Facebook official now?"

"Okay."

Chapter Fourteen

Pate

"You're going to share a room with her?" Oakley asked after class one day. Jody's next performance was scheduled, and I had ordered us two rooms at a hotel in Billings that was affordable but not overly cheap. It had a bar, a pool and a hot tub, even though I never wore bathing suits.

"Share a room with who?"

We both turned around to see Stormy behind us.

"With Maybelle," I answered, slowing down enough to let him walk beside us.

"Where y'all going?"

Oakley and I hesitated and flashed each other a look for guidance only to find neither of us had any to give. "To Billings," I responded.

"For what?"

"Um," Oakley cleared his throat and proceeded in a soft tone, "to a drag show. My boyfriend is performing."

Stormy stopped halfway through lighting a cigarette. "Boyfriend?" He glanced at me. "I thought you said he wasn't gay."

"And according to Pate," Oakley interrupted, "you're cool, right?"

"Don't worry, man. I don't care if you have a boyfriend." Stormy smiled assuredly. "I'm just confused. Pate said that you weren't gay. Oh, but you're that other word. What is it? Beesexual?"

"You told him that I'm bisexual?" Oakley asked me.

"Well, yeah, I guess. I mean, aren't you? You've dated girls and now you're dating a guy. I feel that it would at least put you on the bisexual spectrum," I asserted.

"Sorry, Stormy." Oakley motioned. "It's kind of a new thing for me, you know? I guess I'm weird about labeling it."

Stormy looked puzzled. "But you two had sex, right? So, it wouldn't be new, would it? You've been with guys before."

Oakley rolled his eyes.

"No," I interjected. "That was just...experimentation. Young people experiment. I think this time he's actually dating a guy. It's not just...sex." *Christ, I sound like a crazy nympho with this outrageously diverse sex life, when in reality, it's been years since I've had sex with another person.*

"Oh," Stormy replied, inhaling smoke from his cigarette. "That's cool. Who is your boyfriend?"

"Can you keep this secret? I only told you because Pate already said that you knew some things and seemed good about keeping your mouth shut," Oakley told him.

"I don't really sit around gossiping with my roommates if that's what you're thinking. That's not what we ranch guys do." Stormy winked at me. "Besides, I thought we were friends."

"We're friends," I said, more to Oakley than to Stormy. "Do you want to come with us?"

Oakley shot me a cringing look.

"Really?" Stormy's eyes grew large with excitement. "To a drag show? What is a drag show?"

Both Oakley and I laughed.

"It's a performance show where guys who dress like women sing and dance. They interact a lot with the audience, too. It's pretty fun. That's where Oakley met Jody. Jody Faucet."

"Jody Faucet. Don't think I know him. Guys dressing like women? Like all dolled up and stuff?" Stormy clarified.

"Yeah, they're pretty dolled up, you can say," Oakley responded.

"Um, okay. I'll go. What do I have to wear?"

"Clothes," I replied.

"Do I have to dress up? Is this okay?" he asked, motioning to his standard wardrobe of super-tight jeans over dirty boots and worn-out T-shirts and vests.

"You don't wear cowboy hats, do you?" I asked. "I just can't do the big belt buckles and cowboy hats thing. No offense."

"No, I don't do the hat and belts. I'm a beanie guy," Stormy said as he pulled on his black beanie. "So if you and Maybelle share a room, where am I staying? With you and your guy?" He asked Oakley.

"I don't know. Where is he staying, Pate?" Oakley turned to me with all ears.

"Um, you can stay with me and Maybelle," I suggested. "I think there's two beds in the room. If that doesn't weird you out."

"No, I've stayed with dudes and their girls before. As long as you guys don't have sex beside me. That would be weird."

"You don't have to worry about that," Oakley retorted, nudging me with his elbow.

"Awesome! Message me the details. I'll see you guys later." The large beast stomped off into the distance, always leaving some folks turning heads at his enormous stature and incredibly awkward gait.

"Maybelle is going to be okay with this guy sharing a room with you?" Oakley questioned. "What'd you invite him for?"

I sighed. "I don't know."

"Gosh, Pate, you don't think," Oakley snapped. "You just blurt things out. Give us another month here and the whole state of Montana will know you're trans, I'm gay, whatever."

I hadn't shared the mysterious letter with Oakley. I was afraid that he would assume it was bait for a joke and blame me again for opening my big mouth. He typically went immediately into paranoid deliriums that would only rub off on me, freaking me out more. I felt it was best to keep it to myself for now.

The truth was that I was terrified to be alone with Maybelle. Things had stayed safe while also progressing. We kissed, *a lot*. I had felt her full, soft breasts both in my hands and in my mouth. But I hadn't touched her below the waist because I was scared that would entice her to follow suit. However, being alone in a hotel room seemed too risky. She had already used the word "romantic." At the same time, I knew that she'd be angry with me for bringing Stormy. After all, she already felt that she was doing me a favor by going.

My suspicions were proven right when I talked to her on the phone later that evening.

"Why'd you invite him?" she whined. "In our room? I don't want to stay in a room with that guy—or two guys. Do you not know how awkward that is for a girl?"

Damn! I didn't think about that. Being a young girl and staying with two guys would be awkward as fuck. My tendency to avoid gendering people was proving problematic as I realized that I was ignoring authentic gender issues.

"I'm sorry. If you really don't feel comfortable, he can stay with Oakley and Jody." My stomach churned as I didn't want to push Stormy on Oakley but also didn't want to be alone with Maybelle. I was hoping she'd cave.

"We'll just see. I don't want him thinking he can't stay because of *me*. I guess I've stayed with Bullet and his friends before. I just don't like Stormy."

"Why not?"

"There's just something about him. He's super judgmental. Seems to think he's better than everyone. Plus, I wanted to be alone with you. I thought we could...you know?"

"It hasn't been four months," I blurted out.

"I know! But I thought we could do...more. I want to do more. I was looking forward to it. It's why I agreed to go."

My heart ached and burned with passion. I wanted more, too. I would have given anything to make love to Maybelle. To feel her naked body from head to toe and squeeze it against mine. Staring at my empty couch, I longed to penetrate her, to feel connected to her. It was tragic to have all this love festering inside me without any way to express it to her while also fearing that I never would.

"I want to do more, too," I admitted. "But I was afraid that being alone in the room might make it hard to resist the urge. I didn't want things to get awkward or to cause a fight." *My attempt at honesty…somewhat.*

"Doesn't it drive you crazy, though?" Maybelle insisted. "Like, I'm ready to go. I'm set on you. You're what I want, and I just want to go for it. Do you?"

"More than anything. I think I'm falling in love with you." *Too much information! Honesty is a contagious trap!*

"I love you, too." She giggled nervously. "Can't we just…try? I'll be careful, and we can stop if it hurts."

"It's just too risky. If I do something too early, we may be waiting even longer." *Yes! Perfect!*

"I guess you're right," she conceded. "I just love you."

"I love you, too" When I hung up the phone, I pulled the letter out of my biology book.

The raging, roaring winds of East Montana blister the skin

The Herculean, frigid winters freeze the toes

But when you enter the room, summer breathes into me again

Through the radiant warmth of your splendored spirit that blows

Somehow, I just knew that everything was going to work, and I was the happiest that I had ever been.

* * * *

Oakley

I didn't think that Jody, Pate, Maybelle or myself were prepared for the never-ending word vomit that spewed from Stormy's mouth the entire drive to Billings. We learned how to bale hay, how to brand cows and the differences in various tractor equipment. Then we learned about grass-fed beef and why Montana housed happy, free-roaming cows whose joyful spirits influenced the taste of the meat, at least according to his theories.

"One time for Halloween, I dressed up like a John Deere tractor. It was awesome! I made the costume myself," he told us proudly.

"Did you really, sweetie?" Jody turned around. Jody and I rode in the front seat of my small car, letting Pate, Maybelle and Stormy squeeze in the back. Stormy's huge legs nearly reached my headrest.

"I think it's cool to make your own clothes," Jody commented. "I make all my own outfits. I do my own makeup, too. I have some YouTube videos that are tutorials for other drag queens — and girls, of course. But with drag queen makeup, there are certain tricks you can do if you have a masculine face. It has different techniques."

"You don't have a masculine face," I told him.

"Maybe you can do my makeup," Maybelle suggested.

"Sure! I love makeovers!" Jody exclaimed.

"Can you make me look like a drag queen?" Stormy laughed.

"Uh-oh," I muttered. Jody had begged many times already to "do me up." I could sense his burst of excitement at the challenge of turning someone like Stormy into a woman.

"I don't think he can do that." Maybelle giggled.

"I can do anything!" Jody claimed. "This girl can work miracles."

"You can be a drag queen for the Halloween party," Maybelle told Stormy.

"What Halloween party?" I asked.

"The one at your guys' house," she responded.

"What?" I found Pate in the rearview mirror. "What's this, Pate?"

"I was going to talk to you about it. It wasn't decided or anything," he stuttered. I forced a small smile even though I was furious with him. He always did this shit to me. Every conversation I had with Pate, I could guess that the information shared was at least three or four weeks old. Of course, I also knew that Pate was such a people-pleaser, which was why he agreed to things and avoided informing me about them.

"It wouldn't be a *party* party," he promised me. "Maybe we can get twenty to thirty people? You have that big barn and that big ranch. It's great for a party."

"It will be cold then," I said.

"That's why you have the barn!" Maybelle insisted. "Besides, don't you have to heat it if you're going to still dance in it?" she asked Pate.

"Like a party with drinking?" I inquired.

"Of course!" she squealed. "What would a party be without drinking?"

"I don't know twenty or thirty people in town," I argued. "It makes me wary about having people I don't know drink at my place. They *definitely* cannot stay the night. There better be designated drivers. And Bullet *can't* come."

"Why not? He'll come anyway. I'd like to see someone try to throw him out," Maybelle contended. "You might as well just let him be."

I had managed civility during our biology labs. Bullet mostly fiddled with stuff like he was contributing, but he never really did anything but just copy my work. I let it be to avoid any drama. However, having that guy at my house was different. I saw the way he stared at Maybelle and Pate, and it would only take a few drinks in him to cause something to explode that had obviously been lingering there since summer.

Jody must have sensed my concern. "I got it," he chimed in calmly. "We do the party but on one condition. It's a disguise or masquerade party. Your costume has to hide who you are."

"Then we can have people try to guess who people are! Like a contest for best disguise," Maybelle exclaimed.

"Now you're talking, sweetheart." Jody placed his hand on my leg. "It'll be okay. I'll help you guys decorate."

"I'll help, too," Stormy offered.

When we arrived at the hotel, Maybelle took off to the restrooms while Pate and I checked us in. Stormy came up from behind us as we were filling out the guest information.

"I'm going to be staying with you, right?" he asked Pate with a serious expression on his already stern face.

"You want to?" Pate probed.

"Yes. No offense, Oakley."

"None taken," I responded. I definitely was happy to hear that he would stay with Pate considering he was Pate's friend. I had only spoken to him here and there during classes. I wasn't sure how he would react to

Grayality

Jody and me. I wasn't completely trusting of his motives the same as Pate was. There was just something too eager about him.

We located our rooms and agreed to meet later. Jody needed rest followed by an apparently long-ass period of time to transform himself into Sadie. I lay on the bed, fiddling on my phone and watching *Ridiculousness* while also inspecting him as he placed fake eyelashes on his eyelids and shaded his cheeks with red blush that accentuated his cheekbones, giving him less of a male facial structure. Then he spent a whole thirty minutes trying to get his bra stuffed "just right."

"I didn't know you were so high maintenance," I acknowledged.

"Only when I'm Sadie, my dear." He smiled at me.

"What are you going to sing?"

"It's a surprise, darling. I never reveal my art before it's performed."

We met the group downstairs. Jody had to arrive to the club early to put on his dress and wig, as well as help some other performers finesse their final looks. The club was empty, but the kitchen was running, so we decided to have dinner while waiting for the show to begin. Stormy ordered a large buffalo burger only to have most of it fall out of his mouth as he constantly darted his eyes back and forth, mesmerized. Pate had loaned him an old Ramones shirt, a Metallica beanie, and some studded bracelets to help him fit into the group.

"Wow, I've never been in a club," Stormy shared as he surveyed the room. "How many people do you think will be in here? Is this stuff popular? The food is good. Do people dance on the floor over there? How did you meet Jody? Was Maybelle here, too?"

I couldn't keep up with his questions. He was like a little kid entering a toy store for the first time. I kicked Pate with my foot to get him to tend to his friend.

Pate answered all his questions one by one. "It was packed last time we were here. Yes, I think drag shows are popular. I agree, the food is great! Some people danced on the floor in between shows last time. Oakley met Jody because she performed here when we came. Yes, both me and Maybelle were here."

"It was *my* idea," Maybelle claimed. "See, I'm edgier than you two." She motioned to me and Pate.

"What made you want to ask Jody out?" he asked me.

"He's a really good singer—and entertainer. You'll see," I replied. "I also perform, so I respect that kind of thing."

"He thought he was a girl when he asked him out," Maybelle corrected me.

"Yes, I thought he was a girl," I agreed.

"But you still dated him when you found out he was a boy?" Stormy inquired.

"Yeah, I did."

"What made you do that?"

I paused. "Because he's Jody," I answered with a slight smile. "There's not many people like him out there."

"He intrigued you?" Stormy asked.

"He intrigued me," I confirmed. "That's a good way to put it."

"Wow." Stormy finished his beer. "You guys are so cool."

"You think it's cool?" Maybelle asked, surprised.

Stormy nodded. "I've always been fascinated by city folks. You guys just live your life. You don't care about what other people think. You put yourselves out there. It must be really great to have lived in places where you can do that so easily."

"Maybe you should move to a city," Pate remarked.

"Nah." Stormy dismissed me with a wave of his hand. "I love the wide open skies and fields too much."

"He'd miss his cows," Pate joked.

* * * *

A few hours later, the show was set to begin. We weren't sure when Jody's time would come, so I sneaked backstage to give him a good luck hug and kiss. When I walked back to the original room where we had talked, I saw Sadie in full form. This time, he wore a long, blond wig with wavy curls that went all the way down to his waist. He had a flowing black shirt with red heart sequins and a tight-fitting red-laced bustier. A matching red heart choker lay along his chest, sending attention down to his cleavage.

"Hey, you're not supposed to see me before the show!" Jody argued, pushing me out.

"It's not a wedding. I just wanted to wish you luck. You look amazing."

"Thanks, sweetie." He gave me a light peck on the mouth. "I can't mess up my lipstick!" He pushed me out the door.

I didn't know what was more entertaining, watching the queens perform or watching Stormy. His eyes never left the stage, and they were so wide that I swore he never blinked.

"Watch this," Pate leaned over and whispered to me. The current performer was a full-figured woman with puffy curly hair in a tight, bright blue evening gown who stood over six feet tall. Pate waved for her to come to our table. She was singing *Naughty Girls (Need Love Too)* by Samantha Fox.

When she approached our table, Pate pointed at Stormy, who was oblivious, his eyes getting wider as she neared. She sang to Stormy, twirling around and sometimes squeezing his chin. His face grew red, and sweat beaded on his forehead, but his mouth stretched open in a large grin, making me realize that I had never seen him do an open-mouthed smile.

"I thought he'd freak out," I told Pate.

"I think this is the most fun he's had off the ranch!" Pate joked.

The song finished, and the queen gave Stormy a hug before walking toward the bar. I asked Pate to order us another round of drinks.

"That was so crazy!" Stormy exclaimed, still grinning from ear to ear.

"We popped his cherry," Pate said to me.

"*You* did that?" Stormy asked, pointing at Pate. "Ha ha, I thought she just came over because I'm probably the only person here that's her height."

"Bigfoots in love," Pate teased.

"I don't know about *that*. It was fun. More beer!" Stormy hollered as he pounded his fist on the table.

Pate leaned over to me. "We should get him high next."

"Oh lord, is he your new groupie or something?" I snorted.

"It'll be fun," Pate insisted. "I'd love to see this dude high!" He faced Stormy with a big grin on his face.

"As long as he doesn't go off on cattle tangents," I commented.

The lights dimmed again, and a purple spotlight fell on the stage. The announcer introduced Sadie, who walked on stage followed by a light red spotlight that made her nearly glow. *I wish she were wearing a red wig like her red hair.*

The song began and the lights flickered matching the beat. She sang *I Wanna Dance with Somebody* by Whitney Houston. It took a lot of bravery to attempt to master a Whitney Houston song with her radiating, Broadway-style voice, but Sadie pulled it off. She was an extremely talented singer.

"Wow, he can sing!" Maybelle noted.

Sadie made her way to our table and shimmied up to me, taking my hand and placing it on her heart.

I remembered how tense I had been when we were at the show last time, but now in the crowded room with Sadie singing in an eerily feminine voice and locking her green eyes dead on mine, it was like we were the only two people in the room. I smiled back at her. The sexual chemistry bubbled through my brain, down along my gut and into my loins. I wanted to grab her, pull her hair back and kiss her neck while pressing my hardened penis against her pelvis. Or maybe I could come up and take her from behind.

Sadie pinched my chin before dancing off to another table. The whole crowd was focused on her, even applauding when she hit the really high notes perfectly. The song finished, and she blew me a kiss before heading backstage.

"Wow," Stormy muttered. "He's really good. He does look just like a girl! And sings like one, too!"

"He should perform at the Halloween party," Maybelle suggested.

"In front of *your* friends?" Pate asked with wide eyes.

"What's wrong with my friends?" Maybelle asked, hurt.

"They're assholes," Stormy mumbled.

"No, they're not!" Maybelle snapped at him. "Don't talk that way about my friends. You don't know any of them."

"Yeah, I do," Stormy asserted, making full eye contact with her.

"I don't think it would be a good idea," Pate said firmly.

"Why not?" Maybelle whined. "Why do you think my friends aren't cool?"

"Because they're not," Stormy interrupted again. "Didn't you say that she and her friends were calling Oakley a fag?" he asked Pate.

Maybelle met eyes with me, but I sipped my beer in silence. There was no way that I was going to involve myself in Pate's romantic business even if it was about me or Jody.

"It wasn't like that," Maybelle argued. "They didn't mean anything by it."

"Yeah, and if I say bitch, I guess I don't mean anything either," Stormy blurted out, leaning back in his chair while still maintaining his gaze on her.

"Why are you all ganging up on me!" she yelled, grabbing Pate's hand. "You're going to let your friends talk to me that way?"

"I didn't call *you* a bitch," Stormy corrected her. "I just said that if someone was using a word like bitch — or cunt — how do you *not* mean anything by it? Fag is an insult. It's a slur, really."

"I didn't call Oakley or Jody a fag! You're mixing my words up!" She slung her chair back, running out of the club.

"Thanks." Pate gestured to Stormy before chasing after her.

"I'm just saying that I would *not* subject Jody to Maybelle or her friends. It's just a spectacle to her," Stormy explained to me.

"Dude, you're staying in the same room with them tonight," I reminded him.

He chuckled. His smile and laugh actually gave him a boyish charm. "It's fine," he assured me. "She just doesn't like being called out on her shit."

"You know her well?"

"I've known her for some time now. You don't go far without hearing about her and Bullet's drama."

"Do you trust her?" I questioned.

He thought for a moment. "I guess I trust her as much as any girl like that, you know? She's immature. I guess I can't blame her at that age. But I don't think that she or her friends should be calling you guys fags."

"Thanks," I told him. "I didn't want to say anything and chance messing things up for Pate."

"He's smitten with her, isn't he?" Stormy asked with a serious look.

"Yes, he is."

Stormy shook his head. "Too bad."

I didn't know what Pate said to Maybelle, but she was pacified enough for them to hold hands on the car ride home, yet things were awkwardly silent. Jody had whispered to me, wondering what happened, but I only shrugged my shoulders. Stormy sat in the back playing with his phone peacefully as if nothing had occurred.

We arrived at the hotel, and I pulled Pate aside.

"Are you okay staying with them?" I asked.

"Yeah," he said unconvincingly. "They'll both cool off tomorrow."

"What happened? Is she upset?"

"She cried," he said with a long sigh. "She claimed that I was letting y'all gang up on her and that Stormy called her a bitch."

"He kind of did," I agreed.

"I know."

"Did you let them call us fags?"

He gasped, throwing his arms up in defeat. "I told you already that I told them not to talk about you guys that way. But it didn't do any good."

"It's fine. Your new friend has just as big of a mouth as you do! And even less of a filter!" I snorted.

Pate laughed. "It's okay. I feel pretty secure with Maybelle. It's just a fight. We love each other."

"You didn't use the L-word, did you?" I groaned.

"Yeah. Why not? She loves me, too. It's a good thing."

I placed my hand on his shoulder. "Don't you think you're moving a little too fast? She doesn't even... know, yet."

"Maybe you're moving too fast. You don't even know if you're gay, yet," he snapped.

"Don't get defensive," I stressed. "But she's really young. I don't know if she is mature enough to handle it."

"Don't rain on my shit," he retorted.

"Okay, okay." I backed away from him.

We said goodnight, and I watched Maybelle walk ahead of the boys to the room with her arms crossed while Stormy leaned on Pate's shoulder with his arm to show him a YouTube video.

"Well, they should have an interesting night," Jody remarked.

"Right?" I agreed.

We went to our room. Jody had taken off his outfit and was carrying it in a dry-cleaner bag that he carefully hung in the hotel closet. He was placing his wig box on the counter when I stopped him.

"Put the wig on."

Quietly, he took the wig out of the box and fitted it carefully over his head. His makeup had faded slightly due to sweating, but it added a glittery shimmer to his skin that glistened in the dim hotel light. He still had his stuffed bra on under a white T-shirt.

"Do you want a private dance?" he offered with a sly smile.

"We don't have any music."

Jody took out his cell phone and after a few clicks, ABBA's *Mamma Mia!* emerged. He walked up and pushed me so that I fell slightly on the armchair in the room. Jody sang along softly and moved around the room, jerking his hips and swinging the hair. He looked just like a teenage girl twirling around.

He came up and straddled me, still singing and swinging his hair that flowed all around my shoulders and head. Then he leaned all the way back so that his body was spread out before mine, and I rubbed my hand down his torso. Suddenly, he snapped up.

"I think I feel something. A little something down there," he said with his face a few inches from mine and his hand gliding gently over my crotch.

"Yeah, maybe do that again," I urged him.

Jody smiled and stretched all the way back, and I pulled his legs around my body, continuing to rub his torso and his fake breasts with my hands. I wanted to pick him up and penetrate him until he screamed. My hands dangled downward until I felt a hardened lump. Instinctively, I leaped up, pushing him off me onto the hotel floor.

"Ow, darling," Jody hollered.

I stomped to the bathroom, splashing cold water on my face and adjusting my pants. When I reentered the room, Jody was sitting on the chair, caressing the wig as he held it in his hands. The music was off.

"You know," he began, "I don't typically dirty up my wigs for people. They're expensive."

"I'm sorry. I didn't mean to knock you off."

"You sure seemed like you did. What happened?" His green eyes showed hurt, and they pierced me with guilt and shame.

I wanted to go hug him and promise that I would never throw him down again. But instead, I just mumbled, "Nothing. I'm just not in the mood." I plopped down on the bed.

"You were five seconds ago. I could feel it pressing against my legs," Jody pointed out.

I shook my head. "I'm not ready."

"Is it because you felt my erection?" Jody asked.

I groaned. Before meeting Pate, I had never thought that I would hear so much talk about penises and vaginas. I was utterly sick of all these genitalia.

Jody got on his knees and moved over between my legs, resting his elbows on my knees. "Is it?" he pressed.

"Yes," I mumbled, afraid to look at him.

"Why?"

I leaned back on the bed and rubbed my temples. "Why do we have to talk about it?" I asked, frustrated.

"Because we do," Jody stated, rubbing my knees with his hands. "We're in a relationship, and couples talk about things. We're having a good time, and you just throw me like trash on the floor. Like...I'm not a person."

"You know why, Jody."

He shook my knees. "No, I don't. I need to hear it from you. Just say it. You won't hurt my feelings."

"Umm...I don't know," I pleaded.

"Were you aroused, Oakman? By me?" He pulled at my arms, forcing me to sit up and look at him.

"Yes, I was," I admitted, nodding my head.

"Did you think about having sex with me?"

"I thought about having sex with you like a girl. Like penetration."

"There's a lot we can do that is penetrative. What really changed?" he asked.

I covered my face with my hands. "When I felt your—you know, I thought that I would have to...you know...reciprocate."

"That you would have to touch my penis? That you would have to make sure that I enjoyed the sex, too?" he asked.

My throat was tight. "It's not that I don't want you to enjoy the sex. I don't think I can...do that."

"You can't make sure that I will enjoy the sex. So you're lousy in bed?"

"No!" I snapped.

"Sorry, honey. Just teasing." He smiled. "Got to lighten things up sometimes. You didn't think you would be willing to do that for me, is that it?"

"Yes. It scared me," I confessed.

"My little pecker scared you! I don't think that's happened before." Jody cupped his hands over mine. "Foremost, don't ever shove me on the floor again, baby. I deserve better than to have someone act repulsed with me or discard me like some…thing."

"I'm sorry," I apologized, my face burning with embarrassment.

"However, I am willing to work with you." He gave a slight smile.

"How?" I asked, dumbfounded.

"Let me pleasure you."

I jerked my hands away from his. "I don't think so."

"You thought so a few minutes ago. Come on. If you need to work in stages, okay. Stage one, just let me touch you. No strings attached." He rubbed his hands further up my thighs, filling me with both fear and excitement.

"Jody—"

"No, Jody." He wagged his finger at me. "Look, at least let me touch you, and if you don't want to continue until you come, that's fine. No orgasm required."

"Can I close my eyes?" I asked, carefully. Somehow closing my eyes made it feel easier.

Jody got up and placed his wig carefully back in the box. Then he took his shirt and bra off before walking back over and kneeling between my legs. "No, you can't. If we are going to move on to stage two, then you need to be able to look at me during sex."

He unzipped my jeans and pulled them off. My gut tightened so much that I thought there was no way any blood was getting down there. But at the same time, I wanted Jody to touch me. I just hoped that my feelings wouldn't change halfway into things, possibly hurting him even more than I already had. I wasn't sure how far I was going to be able to go. His fingers pulled on my briefs.

"Can I leave them on?" I asked, stopping his hands.

"Okay. But I want you to watch and look at me."

I watched his delicate hands and fake nails open the front flap and enter my groin area. The first touch tickled me, causing me to jerk.

"Relax," he assured me.

I took a deep breath. His fingers gently brushed against my penis, only very barely touching me. It caused tingling sensations, and I felt my penis swelling.

"Seems like it's working to me," Jody encouraged me.

"That's what it does if someone touches it like that. What'd you expect?"

"That's the point, Oakley. It does that when someone touches it — when anyone touches it. Even a guy."

Jody wrapped his fingers around my penis and slide his hand down to my shaft. Erotic sensations fluttered all over my body. He leaned forward.

"What are you doing?" I demanded, jerking away.

"Kiss me," he whispered.

"Now?" I asked. I was just starting to savor his hands touching me. Kissing him emphasized that I was in fact having sex with a guy. While my body and feelings for Jody consented, something in my brain still said that somehow this was wrong.

"Well what kind of sexual experiences do you typically have? Yes, now!" Jody insisted.

I went to kiss him.

"Eyes open!" he ordered firmly.

I reluctantly opened my eyes and kissed him. My lips were reserved, but Jody's were passionate. His tongue bullied its way past my closed lips, and he jerked even harder on my erect penis. I opened my mouth, seizing his tongue with mine, leaning into it.

"What if I laid on top of you?" he proposed. "Take your shirt off."

"My shirt! But you said—"

"I didn't say that you had to have sex. We laid together with our shirts off before," he reminded me.

I took my shirt off and lay down. Jody climbed on top of me but a little over to the side so that he could keep caressing my cock. My brain was telling me that something grotesque was on me, but the weight of his body and the ways that his breath tickled my neck hairs seemed to interest my penis more in the activity. It felt good.

He kissed me hard again. "Relax. Just let it feel good. Don't analyze it. Don't think about what you've been taught about sex with men. But I'll stop whenever you want me to, okay?"

But that was all my brain wanted to do. *What if I like it? Will I ever be able to go back or will he demand sex all the time?* I realized that the potential for sexual freedom that Jody offered might also manifest into a sexually demanding situation that I couldn't handle. I needed things to move slowly.

"Come on," he coached me. "You don't have to come. Just let yourself become fully aroused. Like you were earlier. Just let me know when you want me to stop."

I started taking deep breaths. Even though it was awkward, there was something erotically intimate about it, as if it was my first time, and Jody was lovingly taking my virginity. In a way, I also found my innocence arousing.

"Look at me," Jody reminded me.

I stared at his eyes, still breathing in and out only to find that the breathing reminded my body too much of orgasms, and my little guy poked upward.

"There you are." Jody smiled. "Do you want me to stop now?"

"I...I...don't know." I wasn't ready to just say yes.

"Gosh, Oakman, do you know anything?" He pinched my cheek.

"No."

"I would like to keep going. Do I have your permission?"

"Can I close my eyes?" I begged again.

"Yes, but I get to take your briefs off. Deal?"

I nodded and closed my eyes, continuing my breathing, *In and out. In and out. In and out.* I felt Jody slip off my boxers, and the cool air of the room sensitized my penis more. *In and out. In and out. In and out.* I felt his mouth close around my penis. There was only wet, warm softness pressing up and down along me, and a wave of pleasure circulated all over my body. I felt a little pull and tickle as his tongue circulated around my Prince Albert piercing. I pictured Jody's red curls, full lips and his head bobbing up and down in my mind. A moan escaped my mouth.

"Sorry," I stuttered.

"For enjoying it?" Jody whispered.

In and out. In and out. In and out. I put my hand on Jody's head. His hair was thick and curly like a girl, so I fiddled with his locks as I felt his head bob up and down faster. *In and out. In and out. In and out.*

Then I came.

Chapter Fifteen

Pate

"You got me in some shit, man," I scolded Stormy in class the following week. "I had to spend the whole weekend apologizing."

"Yeah, but what I said was true," he argued. "Did you see this? I got an A on my paper! That's awesome!"

We were hanging out in the library at our usual study room space. It had been a long night at the hotel with Stormy and Maybelle. She basically gave me the silent treatment, washing her face and immediately going to bed while Stormy begged me to walk around the hotel neighborhood with him so that he could smoke and explore. The tension in the room didn't seem to faze him, but I walked around with him to avoid having another person angry at me. Fortunately, Jody carried on most of the conversations with him on the car ride home while Maybelle and I fought through text messages. I squeezed up all the leftover money I could find after paying for the trip to send her flowers, which seemed to ease things over.

"Just never invite him anywhere again," Maybelle ordered me on the phone.

"He's my friend," I reasoned with her.

"Well, keep your friend and his stupid opinions away from me."

The typical me would have immediately ceased all interactions with Stormy in order to appease her, but I couldn't do it. He was the only person who knew something about the "real" me, and he had accepted me. It was too much to give up a support like that, especially when he could beat people up, including Bullet.

"Just don't antagonize my girlfriend, okay?" I asked Stormy.

"Okay, man, I'm sorry. But I got an A! Look!" He was holding up his paper like some kind of trophy. "I couldn't have done it without your help."

"You're welcome."

"So what about this Halloween party? I've never been to a party. I'm excited," he stated, still admiring the paper.

"You're pretty excited about anything. Why don't you hang out with us this weekend? Come over to the ranch," I suggested.

"Sure, I'm free most weekends now that it's getting cold."

We were three weeks from Halloween, and the pressure to have the party to make things up to Maybelle was high. Oakley was still reluctant, but Jody's assuredness seemed to cool him off. He had also been quiet on the drive home and hadn't spoken to me much since we returned. I figured an evening of getting

Stormy high was just the entertainment we both needed.

When I returned home later that day, there was another mysterious letter lying on my bed. It had no return address, and the handwriting on the front was the same as the previous one. I opened it and pulled out a small purple letter with typed writing.

The summers in Montana are sudden, hot and dry
The ravenous Jurassic mosquitoes will torment your soul
But the swiftness of your unique smile makes the warm, long days pass by
Causing your spirit to shine through like a single diamond nestled in a pool of coal

I still hadn't told anyone about the first letter — not even Maybelle. I figured she was working up to something with me by dropping these random poems in the mail, so I didn't want to ruin any surprise. *But what if she thinks I don't like them?*

No one had ever bestowed any romance on me. Oakley and I had dated in high school where we were just figuring out how to do couple things, and none of the other guys I'd dated had ever taken the time or figured I needed it. Secret love letters resembled acts of affection from middle schoolers, so the only possible option was Maybelle, knowing her sweet immaturity. Or worse, it was a joke. The latter was another major reason that I kept the letters to myself.

I spent a few hours studying the letter in my bed and daydreaming about Maybelle. The weeks were flying by. By December, she'd want to have sex. I concocted many scenarios in my brain. One, she would tell me I was gross and slap me for trying to date someone like her. Then I imagined all the gossip and rumors that would likely drive me out of school, and perhaps away from Montana altogether, leaving poor Oakley behind to fight his own battles.

But then I thought of hope. Maybelle would be confused, but her love for me would overpower any doubt, and she would learn to make love to me as a man with a vagina. After all, girls were often more fluid in their sexuality. December bought me more time to woo her and strengthen our bond so that it could withstand any obstacle that a vagina might send my way. *You can't love someone and just throw it all away, can you?*

Oakley came home later, throwing his bookbag on his bed and running his fingers through his brown hair. He looked tired.

"Want to go smoke?" I asked. Relaxing with some weed at the end of the day was a common event for us as long as we weren't working the evening shift at Walmart.

Oakley still didn't say much. He just puffed and stared blankly off at the brown barn walls.

"You've been quiet," I commented.

"Just got a lot to think about." He kicked his feet in the dirt.

"Did something happen with you and Jody?" I asked him. I feared that he had blown it with Jody.

"Happen? Like what do you think happened?"

I shoved the joint in his face. "Geez, smoke this and relax."

He smoked.

"Did you guys get into a fight?" I tried again.

"No. It's actually good—but it's not good. I don't know." He rubbed his temples and grimaced.

I inhaled the sedating smoke deep into my lungs and stretched my legs. We sat in silence for a few moments before he finally spoke.

"He...sucked my dick," Oakley blurted out.

"Oh," I gasped. "How was it? Did you...you know?"

"We didn't have sex!" he asserted strongly.

"A blow job is still sex," I claimed. "If anyone touched my vagina, it would definitely be sex. It just isn't intercourse. You've done more than I have with Maybelle. Did you orgasm?"

"Yeah, I did. But it was...weird." He took a long puff, staring off in the distance. "It's still weird. I don't know how to feel about it."

"But you liked it?" I asked, raising my eyebrows.

Oakley shrugged. "I like getting blow jobs, yes! They feel good. I just...I worry about how far this is going to go. Like, I can't suck a guy off. I don't even know if I can have intercourse with a guy."

"So you didn't do anything back to him? He just got you off," I confirmed. Honestly, I didn't think he was going to make it to any kind of sex with Jody. I was impressed.

"Yeah. Fuck, I pushed him on the floor." He buried his face in his hands in shame.

"You got violent?" My eyes widened in horror.

"No, it was an accident," he pleaded. "He was sitting on me, and I felt his...penis, and it was...hard. It freaked me out."

"It means that he is sexually attracted to you. That's good." I surveyed him for a few moments. "What are you scared of? And please don't say 'I don't know.'"

Oakley puffed some more and stared at his shoes in thought. "I'm afraid that I'm attracted to him, but I'm also afraid that I'm not. Does that make sense?"

I reflected for a moment as I tried to relate to him. "Maybe it's kind of like I was afraid that I wasn't trans even though I am trans. It seemed so surreal at first, like something that only happens to other people. It seems funny but sometimes now I still wonder if I'm trans."

Oakley's eyes flashed a smile. "You're trans." He patted my thigh. "Yeah, I guess it feels something like that. It doesn't seem real. It's not something I ever thought about myself. So, I also worry that it's fleeting. What if I'm only going through a phase? I feel like my life is at this standstill, and I don't know where I want to go. I worry that this is just some distraction."

"What is your status with Jody? He's your boyfriend? Officially?" I asked.

"I made it official," he replied.

"Have you told your dad?"

"No!" He gasped. "Granny's pretty good at keeping her mouth shut. I don't want to tell him unless I know for sure that this is going to be some permanent thing. Why put him through it?"

"But he's your boyfriend. It is permanent," I informed him.

"I need more time to see if it's going somewhere," he explained.

"To see if you can have sex with him, right?" I asked.

"Yes."

* * * *

A couple of nights later, we were both sitting on a swing in Granny's front yard watching Stormy's dirty exhaust-farting truck spew up the driveway. Oakley seemed to have warmed up to Stormy after the Billings trip and agreed that we needed a little harmless amusement in our life. We were both hoping to talk him into some marijuana.

"What's up, guys?" Stormy hollered, practically letting his large body fall out of the truck instead of climbing out.

Jody came walking out of the barn. He had agreed to help us decorate for the Halloween party that was still up in the air, although we were moving forward with planning it. The situation made both me and Oakley nervous. Jody walked up to Stormy, shoving some skull lights in his face.

"Just the job for you. You can hang these in the barn, my friend."

"Okay," Stormy happily agreed.

We all walked into the barn. Jody had brought over a few old tables and had picked out some decorations at Walmart.

"What about refreshments? Do you guys just want to buy things or does anyone cook?" Jody asked.

"I can cook." I raised my hand.

"I vouch for him," Oakley said.

"Good," Jody said. "It's more fun if we make our own cookies and cupcakes. I love decorating them! I'll come over the day before, and Pate and I can make all the food."

"I can help," Stormy volunteered.

"No, because you'll just eat everything," I argued. Hanging out with him over these past weeks, I had watched this guy consume everything around him to nourish that gargantuan stature of his. I didn't trust him around my cupcakes for a minute.

Oakley rolled a joint and motioned for all of us to come join him by our barn swing. He held it up to Stormy. "Are you game?"

Stormy nodded. "Okay."

We all smoked and drank a few beers while talking through party plans. The skull lights added more subtle light to the barn along with the old Christmas lights that had already been hung up. The barn offered the perfect atmosphere for a fall party. However, I hadn't figured out my costume, something that would disguise me. Jody had already decided to dress in a girl costume as a witch, which would be easy for him. I still worried that people would know that it was Jody and there was no way to predict their reaction to Oakley and Jody together.

Stormy played with the skull lights, making a lasso and whipping it over his head. "What if I got one of those light costumes? The ones with the lights all over a black outfit. That would look cool out here."

"Are you going to dance in them?" I asked.

He snickered. "I'm not a dancer."

"It's a party. You got to dance," Jody asserted. "What are you going to do? Just sit on the sidelines watching everyone else?"

"Not everyone here dances. I bet a lot of people won't," he replied.

"Then I don't want them at my party," Jody stated. "I'm not helping decorate a barn and feed folks just to have them stand around and drink beer."

"And smoke weed," Stormy remarked.

"They're not getting my weed," both Oakley and I said together.

"When we invite people, they should know that it's a Halloween dance party. Otherwise, it's lame," Jody persisted.

"I don't know how to dance," Stormy admitted. "Look at me. At this body. It's awkward."

"I can show you how to dance," I offered.

"Yeah! Let's teach Stormy how to dance!" Jody exclaimed. "Pate, go turn on some music."

"I don't know…" Stormy grumbled.

"You're not shy about dancing with a bunch of guys, are you?" I questioned.

"What kind of dancing are we talking about?"

"Don't worry." I winked at him.

I selected The Sugarhill Gang's *Rapper's Delight*. It had an easy, repetitive beat that I thought he could learn to follow. Too many changes in rhythm would throw him off.

I took Stormy's hand and moved to the middle of the barn. Oakley and Jody followed.

"So, just try to hear the beat and match your body movements to it," I instructed.

"I feel stupid." He giggled. His eyes sparkled a little when he laughed, and I noticed that he had dimples in his cheeks. He was a little cute for such a cowboy.

"Come on," Jody encouraged him. Jody was already moving around to the music and jerking Oakley's arm to do the same.

"Watch me." I moved my hips from side to side without moving my feet. "See, this is a very simple movement."

"I don't want to swing my hips," Stormy said shyly.

I grabbed his shoulders and turned him around, standing behind him. "Okay, I'm going to put my hands on your hips and help you find the rhythm. Is that okay? Not too weird?"

He nodded in agreement while sniggering. I squeezed his hips and moved his torso around. He started laughing more.

"I can't do this." He snorted. His face grew red.

"Come on," Jody chimed in. He got in front of Stormy and took his hands, swinging them along with my hip movements.

Oakley was laughing hard, too. "He looks like some lanky Sasquatch! Oh, that's what you should be, man. Be Bigfoot."

"'Cause I don't get called that all the time," Stormy retorted.

"Yeah, but it matches your general awkwardness well," Oakley suggested. "No one's going to think anything about an awkward dancing ape man. Hell, I'd pay to see that shit!"

"I'm going to let go," I said in Stormy's ear. "Can you keep moving on your own?"

I removed my hands from his hips, and Jody released his hands. We both danced around him, and Stormy attempted to keep his stiff frame moving in between giggling spells.

"The whole point is to just let loose and have fun," I urged.

"I guess I'm having fun, then." He winked at me.

Oakley was still pointing and laughing at Stormy's utter lack of rhythm and the way his stiff hips shook.

"You're not helping," I yelled at Oakley.

"You guys won't let me dance alone, right?" Stormy asked.

"No, man. You won't be alone. We'll all dance with you," I promised him.

"We'll all be disguised anyway. No one's going to know it's a bunch of dudes dancing together," Jody said.

"I think everyone's going to know *he's* a dude," Oakley interjected, pointing at Stormy.

"Can I see you dance?" Stormy asked me.

"Yeah, I'd like to see you dance, too. Oakley's talked about it a lot," Jody agreed.

They all went to sit back on the swing while I changed songs. I changed the tunes to Kenny Loggins' *Footloose*. It was one of my favorites to dance to. I could include a multitude of various dance moves from robot to river-dancing to breakdance. They cheered as I moved around the barn and occasionally danced up to them.

I grabbed Stormy by the hands again and pulled him back on the floor. "I've got it," I told him.

I showed him some of the robot moves, and with his awkward figure and long limbs, the dance worked perfectly for a beginner.

"You got it!" Jody said as he rejoined us. "He looks great!"

"That's it! I'm going to be a robot." Stormy cheered, clapping his hands together. He continued to practice the few robotic moves I showed him.

The night fell upon the prairie, and we all sat outside on Granny's porch sipping wine and beers. Jody pleaded with me to enter the talent show that was scheduled for December.

"You're really good. You should do it. Hell, if I could doll you up, you'd make an excellent drag queen. You've got a lot of feminine features," Jody commented.

I blushed. "Yeah, I've been told that before."

"You should do it," Stormy agreed. "You're really talented. Hell, you should be doing it professionally."

"I think it would be good for you to do the show," Oakley encouraged me.

"Maybe you guys are right," I replied. "I haven't performed in a long time."

"What made you stop?" Jody asked.

"Just lost some confidence in myself, I guess. You know what I mean?" I implied to Jody. Oakley had informed me that Jody knew that I was trans, but I wasn't ready to reveal that to Stormy.

Jody nodded.

"What do you mean?" Stormy inquired. "You're not confident in yourself?"

"Nothing. I just changed after high school, that's all," I told him.

When the evening ended, Oakley drove Jody home, and Stormy took off in his truck. It gave me time to read the letter again. *Would Maybelle find me more attractive if I danced in the show?* I was my most confident when I danced. The show was in December, the four-month mark. Perhaps performing again was the boost I needed before I would have to come out to her. Perhaps she would see me differently when I was on stage. Maybe my performance would make her want to stay with me.

At least, that was what I hoped.

* * * *

Oakley

I had noticed changes on campus. Whispers seemed to flourish when I walked by, and conversations ceased when I entered a room. I was never too social, so it was easy to just focus on hanging out with Pate and Stormy, but something hung in the air. This inevitable tension kept building. I didn't know when it would explode, but I knew it was coming.

Jody started having lunch with me on Thursdays before my afternoon shift at Walmart. We had to meet on campus because he had back-to-back classes. The weather had gotten too cold to eat outside or in the car, so we ate in the student cafeteria. The noise and voices always left me feeling tense, and I started realizing what Pate meant with his social anxiety issues.

Jody was always calm. He chatted away about his classes and possible jobs after graduation. We'd had a few more sexual encounters since Billings with hand jobs and blow jobs, but I was always the recipient. However, it had gotten easier and a lot less stressful for me to relax and lean into it. I knew that it wouldn't continue that way forever. At some point, he'd want more.

"Have you told your parents about us?" Jody suddenly asked.

"Huh?" I had been lost in the social chaos around me. "My parents? No. I'm not ready for that. That's like coming out as gay."

Jody raised his eyebrow. "I thought we were in a relationship, though? And you haven't told your parents about me?"

"I thought we'd wait to see where things are going. I don't want to stress them out if I don't have to."

Jody sighed and gazed seriously at me. "So to you, things aren't going anywhere. You don't think there's a future here?"

"I don't—"

"Damn it, Oakman." Jody pounded his fist on the table. "Stop claiming that you don't know. I have the right to know how you feel about me. How you feel about *us*."

I gulped. "I really like you. I want to keep seeing you."

"Do you see a future with us, though? Something long-term, committed?" he asked.

"I don—I would prefer if there could be a future. That's what I hope happens."

"I hope so, too." Jody smiled. He reached for my hand, but I yanked it away and moved back.

"I see," he said sadly.

He got up and tossed his paper bag in the trash.

"Wait," I said, holding up my hand.

Jody didn't respond but walked out of the building. I threw my trash away and ran after him.

I caught up to him and grabbed him by the shoulders. "Wait, Jody. What's wrong?"

For the first time, he didn't make eye contact with me. He was usually adamant about staring at people head-on with those green eyes, something he said he learned to do to assert himself more. This time, he looked away as if purposely avoiding me. I could see tears in his eyes.

"Do you *not* realize that all these things you do hurt me?" he asked. "How would you feel if some girl pushed you on the floor just because you got an erection?"

"I apologized for that. I thought we were over that," I pleaded.

"Then you call me your boyfriend, but you don't tell your parents," he continued. "And you know that people around here already know about us, yet you won't hold my hand at lunch. Not to mention that you still won't touch me."

I looked down in shame. "I told you it's hard for me."

"So when does it get hard for me, Oakley? How long am I supposed to date someone who seems repulsed by me?"

I shook my head. "I don't know what to say. You know I'm straight."

Jody wiped some tears from his eyes. "Maybe that's the problem. I shouldn't be wasting my time on a straight guy, or at least a guy who keeps insisting that he is straight. I told you upfront that we could be friends and that if you wanted to pursue this, then you needed to be ready to actually do it."

"Are you breaking up with me?" I asked desperately.

Jody finally made eye contact. "No, not yet anyway. But I'm not waiting for you, Oakley. You need to figure this out because my heart isn't a tool for you to figure out your sexual orientation."

"I promise. I'll try harder. Don't give up on us yet." I grabbed his hands.

Jody smiled and went to touch my cheek with his hand, but I pulled away. He shook his head in disappointment.

"I guess I'm at the point where I'm going to start not believing you, Oakley."

"I'll call you later," I said.

"Whatever," Jody mumbled and coldly walked away.

* * * *

"So you're having a party?"

Bullet rarely spoke to me. We had worked out a system in lab where we didn't speak but somehow navigated the tasks. So, when I heard that deep, raspy voice, it caused me to jerk.

"Maybelle says you're having a party." He peered at me.

"Yes. That's true."

"Is it a fag party only or are other people invited?" he asked menacingly.

"Is this supposed to be your polite way of asking me to invite you? Because if it is, you're not very good at convincing me." I returned my focus back to the lab assignment.

Bullet snickered. "You think I give a rat's ass if you invite me? I'll come if I want to. I know where you faggots live."

I tossed down my pencil. "So...if Pate's dating Maybelle, how does that make him a faggot?"

"Because he is one." He snorted. "He looks like a pussy. You really believe that a girl like Maybelle is going to stay with him? Girls like tough guys around here. Guys who work with their hands, not pussies who dance."

Hearing that Bullet was aware that Pate danced only proved that Bullet talked to Maybelle more than we'd believed.

"Look at your little pussy hands, too," he continued. "I bet you guys never done any real man's work. I guess you need hands like that if you're playing with dick, right?"

"Let's just do the lab," I ordered, returning to the lab worksheet. "I don't like you. You don't like me and Pate. That's it. Let's just get this done."

"You can tell your friend that she still loves me," he continued. "She never stopped. We talk every day before bed. He's just a rebound. She's just punishing me."

"I thought real men wouldn't let a girl have so much power over them," I blurted out.

"I can take her back any time I want. You remember that," he promised, waving his finger at me. "Besides, he won't even fuck her. She'll be running back in no time."

"Just mind your own business," I snapped.

Bullet laughed. "It's hard when that little girl tells me everything! There's nothing that happens in this place that I don't know about. You two remember that. I'll be at your fucking little party, and there's nothing either of you are going to do about it."

"Stormy is coming. Maybe *he'll* do something about it," I threatened, clenching my fists tightly.

Bullet's smile faded, and he turned around, examining Stormy and Pate together in the back of the room. "Let that motherfucker try," he said.

"He isn't afraid to," I retorted.

* * * *

I called Jody several times that evening, but he wouldn't answer. Pate was home and typing up a paper for class, but I was hesitant to talk to him about it. He always seemed to gravitate toward Jody's side, and I wasn't in the mood. I needed empathy. I felt like I was being crushed by all the pro-gay jargon and the pressure to expand my sexuality, as if that somehow made them all better people than me. It wasn't fair for them all to judge me for being straight. But then again, as Jody said, maybe a straight guy shouldn't date a gay guy.

"Pate?"

"Yeah. What's up?" he answered.

"Bullet's probably coming to the party."

"I figured he'd show up," he responded nonchalantly.

"But there's more to it," I told him. "He was talking in lab today, and he knows an awful lot about you and Maybelle. He knows you haven't had sex with her."

Pate closed his laptop. "What did he say to you?"

I took a deep breath. I didn't want to make Pate go into a panic attack, but I also felt he needed to know. "He was talking shit about it not working out between you two and that you're not fucking her. That seems like a really personal thing to tell him, don't you think so?"

"Yeah, it is. It's embarrassing." His tone was soft, more sad than angry.

"Aren't you upset with her?" I asked.

"Yeah, but what do I do?" He shrugged. "I don't want to lose her. I love her."

I went over and sat on his bed next to him. "Do you think that maybe you're in love with the idea of her? I mean, she doesn't know the truth. It might change everything."

Pate rubbed his chin in deep thought. "But it might not. Why do you have to be so negative? You're sitting here pushing me to disclose that I'm trans, yet you won't even have sex with Jody. You're accusing me of pursuing a doomed relationship, yet here you are pretending like you're gay, and you're not—or at least you keep convincing us that you're not. So leave me alone."

I rolled my eyes. "You know, Pate, you always defend anyone who's gay or trans. Well, what about straight people? Are you not playing around with Maybelle's feelings? Do you not think *she* can get hurt? Have you even considered it?"

Pate sat in silence.

"Just because she doesn't stay with you doesn't mean that she couldn't love you," I suggested. "You could break up and both be brokenhearted. It's not always about you. And…maybe it's possible that I can't make it work with Jody and that I could be brokenhearted, too."

We both went back to working on homework. After about twenty minutes, Pate closed his laptop again.

"Oakley?"

"Yes."

"When I transitioned, I had to decide that my own happiness was more important than what society thought I should be. I understand what you're saying, but if Maybelle rejects me but still loves me, isn't she choosing society over her and my happiness? If you leave Jody but love him, isn't that the same? I've gone through too much to move backward. I guess that's why I'm so stubborn about it."

"I'm sorry," I said. "I forget sometimes that you've had to fight."

"I know that she might dump me. I *know* it." His voice choked up a little. "I think about it constantly. I'm foolishly hoping that with time, our love will be strong enough for her to overcome it. Just as I feel that Jody is hoping the same for you. Is that stupid?"

"No, it's not stupid," I assured him with a slight smile.

When I laid down to sleep, I reflected on Pate's words. Maybe like Pate, Jody was being patient with me in the hopes that my feelings for him would overcome the physical issues. On the other hand, maybe I was hoping for the same thing.

Chapter Sixteen

Pate

I threw the flannel shirt across the room into the pile of three other shirts that weren't good enough, either. I fell back onto the bed in insecure misery. *Why the fuck am I having a party? I don't even like people or parties.*

"What's the deal?" Oakley asked. He had settled on a werewolf mask and a ripped shirt for effect. I had decided to be a scarecrow, an entity that was meant to scare birds away. In this case, perhaps to scare people away.

"I'm in over my head," I murmured. "I don't think I can handle all this responsibility."

"Jody and Stormy already did the decorating. The food is made. It's just showing up and cleaning up now."

I knew that, yet something was eating at me—a twisting dread in my temples and stomach. I didn't want to do it.

"Are you worried about Bullet showing up?" Oakley probed.

"Maybe. I don't know."

Oakley came over and sat on the bed beside me. He placed his hand on my bare stomach and rubbed it, something he often did to comfort me. I'd always teased him for treating me like a dog.

"Jody wants me to tell my parents about us," he said, continuing to stare down at my belly. "I don't think I can do that."

"What does that mean? If you can't?"

"I don't know," he said with a nervous smile. "I really don't know."

I sat up and took his hand. "Why did we get ourselves into doomed relationships? Are we that self-destructive?"

Silence.

"I feel like we're both afraid to discover who we really are," Oakley stated.

* * * *

Jody and Stormy had done an amazing job with the décor. It was all mostly Jody's design, but Stormy's height had played a vital role in getting everything where it needed to be. Jody was dressing up like Lady Gaga and had spent hours perfecting his makeup, wig and costume. Stormy had decided to forgo being a robot and instead was dressed like a meat packer with red paint splashed on his white coat and large black latex butcher glove, carrying a fake meat cleaver. He wore a facemask over his mouth and nose to disguise his identity, but I didn't think anyone would miss the behemoth in the room, making him easily identifiable. Quite scary, also.

My scarecrow mask was hot and stuffy, but I was determined to keep it glued to my face. It provided a comforting shield to hide behind throughout the party. Maybelle was wearing a plague doctor costume, which gave off a radiating masculinity that really turned me on. I was so accustomed to seeing her in girly clothes and not something so dark and creepy.

Fortunately, the party was not crowded. We had around fifteen people show up who mostly sat around, chilling to music, drinking some homebrewed Montana beer and having fun. Oakley and I didn't know the other people, but Maybelle had gone to school with them. She fluttered back and forth between my crew and the guests, often removing her mask. I envied her social confidence.

"I thought you'd be dancing at a party," Stormy teased me.

"Not with all these folks around!" I responded, watching the four people who were having fun on the dance floor.

"I'd dance with you," he offered with a grin. "If you want. I'm not weirded out. Unless you think I would embarrass you with my dancing."

"Nah."

"Come on." He extended his hand.

"I really don't feel comfortable."

"We could step outside and smoke a joint? Maybe that would loosen you up?" he offered.

Silence.

"You're really self-conscious, aren't you?" he inquired.

I nodded. "Yes."

"I can understand." He smiled. "It's not easy being this size. I stood out way early in elementary school. People always ask why I don't play basketball. It's difficult. Sometimes I intimidate people without even meaning to."

"Were you teased for it?" I asked.

"Yeah, but not in a strict bullying way, you could say. I mean, yes, it was teasing that made me feel different. But no one avoided talking to me or being my friend, necessarily. I've always kind of been a social recluse, though. I never had many friends."

"Me, neither. At least, not after transitioning—" My heart stopped.

"Transitioning?" He took off his mask. His skin shimmered with a few sweat droplets, and his hair was matted down. He almost looked like a different person.

"Um, you know"—I grabbed his arm—"maybe I will dance with you. Come on."

I pulled him out on the floor, and we started dancing to the *Monster Mash*. Stormy retreated into his physically awkward self, laughing and amusing himself with his clumsy attempts to dance. I laughed. The dread that was simmering in my gut started to steam, though. *Maybe we should get drunk. He won't remember what I just said.*

Just when I felt my body loosen and my mood relax, Bullet walked in. He had three friends with him, and they all appeared intoxicated. My eyes scanned the room for Oakley, but he was nowhere to be seen.

"Where's Oakley? Have you seen him?" I asked Stormy.

"I think he and Jody took a walk or something. Private time, I guess." His eyes found Bullet. "Is that what you're worried about?"

Maybelle walked up from behind, throwing her arms around me. "Ugh, he actually came. I told him not to. But I did make him promise that if he did, he would be good. So don't worry. I'll handle him if he gets mean. I know how to handle Bullet."

"You sure do," muttered Stormy.

Maybelle rolled her eyes. "Maybe we should go to your room for a while?"

"Why?" I gasped.

Stormy laughed.

"To spend some time together as a couple," Maybelle insisted as she shot a mean glare at Stormy. "Geez, I guess girls' parents didn't have to worry about you trying to get in their daughters' pants in high school, did they?" She giggled, taking my hand to lead me outside the barn.

"I don't want to leave this unsupervised." *First, I tell Stormy that I transitioned, and now Maybelle wants to go to my room.* My entire body burned in fear.

"What are you, a cop?" she joked. "Stormy can watch things. Come on."

We quietly crept into the house. Granny had gone to bed, but there were a few lights on for Oakley and me. We walked upstairs to my room, carefully stepping to avoid the loud creaks that often emerged from the stairs.

"Wow, this is pretty cool. It's private," Maybelle remarked, walking around the room.

"Where would you like to sit?" I asked.

She sat on Oakley's bed.

"That's Oak's bed."

"Oh." She moved over to the other bed. "Come over here," she said, patting the space beside her.

I removed my mask, setting it on the desk.

"Pate?"

"Yes."

"Are you a virgin?"

"What? No!" I snapped.

"You just seem so stiff. Are you…I mean, you're not… I don't want to be rude, but…"

"What is it?" My eyes had locked so firmly on the floor like a chain connected them to it.

"Are you…gay? I mean, I only ask because your friend is gay—"

Shit. Complicated question. "No. Oak is not gay, and if he was, it wouldn't make me gay." The dread bubbled in my gut. *Damn, she'll think I have diarrhea.*

"Okay." Her soft, manicured hands gently grabbed my chin and turned my head toward hers. Her lips curled in the sweet, intoxicating smile that she always seemed to have on her face. We kissed.

"Can you at least take off your shirts?" she asked with a hopeful smile.

"I don't think this is the place or time. I mean, we're hosting a party outside," I argued. I had never felt both this rush of excitement to be alone with her, yet this poignant dread of her potentially discovering me.

"It's the perfect time," she whispered seductively. "It's romantic. It's Halloween. I'm not pressuring to have sex. I just want to go a little further. I'll take off my shirt," she teased, tugging at her shirt collar.

Only a study lamp lit the room, causing shadows that could easily hide body parts as long as I kept my body turned at the right angle. My scars from top surgery had healed amazingly, but they were still visible. *But maybe, maybe, in this light, she won't notice.*

"Okay," I stuttered reluctantly.

"Geez, don't get excited or anything." She pulled away from me.

"No!" I grabbed her by the waist and pulled her close. "I'm sorry. I'm just insecure."

"No kidding."

We kissed as she unbuttoned my flannel and softly pulled it off my shoulders. I jiggled my hands to escape from the shirt. She stood up to remove her costume. She was wearing a T-shirt and jeans underneath.

"Take off my shirt," she ordered.

I carefully grabbed the bottom of her T-shirt and pulled it over her head. I knew she was wearing a colorful bra. I knew that she had wonderful, firm breasts. Yet I didn't see anything in front of me. The dread had entered my veins and crept up into my brain, blocking my sense of vision. My temples pressed so hard into my skull that I wrinkled my forehead in pain.

Her hands found the bottom of my T-shirt and started to pull it upward. I began twisting my torso around, searching for the right angle of shadow and protection.

Then, the shirt was gone.

The chilly October air tickled my skin as I sat exposed.

"Why are your eyes closed?" Maybelle asked.

I hadn't realized.

"You are the weirdest guy I've ever known." She giggled and kissed me, pressing her chest against me. The wire in her bra pinched my skin. Her hands moved from my back, around to my sides then to my chest. She pulled away.

"What? What is it?" I asked frantically.

The skin above her eyes crinkled, and her mouth frowned.

"What?" I questioned again, desperately.

Her little hand touched my chest again, but it wasn't an affectionate touch. It was an inquisitive, confused touch.

"Your chest feels…different. Wait…" Her fingers hit a scar. "What is that? The skin feels different there."

I grabbed her hands, pulling them away from my chest, but when I did, my torso leaned back, and the lamplight hit my chest.

"Wait, are those scars?" Maybelle leaned forward in surprise. I tried to twist away again, but her head was already inches away from my scars. There was no hiding.

"Why would you have scars like that?" she asked, confused.

I had no response.

"Are you not going to answer me?" she demanded.

"I don't have a good answer."

"I don't understand, Pate. I'm just asking why you have scars like this. I've never seen this. Did you have cancer or something? Why don't you just tell me?"

My hands started shaking rapidly. My head was dizzy.

"Pate, are you okay? What's wrong?" She placed her hand on my inner thigh. I immediately tried to stand, causing her hand to fall closer to my crotch. Her hand squeezed my thigh to stop me from standing and accidently squeezed the hollow gap between my legs. She released me.

"What's going on?" she asked with a bewildered gaze.

I escaped to the computer desk, resting my hands on the counter to stable myself from falling over. My heart raced so relentlessly that I could hardly catch my breath. Tears swelled my eyes, pinching out of the corners.

"I have to tell you something. But I'm not sure if you will still love me." The words almost choked out of me as I fought back tears and a panic attack.

"What?" Her tone was cold.

"I'm..." My throat was choking me. "I'm transgender. I'm a transgender man."

"What is that?"

Shaking and still not looking at her, I said, "It means that I was assigned female at birth. I used to...look like a woman."

"You used to *look* like a woman. What does that even mean, Pate? Assigned female at birth..." She stood up and walked over to me, grabbing me by the shoulders and twisting me around to face her. Her eyes appeared angry. "Are you a fucking girl?"

I gulped, but my mouth was so dry that I could hardly swallow. I couldn't stop the tears from flowing down my cheeks. "I'm not a girl." I could hardly speak. "I'm not a girl, Maybelle. I was just born in a girl's body."

Her eyes widened in horror. "You're a girl!" she yelled.

"Shhh." I put my finger to my lips. I didn't want her to wake Granny.

"How could you fucking do this to me?" She walked back to the bed and started putting her shirt back on. "Eww, a fucking girl? I was making out with a dyke? You fucking tricked me!"

I ran to her and tried to grab her hand, but she pulled away. "Don't you fucking touch me, you...you pervert! I don't date pedophiles."

"Maybelle, please," I begged. "I love you. You said that you love me —"

"Don't you dare make this about me! You tricked me this whole time. I would never, ugh, never fuck a girl. I told you that! And you just stood there and said nothing. That's exactly what you sexual predators do. You lie!" She turned to leave.

"Maybelle, no!" I sobbed, grabbing her arm, but she violently snatched it from my grasp, nearly causing me to fall over. I fell to my knees, trying to grab her legs to stop her from leaving. "Please don't do this. I'm a man! Believe me, I'm a man!"

She kicked my hands away. "How dare you do this to me? Oh God, what would my parents say? What if they find out? What if the whole town knows…you've ruined my life!"

She stormed out of the room, leaving me a kneeling mess on the ground and nearly choking on my own tears.

"No," I said to myself, cradling my head in my hands. Inside my chest, a sharp, agonizing pain exploded as my heart broke.

* * * *

Oakley

Jody and I had decided to walk around the ranch with a little flashlight and a few beers. Jody had removed his heels and was walking barefoot, carrying his long blue dress in his hands to prevent it from touching the ground.

"You look beautiful." I squeezed his hand.

"Because I'm a girl tonight?" He smiled.

I looked away from him.

"Oak, our relationship is like a seesaw. It's really good. Then it's really bad."

"Bad?"

Jody sighed. "It hurts me to say it, but yes."

"What makes it bad?" I was shocked. *Being with me is bad? Really bad?* "Just because I'm not ready to tell my parents?"

"Because you don't reciprocate. I tell everyone about us. You don't. I make love to you. You don't make love to me. It's not healthy. At least, not for me."

"Wait, what are you saying?" I stopped walking, releasing his hand.

Jody looked flustered. "Damn, Oak. We keep going around in circles. Honestly, I don't understand why you keep pursing me. Why are you doing this?"

"I...I don't know," I insisted. "I don't have a good answer."

"That's bullshit. You *do* know," he argued. Suddenly, he got very emotional, making me realize that he had been bottling up his feelings about this. "And I have the right for you to tell me. Why do you want to be with me? What do you want? What are we doing?" When he sighed again, I could hear the pain and disappointment cracking in his throat.

"I'm not sure what I want, Jody. That's honest. I need some time to...figure it out. This is all new for me. I've never dated a guy," I told him, hoping he could just understand.

"Do you have feelings for me?"

"Yes."

"Well, that's a cop-out," he replied. "Anyone can have feelings for friends. Do you love me or do you see yourself loving me? Because that's the only relationship I want. I want love. I'm not an experiment."

"Stop accusing me of experimenting with you," I scolded him. "I'm not using you."

"Then what is it, Oak? What?"

I never knew how loud silence could be when tension hovers in the air. I searched myself for the words, the reasons, the excuses...my mind was blank.

Jody took my hands. "Make love to me tonight, Oak. I mean, make love *to me*. I want to get closer to you."

We kissed, but there was fear causing our lips to tremble when they met. Jody slowly moved my hand under his dress and over his genitals. I jerked away.

"No! Sorry...I can't. I just can't do it," I insisted.

"What are you afraid of? Does it disgust you?"

"Not exactly," I responded.

"Then what? Tell me. Be honest. Damn it, Oak. *Talk* to me!" He grabbed the sides of my face with his hands. "Talk to me. Please."

"It's...I'm not attracted to it," I admitted

"You're not attracted to my penis?"

"Yes."

He let go of my face. We stood lost in the ocean of darkness that engulfed the small ranch.

"Then I can't do this with you anymore," he told me with tears running down his cheeks.

"You're breaking up with me?" I asked, horrified.

"How do you propose for this to work? You're not attracted to me. You said it yourself."

Inside, I wanted to grab him and hold him. I wanted to make him understand. But then I thought of touching his penis...I just stood silently in shame at my own inability to move past it.

"That's what I thought. I'm sorry, Oak. I'm not some sidekick or fling or friend with benefits. I'm a person who fell in love with you. Yes, I'm in love with you. I've been in love with you since I met you. But you're lost. You don't know what you want or even who you are. Pate may seem like an anxious wreck, but he knows more about himself than you ever will, it seems. At least he doesn't hide from who he is. I've worked so hard in my life—" He stumbled as he began to cry more. "I've worked so hard to learn to love myself. I refuse to be with someone who doesn't love me but uses me."

"I didn't use you," I argued. "You're too harsh on me."

"Yes, you did. You used me for some self-experiment. To give you something to occupy your time with so that you don't have to commit or do anything with your life. Maybe you even used me to get closer to Pate."

"I haven't been in love with Pate for years! That's bullshit!" I shouted, smashing one of the beer bottles against the ground.

"There's only one thing that's bullshit. That's this relationship. It's over," he stated firmly.

"So we're not together now?" I gasped. "We're not even friends? You do this at my fucking party? The fucking party that *you* wanted me to throw?"

"You had your choice of just being my friend. You don't get to go backwards just to soothe your own conscience." He walked away, wrapping his arms around himself.

"That's not fair!" I yelled. "I'm not a bad person! You're making me out to be some asshole. It's not fair!

I tried, damn it! Doesn't that fucking count? You should be lucky that I tried to date y —"

"Fuck you," he hollered as his figure disappeared in the darkness.

I hovered around the ranch for another thirty minutes, hoping that Jody would be long gone by then. I headed back to the barn with the sole intention of kicking everyone the fuck out. When I got closer, I heard yelling. I started to run.

When I arrived, Pate and Maybelle were nowhere to be seen. Bullet was drunk, yelling and ripping off the décor. Stormy was pushing him back, and Bullet's friends were screaming in Bullet's defense.

"Get his drunk ass out of here!" Stormy ordered Bullet's friends.

"Where my girl?" Bullet slurred. "I'm not leaving without my girl. Where is she? Is she with that faggot?"

I turned off the music. "Everyone go! Party's over. Get out!"

"Where's my girl?" Bullet kept whining.

"She isn't here," I yelled back at him. "Now get the fuck out of my house!" Bullet was twice my size but the energy burning in me, full of pain and anger, was so strong that I was willing to take him on.

"She went home. Yeah, she went home with Kelly. You can find her there," Stormy said as he winked at me.

"She went home?" Bullet groaned like a little kid.

"Yeah, man. She went home hours ago. If you want to see her, go to her house."

Bullet's friends helped steady him on his feet. They slowly carried his large body out of the barn. His constant mumbles about Maybelle and going home trailed behind him.

"What a mess," Stormy declared. "I can't stand that guy."

"Where are Pate and Maybelle?" I asked him.

"I don't know. They've been gone a while."

I wanted to imagine Pate as a confident guy who took Maybelle out for a romantic excursion during the party. However, I knew better. If he was alone with her, I was worried. "Let's go check around," I suggested.

Stormy and I walked around the ranch first, but we didn't see them. Glancing up at the bedroom window, I saw a lamp light.

"I think maybe they're up there." I pointed.

"Oh…" Stormy mumbled. "Then better not disturb them."

"It's okay. Go on home. I'll check on him."

"What about the cleanup?" he asked. "I don't mind helping. I can always lock it up for you when I'm done."

I was antsy to just be alone and rid of everyone. On the other hand, I was in no mood for party cleanup.

"Sure, man. That'd be really nice."

"Cool. Tell Pate I'll hit him up tomorrow," he said somberly without the usual grin on his face. Even Stormy's spirits seemed down.

I carefully and slowly walked up the stairs, trying to detect any noises that might indicate conversation, kissing or even sex. It was dead silent. When I was able to poke my head up enough to scour the room, I saw Pate curled up in the fetal position on his bed. He was only wearing his jeans.

"Pate?" I whispered cautiously.

No answer. I walked closer and could see him trembling. "Pate?"

"She knows." He burst out with a flood of fresh tears that immediately started cleaning away the dried, salty trails on his face. "She knows, and she…she freaked out."

He could hardly speak, the sobbing and trembling were so intense. I took off my shoes and costume and climbed on the bed beside him, spooning him from behind like we always did. I squeezed him.

"She…she freaked out," he cried. "She said that I tricked her. That I'm a lesbian that conned her into dating me. That I'm some pervert, a pedophile. She ran out of here. She was so cold!"

I didn't say sorry. I knew it wouldn't do any good. Nothing would do any good. Pate's anguish only triggered the agony festering inside of me. My tears slid down, leaving a wet spot on his comforter as they ran from my cheeks. He didn't respond or seem to notice. The warm tears leaked from my eyes onto his shoulder and back. We just lay there together, drowning in our own misery and disappointment. But it was better than suffering alone.

Chapter Seventeen

Pate

Disgusting. Pervert. Lesbian predator. Pedophile. Those were all the words that circulated in my mind from Maybelle's reaction. I thought she loved me. She *told* me that she loved me. *Should I be angry at her?* I wished I could be. Honestly, I was more outraged at myself. The dread that lingered inside of me knew that she would reject me. I *knew* it the whole time. Yet I hid from it. I carried on in the fantasy that somehow love would conquer all. But I was a fool. For me, it was just indicative that I would always be rejected.

Oakley had told me about Jody breaking up with him that same night, but he didn't show much emotion about it. He just brought me water and soup and sometimes would crawl into bed with me and hold me. Neither of us spoke much about it. Part of me wanted to yell at him. I wanted to slap him against the wall for letting his own prejudice prevent him from experiencing love. For doing to Jody what Maybelle had done to me. *How can I forgive him for such a thing?* However, Oakley wasn't that way. He was a good person. He was just scared to be happy.

My phone didn't ring. My text notifications didn't beep. No cars drove up our long driveway. Everything we had worked so hard to build in these past few months seemed lost. I was lost.

The mail piled up on the table, and Oakley asked if I wanted him to open it for me. I merely grunted in approval. I sat starting at the wall as I heard paper tearing open and envelopes falling into the trashcan. Then I heard silence. A few minutes later, a small purple paper appeared before my eyes.

I know that I'm not good at poetry
I've never been blessed with a flair for words
Romantic charm was never kind enough to knock on my rugged door
But your presence is the poetry in me
But your presence is the words I've been searching for
It's your presence that romanticizes me
I only have to be good at loving you
I only have to be good at loving you

The words were beautiful but fake. I crumbled the piece of purple lies in my hand and tossed it across the room.

"Who's this from? There's no name." Oakley asked.

"Maybelle," I mumbled.

"Oh, she wrote you love poems?"

"Yeah."

"Why'd she mail them? Why didn't she just give them to you?"

"I don't know. I don't care. It doesn't mean anything now." I shoved my head back in my pillow in misery.

Oakley picked up the envelope out of the trashcan. "It says it was postmarked yesterday. The party was five days ago."

"What do you mean?" I snatched the envelope. The postmark *was* from yesterday. *What does this mean?*

"Is this a sign? Do you think she wants to get back together? Should I call her?" My heart started thumping in my chest with a new flow of hope.

"Maybe," Oakley shrugged. "If she writes you love poems, and she sent this yesterday, then maybe. Why else would she send a love poem? I would at least text her."

I leaped over to my phone and my fingers started texting rapidly, but then stopped. "I don't know if I should text her."

"Why not?"

"Because I don't know for sure if she wrote that poem," I admitted.

"But you said that she was sending you love poems," Oakey said, confused.

"I assumed. I mean, these letters came in the mail. Who else would send them?" I asked.

"But you don't know? You didn't ask her about them?"

I shook my head. "No."

Oakley stared at me for a moment. "Why wouldn't you?"

"I don't know," I moaned. "I was afraid. I don't know why I was afraid, but I was afraid."

"Afraid that they might not be from Maybelle?" Oakley suggested.

"Yeah," I affirmed. "They were so nice. No one ever wrote me love letters or poems. I wanted them to be from her, and I was scared that they might all just be a big joke. A big joke on me. Like from Bullet. So, I didn't say anything. I just wanted to believe it was her. I certainly didn't want to say anything if it was all a joke."

"Well, shit. He probably knows now. I wouldn't put it past that motherfucker to do something like this," Oakley scolded angrily.

"So, you don't think I should text her then?" Deep inside, I wanted him to say yes. I just needed approval from someone to text her.

"I really don't know, Pate. I don't think I'm qualified for relationship advice. I'm certainly no good at predicting people."

"Okay."

Oakley stood silent before pulling his desk chair over to the side of the bed to face me. "Can I talk to you. Like directly?"

"Okay."

"If you don't want to talk about it, it's cool. I don't want to cause any more pain. I just want to understand." He sat silent for a few moments. "But what was it like to be rejected like that?"

I paused as I collected the overpowering emotions that crept up in me when I heard the word "rejection."

"Powerless," I choked. "Defeating. I know that I moved too fast with Maybelle. I see it now. You were right. I should have been honest. I wanted to believe that I could make her love me. I could be the best boyfriend to her and treat her like she deserves and not like guys like Bullet do. I betted that my love was enough." I stopped to cry. "That she would see me as a person and not as something different or gross. Or that the physical wouldn't even matter. I believed that if the romantic connection was there and was strong, she could move past the physical stuff. I mean, what's the big fucking deal anyway? People get married and their spouse becomes disabled. It doesn't change the romantic love. So why does this have to be so different? Why is everyone so obsessed with genitals?"

Oakley rubbed his eyes. "Do you think she loved you? Like, do you think the romantic love was there?"

I cried some more. "Now I don't know, which hurts even more. Part of me says it must not have been for her to react that way. The other part of me says yes, but she can't overcome the physical conflict. Like you with Jody. You couldn't overcome it. But I think you...I think you may be in love with Jody."

Oakley stared down, fiddling with his fingernails. "Are you saying," he began after a long pause, "that romantic love is different than physical love?"

Despite my poignant sadness, I was surprised. This was the first time Oakley had ever really listened to me when I talked about such matters. "Romantic attraction and sexual attraction are different, I feel. I can be sexually attracted to people without loving them or wanting to have a relationship with them. I even prefer to have the romantic attraction first before I feel like I want to have sex with someone. I guess I'm more demisexual."

"I never thought about that," he stated, still picking at his fingernails. "How can the romantic love overpower the physical then? Can it?"

"Is the physical really that big of a problem for you?" I asked him. "Is there really no way?"

"I'm starting to second-guess that myself," he mumbled.

He didn't say much else.

* * * *

I had avoided campus for over a week but knew that I had to return. I had emailed my professors and told them that I had the flu. They were understanding, but I had to get to the library to do the research I needed for a paper. I decided to wait until evening. I knew all of Maybelle's classes were during the day, and fewer students were walking around in the cold November evenings in Montana. I would be safe?

The campus was mostly empty. A winter storm had come in over the week, leaving behind snow and ice and a sixty-mile-per-hour wind gust that scared most people indoors. I was thankful for the weather in a way that I had never thought possible. I had borrowed Oakley's car and parked near the student center and made my way inconspicuously to the library. It was also bare. Shoving my hoodie over my head, I found the reference books needed and made my copies. It was around nine p.m. when I left, and the campus looked even more isolated and cold.

The walkway back across campus was a sidewalk that wove in and out around the various buildings. There were only a few streetlights to illuminate the way. I pulled my hoodie tighter and kept my eyes on the ground to avoid the ice. I didn't even hear them coming.

One moment I was dodging an ice patch, and the next, I felt a hard object slam against the back of my head. I slipped, falling onto the ice. All my papers and notebook flew into the neighboring snow pile. When I turned my head, I was punched in the jaw and kicked in the gut. The air in my lungs gushed out, leaving me gasping for air but finding it impossible to breathe. The pain shot all over my body, and I gave a yelp.

"That's what you get, you fucking pervert!"

"Fucking rapist!"

I knew one voice was Bullet, and I could see two other figures in the darkness. Another punch hit me in the forehead, bashing my back into the ground. I curled up and squeezed my head as tight as I could between my arms, but the fists hit the exposed skin of my hands and arms.

"Don't you ever touch Maybelle again, you fucking freak! You fucking tranny!"

I sensed another foot sliding in and cringed as I prepared for the painful blow. But it didn't come. I heard scuffling. Carefully peeking out from my arms, I saw a gargantuan black silhouette throwing Bullet into the ground.

"Get the fuck off him!" Stormy yelled.

"What the fuck, man!" Bullet got back up. "He's a fucking pervert, man. A pedophile. He tried to molest Maybelle."

"He didn't do any of that shit! Now get the fuck out of here! Go! Or you can fight me, if you like," Stormy threatened.

"You're wrong, man," Bullet's sidekick shouted.

"Get out of here before I call the police. There's enough evidence for assault," Stormy screamed.

"Ain't no police going to care about some pervert. You should let me kill him—it—and do the world a favor."

"Get!" Stormy ordered.

Bullet brushed his clothes off and stomped away. "It's not over," he yelled from the darkness.

Stormy kneeled beside me. "Are you okay? Should I call the hospital?"

"No hospital!" I yelled, only to grimace in pain.

"Are you sure? You're bleeding." He moved some hair away from my face to examine my injuries.

"No hospital," I insisted, pushing his hand away. "Can you help me up?"

Stormy helped me stand and shone his key chain flashlight on my face. "You're really bloody. Come with me."

"No hospital!" I cried. My body was violently shaking, and I could hardly breathe.

"I'm not taking you to the hospital. I'm taking you to my house."

"So your roommates can see me? No!" I refused.

"They're not home. It's just me for the week. Come on. Let's get you out of here."

He grabbed my papers and I leaned against his side as we walked to his truck. He handed me some paper towels. "Here, you can wipe some of it off with these. I always keep some around."

I barely registered the drive to Stormy's house. I blinked and was sitting on a chair in his kitchen while he washed the blood off my face and hands. I was in and out of a daze.

"Why don't you take your shirt off?" he suggested gently. "I think you may be bloody under there, too. There's bloodstains." He pointed at my T-shirt. My arms were scratched and bruised. I touched my hair only to feel it stiff with blood.

"I don't want to. I got in trouble the last time." I started shaking again.

Stormy walked out of the kitchen and returned with a pair of sweatpants and a Grizz sweatshirt. "Follow me." He took my hand and led me to a small bathroom with blue and yellow walls. "Why don't you take a bath or shower? You can borrow these clothes. They're my roommate's. He's about your size. You can leave the bloody clothes on the floor. I'll wash them when you're done." He softly closed the door and left.

I must have sat on the toilet for what seemed like hours just staring at the tub. I didn't want to remove my clothes. The vagina was waiting there. It was to blame. Why couldn't I have just been born a man? Why did I have to be a man born with breasts and a vagina? That was what everyone seemed to hate about me, so in that moment, I loathed it, too. I despised it with all the revulsion capable in my soul. I wanted to grab the Gillette men's razor sitting on the counter and just cut it off. I didn't care if I bled to death.

A gentle knock came on the door. "Are you okay? Do you know how to use the tub?"

I didn't respond. I was too consumed with the dysphoria.

Stormy knocked again and poked his head in. "Are you okay?"

I kept staring at the tub.

Stormy took the clothes off my lap and set them on the counter. "Are you a bath person or a shower person?"

"Shower."

He turned on the shower. Taking my hand to stand me up, he started lifting my shirt.

"What are you doing?" I snapped, grabbing his hand.

"It's okay, Pate," he whispered softly. "Just trust me. I don't mean any harm. I want to help you get cleaned up. May I?"

At this point, I had already been dumped, harassed and beaten up, so it couldn't get any worse. I let him remove my shirt.

I stared at the bloody scrapes and already blackening bruises on my sides. My body trembled so much that I thought I would pass out from exhaustion. My scars were the only part visible.

"Okay, I'm going to take off your pants now. You can keep your boxers on if you want."

I let him help me take the pants off.

"I'm going to remove my clothes and leave my boxers on, too so I can get in and help you, okay?"

I nodded.

Normally, I would have felt so exposed standing there with my chest and scars in plain view and in my underwear with no visible bulge. But I was numb.

Stormy helped me into the shower and stood behind me. With a washcloth, he cleaned my face and chest. It took time because his touch was gentle to avoid pain or additional injury. He shampooed my hair and helped me rinse it, and he even sat on the side of the tub to wash my legs and feet. It hurt too much for me to bend over.

"Okay, I'll step out and let you get the rest. Just toss your underwear out with the other dirty clothes."

"Can you stay?" I requested in a voice so low I wasn't sure *I* even heard it.

"You want me to?" he asked, surprised.

Still facing forward and not looking at him, I choked, "You know what I am?"

There was a long pause. "I know you're transgender. I don't know what all that means. But it's okay with me, Pate."

I sluggishly pulled down my boxers and let them fall into the bottom of the tub. My trembling became even more violent and tears gushed out, causing me to gasp in pain. My face was already swelling. Stormy had to take my arms as I turned to face him to keep me from falling. I stood facing him, shaking and sobbing.

"This is me," I squeaked out in a childlike voice. "I don't want to be alone with it." I cried. "I don't want to be alone."

"It's okay," he said in a calm, low voice. "I'll help you wash it."

Stormy was calm, gentle and sensitive as he carefully washed the area with a washcloth. He often looked up to make sure that I was okay and informed me of anything he was going to do so that I knew what was coming. His large workman's hands were soft and soothing.

After the shower ended and I was dressed, Stormy helped bandage my wounds. The bleeding had finally stopped. My jaw was so swollen that it was nearly impossible to keep my mouth closed. My entire body ached, especially my head and my sides. He ordered me to take a few deep breaths to see if I had broken ribs. He carefully examined my jaw.

"I don't think anything is broken. It's hard to tell," he said afterwards. "But you're not going to sleep any time soon on me. Since you're unwilling to let me take you to the hospital."

"Why?"

"Concussions, my friend. So why don't I grab some Aleve?"

We sat on his sofa, me sipping water through a straw and listening to a punk rock station that Stormy had found just for me. He held a bag of ice in a washcloth against my jaw for me, and I eventually laid my head on his lap to make it easier to ice.

"I know it's hard to talk, but I don't know what transgender means. Would you explain it to me?" he asked.

Moving my mouth the best I could, I shared my story with Stormy. I told him how I'd never felt like a girl but rather a boy always trying to be something he wasn't. I told him about the baggy clothes in high school, the sports bras and binders to squish down my breasts, and Oakley, loving me as a girl but not as a man. I even told him about the suicide attempt. At this point, I figured he had already seen me get assaulted. He had already seen my vagina. Everyone in town already knew. What more could I lose?

He just listened in intent silence. Surprisingly, words flooded out of my swollen jaw, and I kept drooling as I talked. Stormy wiped it away with the washcloth and kept listening. The hours flew by until I saw the sun shining in through his blue curtains and heard the early birds chirping outside. I was exhausted.

"I'm really tired." I moaned.

"I guess it may be okay to let you sleep some. I'd like to watch you, though. Just to be sure."

"Okay."

He took me to his bedroom and helped me into bed.

"I'll just keep the door open and pop in now and then, okay?"

"I don't want to be alone."

He left the room and returned with a throw blanket. He lay down on top of the covers beside me. I painfully shifted my body to the other side to face him. "Can you stay until I fall asleep?"

"Sure," he said.

I closed my eyes. "Stormy?"

"Yeah?"

"Thanks for being my friend."

He reached out and took my hand. "It's my honor," he whispered.

Chapter Eighteen

Oakley

Pate's words haunted me. Romantic love. I didn't know there was any difference. I had assumed romantic love and physical love were one and the same. Pate said that he thought it was the romantic love that was stronger over the physical. *Was he right?* People got older. They lost their youthful attractiveness. Perhaps, the romantic thrived on and had enough power to keep the physical alive. After all, I couldn't imagine leaving a wife because she got old.

I had obsessed so much about the physical aspects of Jody. When he was dressed like a woman, I craved him. His long hair, polished nails and elegant dresses. But it wasn't real. It was real in that moment, but the male Jody was still there underneath. As much as I wanted to imagine that I was attracted to Jody as a woman, I was still attracted to a man the whole time.

What was the physical? A penis was a body part like a breast was a body part. It was just skin. It didn't make a man a man. Pate was still a man without one. I had never been bothered with Jody not having breasts. His small, flat chest was arousing. The freckles that dotted all along his cheeks, neck, back and arms drove me crazy.

I had always assumed that, to be gay, men had to have anal sex. But none of my sexual encounters with Jody had involved anal sex, nor did he ever suggest it. All Jody wanted was for me to reciprocate with hand jobs or oral sex. If those were all I was willing to do sexually, I knew that Jody would accept it. The real problem was my reluctance to try *anything*.

Watching Jody walk away and yell "fuck you" sank my soul. I didn't realize how strong the romantic attraction had been until it was severed. Jody was the most warm-hearted, patient and fun person that I'd ever met. Watching him perform on stage in drag was truly mesmerizing. I couldn't take my eyes off of him. We would stay up late throughout the night just holding each other with our bare chests pressing against the other and talking about our dreams and fears. Other than Pate, Jody had been the only other person that I felt so deeply connected to. It wasn't because he was a good friend. I was in love with his soul and essence that warmed any room. I was in love with Jody.

I dialed my father. He answered after a few long rings.

"Hey, Oak! What's going on? How's Mom?"

We chatted casually for a few minutes as I told him how Granny was doing and how my grades were looking.

"I'm so proud!" he exclaimed on the other end. "I never went to college. Wow! My son is finishing his first semester at college."

"Dad, I really called to tell you something else...or ask you something."

"What is it?"

My hands trembled, reminding me of Pate's anxiety. For the first time, I understood it. "Dad."

"Yes?"

"What if...would it be okay...if I liked a guy?"

"If you like a guy? Like a friend at school?" he asked.

"No, if I like a guy and want to date him," I stuttered.

The phone buzzed loud with silence on the other end.

"Oak, are you telling me that you are dating a man? Are you gay?" He sounded more confused than upset.

"I'm not gay exactly," I explained. "I met a guy here at school, and we've been...dating."

"What does dating mean?"

I took a deep breath. "He's my...boyfriend."

Silence.

"I'm confused with what you are telling me. Are you gay? Is that what you want me to know?"

"I'm not gay," I stammered. "I still like girls. But I like this guy, too. I like him a lot."

"Well, son, I'm not sure what to say." There was a long pause. "It's a surprise. Does he make you happy?"

"I want to date him seriously. I think I can be very happy with him." The fact that he hadn't yelled eased my anxiety some, but I kept waiting for him to flip out. My dad had always been a rather traditional guy. I didn't think he'd go for it.

"What is that like in a small town?" he inquired.

"Dad?"

"Yes?"

"I don't care what it means in a small town. Hell, my best friend is trans. What does it mean to you? That's what I care about." I could feel the tightness swelling in my throat.

After a minute, he responded, "I always thought you would marry Pate, anyway. So, you met another fella instead. It's fine with me, Oakley. It was fine with me when you brought Pate to live with us. It's fine with me if you want to date this man. It's your life. I still love you. I don't know what else to say, son. Is that what you needed to hear from me?"

I nearly burst out into tears. "You said all I needed to know."

I talked to my dad for hours, well into the night. When we finally got off the phone, it was midnight. I should have gone to bed, but I couldn't wait until morning. Pate had taken the car to campus and hadn't returned, so I borrowed Granny's truck. I was too scared to text or call Jody because I was worried that he wouldn't see me. It had been weeks since the party, and not one call or text since. When I arrived outside his dorm building, I called him.

No answer.

I called again.

No answer.

My fists beat the steering wheel in frustration, and tears welled up in my eyes. I called again.

"I thought you'd get the point when I didn't answer," his sleepy voice said over the line.

"I'm outside your dorm. I want to talk to you."

"You're outside? What?" He sounded awake now.

"I'm outside. Please. I want to say something to you, and you can do with it whatever you want. I need to say it in person. I need you to know. Can I please come up?" I begged frantically.

"Wait outside the door. I'll meet you in the entranceway."

It felt like an eternity waiting for him with the bitter cold air tingling my fingers and toes. Finally, I saw his small figure in a hoodie and sweatpants walking toward the door. He let me inside.

"Thanks. It's freezing!" I shook some snow off my clothes.

"Montana winters," he said indifferently.

I could hardly see his face behind the hood. I wondered if he was purposely hiding it.

"What is it, darling? It's late." His voice was dull and somber.

"I don't know how to say it, so I'll just say it." I pulled his hoodie down gently and placed my hands upon his shoulders. "I'm so sorry. I was wrong. I love you," I said with tears swelling up in my eyes.

"What do you mean you love me?"

"I love you." I gently shook him. "I don't think. I know. I was getting so hung up on the physical stuff that is new for me that I completely ignored all the romantic love that was developing."

"Sounds like you've been reading an LGBTQ page," he joked.

"I'm serious." I could see his green eyes gazing drowsily at me. "There's so many wonderful things about us. Our long talks. Our cuddles. The way you make me feel like a better person — the person I want to be. The way you make me grow. The way I feel with you. I took that for granted until I lost it. Or maybe I was even suppressing it because I was scared. I was scared to push myself sexually to explore those feelings. I was afraid to truly discover if those feelings could transcend the physical. Does it make sense?"

"I think I understand you, Oakman. But I don't want to be with someone who feels like they have to force sex with me."

"I won't have to. It's new to me, and I made it bigger than what it is." I squeezed his shoulder harder.

"How do I believe you?"

"Jody." I put my hands around his waist and pulled him closer to me. "I don't want to have anal sex."

He looked puzzled. "Neither do I. I'm a virgin in that sense."

"That's all. I know my sexual boundaries, and I know now that we should talk about it and work out something that works for us. I'm ready now. I promise. I want another chance."

"I don't believe you," he said coolly.

"May I...kiss you?" I asked.

"That's supposed to fix —"

"Please, trust me."

"Okay," he agreed.

"Can I touch you?"

"This is weird, but if you're proving a point —"

I pulled him to me and kissed him hard. His lips were dead at first, but eventually, I felt them start to move along with mine. I reached down and gently rubbed his penis through his pants.

"I want to prove it to you by making love to you," I whispered. "By *me* making love to *you*. No reciprocation needed on your part."

"Look, I don't want to go upstairs and get my feelings hurt when you freak out or change —"

I kissed him hard again, and my hands went up his hoodie and caressed his back. I hugged him, whispering in his ear. "Please, trust me one more time."

"Okay," he replied.

We went upstairs to his room, and I made love to Jody. I caressed his small, petite body. I swallowed his delicate but firm penis in my hands. I kissed his body from his head to his legs and eventually over his manhood. I fell in love with every physical, emotional and spiritual part of Jody. I became more in love and aroused with each touch and kiss and moan. I couldn't hold his body tight enough against mine. He was the most beautiful, sexy person that I had ever made love to.

* * * *

Pate

I stayed the weekend at Stormy's, mostly in his bed. I listened to him run in and out of the house, and he came in occasionally to bring me food or water or to check on my injuries. The swelling on my jaw started to recede after three days, and I could finally close my mouth and speak more easily again. Staring in the mirror, I cringed at the dark, purplish blotches around my forehead and eyes, and my cheeks with red, swollen scrapes around them. I didn't know how to go back to school. I didn't know how to see Oakley. If I could, I would have just hidden in Stormy's bedroom forever.

"You got to go back to school sometime. The semester's almost over anyway. I know you can hammer out the work. You're really smart," Stormy pleaded. "I've kept us up to date on the lab. I told the professor you were in an accident. He understood. He says you can make a date to do the labs."

"I never wanted to go to school anyway. It was all for Oakley," I grumbled.

"I don't want to be there without you. Or Oakley or Jody. You guys are my friends."

"What about your roommates?" I asked him.

He smiled. "You guys are better friends."

Tears started fighting their way into my eyes. "Everyone knows I'm trans. They all probably know I got attacked. I'm not wanted here," I told him.

"You are not alone," he reassured me as he placed his hand on my shoulder. "Trust me. You are *not* alone. If you want me to go to every class with you, I will. Hell, we can go to the professors together and ask that you not be in class with Bullet. I think they can understand."

"Then I look scared. I'll just hide, and things will get worse."

"Maybe you won't have to deal with Bullet anymore," Stormy told me confidently.

Oakley had blown up my phone searching for me and the car, which I informed him was still on campus, but I didn't explain why. With Stormy's encouragement, I decided to reluctantly push myself back to campus to finish. He tried to make me promise to wait for him to return from an important errand, but I decided to call Oakley to pick me up and take me to Granny's so that I could change clothes and get my school materials.

When I climbed into the car, I met a large grin that immediately dissipated into a gaping mouth of horror.

"What happened? Oh my God! Are you okay?" Oakley exclaimed, examining my face.

"I'm okay. I'm just sore."

"Pate, what happened? Did someone do this to you?"

I stared down. "I got jumped. Bullet and his friends."

I could sense Oakley's fury. "That asshole did this? When? Why didn't you call me? Tell me?"

"I didn't want to tell anyone."

"How did you end up at Stormy's?" he asked.

"Thank God, Stormy showed up before they beat me to death." *Death.* It was the first time I had realized that, with how small I was and how big Bullet was, he could have killed me. He might not have intended it, or maybe he had. But he could've killed me. I started to shake.

"I don't want to talk about it right now," I insisted, trying not to break out in a crying fit again. "I just want to get ready for class and figure out how to finish the semester."

I got showered and changed, and Oakley and I went to campus. As soon as I saw the sidewalk, shivers circulated all over my body. When I approached the door to the building, I grabbed the door so tight that my knuckles turned white.

"I don't know if I can do this. This is a bad idea. What am I doing?" I mumbled, terrified.

"You don't have to do it. I'm sure they'd take an incomplete, given the situation," Oakley said, placing his hand on my shoulder.

"I don't want to have to explain to them." I released a big sigh. We were going to biology class, the class with Bullet. It felt impossible.

"We can go in there, and if it's too much, we'll talk to the professor," Oakley instructed me. "I'll be right beside you the whole time."

"Stormy said he told the professor that I was in an accident," I informed him.

"Well, he'll see that, obviously," Oakley said, pointing at my bruises. "So, we don't have to stay. In fact, we can just go talk to him and then leave."

"What about your work? You shouldn't leave," I argued.

"It doesn't matter, Pate. What matters is you."

Oakley held my hand as we walked to class and past all the whispers, stares and gasps. I wore a hoodie with the hood pulled up to hide as much of my face as possible. My fingernails dug into Oakley's skin as I squeezed his hand.

When we entered the classroom, Bullet was already there, but my eyes immediately did a double take. He wasn't his usual self, talking, standing, taking up space. Instead, he was slouched and forlorn. On closer inspection, his right eye was black and bulging out. His upper lip was swollen and cut. His hands were bandaged. He stared blankly at the book on his desk and didn't even acknowledge our entry.

"Whoa…" muttered Oakley.

Stormy was in the back of the classroom, waving for me to join him. As I walked back, people looked at me but were quiet.

When I sat down, I noticed bandages on Stormy's right hand, which looked red and swollen. He smiled at me, which showed a small cut above his right eye.

"What is this?" I asked, pointing at his hand.

"I told you that I had an important errand."

292

"Did you do that to him?" I demanded, gesturing toward Bullet.

"He won't ever mess with you again. I promise. It pays sometimes to be the biggest guy in town." Stormy winked at me. He gave me a side hug. "I'm glad you came."

The professor gave me an extension to complete the work I'd missed. Oakley said Bullet didn't speak to him the whole class. He only followed the instructions for the lab and left as soon as it was over. For the first time, he walked out alone, without his sidekicks right beside him. They seemed to almost linger around on purpose until he had left.

I met with my other professors to make arrangements for my work, and they were all supportive. I didn't know if it was because of my bruises, that they believed I had been in a car accident or if they knew that I had been assaulted. I didn't know if it was because I was transgender. I got a lot of teary eyes, comments about my courage and even a hug from the writing instructor.

When I left the writing instructor's office, Oakley was waiting. He wrapped me in his arms in a large bear hug.

"What are you doing." I grimaced. "Ouch, not so hard. I'm still sore."

He didn't respond. He just continued to hug me.

"Aren't you worried that others will see us?" I asked him.

"I don't care. This whole thing really scared me. I'd die if I lost you. I'm so happy you came today." I could hear him crying as he spoke.

"I'm okay." I pushed him away a little because he was squeezing me so tight I could hardly breathe.

"It just…" He sobbed a little. "I think back to when…when you tried that time to…"

I know he was referring to the suicide attempt. I stepped back and kissed him on the cheek. "I'm okay, Oak. Thanks."

I saw Maybelle standing by the outside door as if she was waiting for someone. She stared at us and smiled.

"Maybelle is over there," I told Oakley.

He turned to see her. "What the hell do you think she wants?"

"I don't know. I don't know if it even has to do with me."

"Let's go." He took my hand and we walked toward the door. Maybelle stopped us.

"Wait, Pate. Can I talk to you? Please," she stammered. She wasn't her usual bubbly, confident self. Instead, she seemed anxious, and her voice squeaked.

"He doesn't want to talk to you," Oakley interjected firmly.

"I just need to talk for a few minutes. We can talk outside. Please?" she begged.

"He's like this because of you!" Oakley shouted, causing people to stop and stare. "We don't need anything you're selling."

She started to cry.

"Wait," I said. "I'll talk to her."

"Pate—" Oakley shook his head at me.

"Just wait over by the benches. It'll only take a minute," I assured him.

"I told Jody that I'd meet him, so I'll go get him and come back. I'll be back in five or ten minutes, okay?" Oakley stated as he scrutinized Maybelle.

"I'm fine, Oak," I promised him.

We stepped outside, and I watched Oakley disappear across campus. Maybelle was wiping her nose, and her hands trembled slightly. Normally, my gut would be boiling, but I just felt numb.

"What do you want?"

"I want to know if you're okay?" she whispered, trying not to cry again.

"What do you care?" I snapped. Bubbles of anger were brewing in me.

"I *do* care."

"You told Bullet! Bullet! Of all the people, you told *him*? You knew what he would do," I yelled, provoking more stares from passersby.

"I never thought he'd go that far. Honestly!" she promised.

"You didn't know a guy prone to violence would get violent?" My hands shook, and my face grew red.

"You don't understand. You don't know him like I do." She stared down, wrapping her arms around herself. "He's not all bad. He really isn't. He had a tough childhood. I needed someone to talk to. I was devastated!" She looked up at me with tears.

"*You* were devastated?" I gaped in shock. I saw Stormy sitting over by the benches watching us. Part of me still expected Bullet to come running out of the bushes and attack me again for talking to Maybelle. Stormy eased that fear. I sighed in frustration, pulling my hoodie down. "You see? You see what he did? If it wasn't for Stormy, I...I don't know what would have happened."

She cried again. "I know he would never truly hurt someone," she sobbed.

"I'm done." I started to walk away.

"Wait!"

"No," I snapped at her. "You want to pull me aside and fucking defend Bullet?" Normally, the tears and anxiety would seize my body now, but instead, only loathing engulfed me. "You have *no* idea what I've been through. You have no idea what I've been through before I met you, and you have no idea what *you* and your fucking boyfriend have done to me."

"Pate, I'm sorry. I didn't know how to react."

"So, Bullet's a good guy, no matter what? But I'm a pervert, a pedophile. Isn't that what you called me?" Remembering those words, I only despised her more.

"I didn't mean it," she claimed.

"Yes, you did. You meant it when you said it. That's how you feel about me."

"Pate, I love you. I do. It's just...it can't happen. I wanted you to know that I have feelings for you, but...it won't work out here. I can't date a transgender person. My parents would never accept it."

I smirked. "You broke my heart. Now, you stand here as if I still want you with your excuses. Don't ever talk to me again."

"Pate! Don't end this way. We can be friends," she pleaded.

"You're not the kind of friend I want."

I walked away toward Stormy. I could sense her behind me, standing, staring. The dread was gone. It was replaced by anger and hatred for her. That fury gave me the power to sever my life from Maybelle.

"Everything okay?" Stormy asked when I approached him.

"Yes. In fact, I got one less problem in my life now."

Chapter Nineteen

Oakley

Jody, Pate, Stormy and I all sat around the barn, smoking joints. Pate struggled to purse his lips enough to inhale right, but he still tried.

"I'm so sorry, dear," Jody told him with tears. "I can't fathom someone doing such a thing to someone like you."

"Thank you," Pate said.

"I'm so thankful that we have this strong, large bodybuilder to protect us," Jody told Stormy.

"I'm not a bodybuilder," Stormy remarked. "Just big. Just strong. Ranching keeps you fit. It doesn't matter. Even if I was smaller, I'd still have helped. I've seen Bullet assault people too many times. People who are defenseless against his size. He deserved to get what was coming to him."

"You did a good job," I replied. "That dude has not said a peep since that happened."

"I didn't even get a chance to congratulate you guys on getting back together. I've been so withdrawn in my own shit," Pate commented.

"It's okay, sweetie," Jody said. "We have lots of time to fall madly in love. It's about helping you heal now."

"Did he say the L-word?" Pate asked.

Jody and I smiled. My cheeks got hot.

"He's blushing. Look!" Stormy pointed.

"Yes, I said the — I love Jody," I confessed proudly.

"And I love Oakman."

"I love you, you love me, homosexuality," Stormy sang. We all laughed.

"Honey, have you thought about the talent show? Didn't you register?" Jody asked Pate.

"Shit! Yeah, I registered. I even had a routine. But I totally spaced out. I haven't practiced in weeks. I don't think so."

"I think you should," I told him.

"Me, too," Jody and Stormy agreed.

"My body's still sore," Pate stated.

"There's still a few weeks. It's not until December first."

"Guys, I don't want to be the trans person dancing on stage. I haven't even danced publicly since before I transitioned," Pate argued.

"You're so talented, Pate," Jody beseeched. "You are *so* talented. Show them that they don't control you. They don't take away that spark that burns inside. Besides, I'm performing. Actually, Oakley and I are performing."

"What?" Pate exclaimed.

It was true. Jody had convinced me to sing a duet with him, and while my old self would have been totally against such a thing, the new me wanted to leave that behind. If Jody could perform, so could I. Though my singing was atrocious beside his enchanting voice.

"What are you doing?" Pate asked.

"We're singing *Nothing's Gonna Stop Us Now.*"

"Wait, the death metal guy is going to sing a sappy love song?" Pate joked.

"Hey," I interjected, pointing my finger at him. "It's considered rock music."

"He's going to play guitar, so there will be some metal added to our version," Jody told them with a large grin. His excitement alone was worth it.

"Yeah, I'm going to add a little metal twist, but of course, keep it light. I don't know if the audience could handle it."

"That's awesome," Pate said. "Wow, I'm proud of you, man." He slapped me on the back.

"So, what about you?" I confronted him. "You should do it. We can all be together."

Pate sighed. "I don't know, guys. It's a lot to deal with. I've already dealt with so much this past month."

"But dancing is your...it's your medium," I stressed "It's your coping. It's what makes you *you.*"

He nodded. "You're right."

"I think you should do it, Pate," Stormy told him. "We'll all be there with you. In fact, it's important to me that you do it."

"I guess I owe you for kicking Bullet's ass," Pate agreed.

"You always told me that you didn't even notice the audience when you were on stage," I reminded him.

"You're right. I don't. I just feel the beat and go to my happy place."

"So will you do it?" Stormy asked.

"Okay," Pate conceded.

* * * *

I didn't understand how some small-town death metal guy got talked into playing guitar at a talent show in Montana while he sang a corny love song with his boyfriend. I hadn't played any music for months and pulling out my black guitar seemed to bring everything together. Playing music with Jody was awesome. Until then, I had only thought that he enjoyed dressing in drag and becoming that character, but as we rehearsed, I saw his true love for music, too. I almost didn't want the rehearsal to end.

"Are you ready to sing our love to the whole world?" Jody said dramatically. "Or at least to Cloverleaf, Montana?"

"Everyone already knows anyway. What difference will it make?" I strummed my guitar.

"It'll make some people uncomfortable. But sometimes that's the whole point. I've lived my life in a lot of discomfort. Let them be uncomfortable for a while."

I nodded. "I'm cool with that."

"Do you want to see my costume?" Jody took out his phone and scrolled. "Here it is." He showed the pictures of his "look." He had bought a bright pink mohawk wig, a tight black dress with spaghetti straps that ended above the knees and fishnet pantyhose with combat boots.

"Wow!" I exclaimed.

"I thought it only fair that I go a little metal for you, my love." He grinned.

"That's awesome! I've always wanted to see you go gothic or punk."

"I know. And afterwards, we can have a little roleplay," he teased as he tugged at my belt.

"I wouldn't have it any other way."

* * * *

Pate

I had no idea what I was doing at the talent show. I didn't think people in this small town would attend a talent show, but apparently, they did. I guess there weren't many entertainment options in town. The medium-sized auditorium was nearly full, and there were ten acts, including mine. I was the second-to-last performer. Jody and Oakley were the second.

Jody and Oakley looked amazing. Oakley had dyed the tips of his hair pink to match Jody's mohawk. He wore a ripped black tank-top with a large red skull and black jeans. Jody marched out with his black dress with silver sequins and fishnet pantyhose. They looked right out of an eighties' metal magazine. Even Stormy looked nice, dressed in black slacks and a sleeveless, button-down black-collared shirt.

"Is this your punk look?" I teased him.

"My attempt to match my posse." He laughed.

I had to have clothes to move in. I wore black nylon pants that were still loose, with a tight black and red tank-top. Oakley and Jody had dyed the tips of my hair red to match. I wore no shoes.

"I'm used to seeing you in baggy clothes," Stormy commented as he examined my outfit.

"Yeah, but they're hard to dance in. It's a big reason why I haven't performed in a long time. It feels weird. I feel exposed."

"You look good." He smiled. "The bruises are nearly gone. You can't see them."

"Thank God for makeup, too."

We walked out to the sitting area for the people performing. It was close to the stage so that we could see the show but sneak backstage when we needed to prepare for our own performances. Stormy and I found a seat in the front row next to two other students who gave us looks but mostly ignored us.

The first act was a poetry reading. A young girl in pigtails and a floral dress that dragged the ground as she walked recited from center stage. The act started stale but transitioned into an expression of emotion and pain. It was quite moving.

"That's what Oakley and Jody are following?" I commented. "Seems like a weird emotional transition."

Jody used a karaoke recording of *Nothing's Gonna Stop Us Now* that boomed from the auditorium's little sound system. Oakley set up his guitar amplifiers next to a sole microphone. Jody used a wireless mic so that he could move around the stage more as Oakley sang and played. When they walked onto stage, mutters could be heard around the crowd, and our two fellow students beside us shot us glances.

"Don't get nervous." Stormy leaned over and whispered, "They'll be great, and you'll be great."

The music started, and it was the best thing ever. Oakley had obviously spent many hours preparing to add the right amount of electric metal guitar to the song, and it sounded great. I was so proud to see him playing his guitar again. I could tell that he loved it, too. Jody danced around but occasionally walked over to Oakley, singing while leaning over on his shoulder. He smiled over at him while strumming away on his guitar. They were really in love.

"Oakley's really good. I mean, so is Jody, but I didn't know that he played so well," Stormy remarked.

"He's always been good. He just fell away from it when we moved here. I'm so glad Jody got him back into it."

"They're great together," he agreed.

"Yes, they are."

The performance ended, and a decent amount of applause emerged from the room. I wasn't surprised that the audience wouldn't have as much appreciation for it as Stormy and I did. But the room was not silent, which was a good sign. Maybe people just had to warm up to us.

Several other acts performed, including a dance act to a country song, a guitar solo and a comedian. They were all really enjoyable, making me wonder if I had missed out on the artsy crowd at the college. Oakley and Jody returned. They were dressed in jeans and sweatshirts with their costumes in a duffel bag.

"What'd y'all think?" Oakley asked.

"I loved it," Stormy said. "I didn't know that metal music was so fast. Your fingers were flying."

"That's a slow song compared to most metal. I'll play for you in the barn some time, and you can see how fast it can really get."

I hugged Oakley. "I'm proud of you. You looked great up there."

"Did it inspire you?" He nudged me in the side.

"Yes."

"So now you can do it, too?

"Yes."

My anxiety rose as my time drew near. I decided to go backstage a few acts ahead to get in the right headspace and forget about the audience. I leaned against the wall backstage and closed my eyes, breathing in and out. A hand touched my shoulder.

"Good luck," Stormy said, and he kissed my forehead.

"Thanks."

I had chosen VNV Nation's *Perpetual*. I knew that no one in the crowd would know the song, and I often chose popular music. But I hadn't danced in so long, and this song hugged me by the soul. It was the strength I needed to truly let myself go to perform the routine right.

Everything was pushed off stage except for the piano for the last act. I started at center stage, squatting down, holding my ankles. As the sound rose, my body slowly moved upward. Then the beat began. It was an interpretative dance but also a freeing one. My hands and face sent out emotions while I moved lightly around the stage. Emotions from the entire semester of anger, love, fear, rejection flew out of my body. I even completed a double kick off the wall and back flawlessly. The crowd clapped. Tears climbed to the surface of my skin, but I let it all go. I let the tears fly off my cheeks as I spun. I did cartwheels and flips. The crowd cheered again. The song ended with me in the same starting position but staring at the audience straight on. The crowd cheered. Some even stood to applaud. It was the best reception all night.

Stormy met me backstage with a towel for the pools of sweat dripping off me. "Thanks. What did you think?"

"You're amazing!" He grinned, hugging me. "I knew you were amazing, but you're breathtaking. I feel like I saw you. The unguarded, unafraid you. It was wonderful." His smile was the biggest that I had ever seen across his face.

"Thanks. I may need to cool off a second. Do you want to step outside a moment? The cold air should work in about five minutes."

"I have to perform," he told me.

"Huh, what?"

"I'm the last act. I have to go on now. Why don't you go up front and watch? I'd like to know what you think."

"You're performing?" I asked, stunned.

He just smiled and winked at me as he walked on stage. I hurried back to our spots in the front row with Oakley and Jody. Their mouths were wide open.

"He's performing? What's he doing?" Oakley asked in bewilderment.

"I don't know. He didn't say anything to me," I told them as I plopped down beside them.

Stormy sat at the piano. I had no idea how his big, fat fingers would play a piano. Surprisingly, it was smooth and graceful. The tone relaxed my muscles that were still riled up from dancing. He began to hum to the tune in a startlingly melodic voice. Then he began to sing.

The raging, roaring winds of East Montana blister the skin

The Herculean, frigid winters freeze the toes

But when you enter the room, summer breaths into me again

Through the radiant warmth of your splendored spirit that blows

The summers in Montana are sudden, hot, and dry

The ravenous, Jurassic mosquitoes will torment your soul

But the swiftness of your unique smile makes the warm, long days pass by

Causing your spirit to shine through like a single diamond nestled in a pool of coal

I know that I'm not good at poetry

I've never been blessed with a flair for words

Romantic charm was never kind enough to knock on my rugged door

But your presence is the poetry in me

But your presence is the words I've been searching for

It's your presence that romanticizes me

I only have to be good at loving you

I only have to be good at loving you

Stormy's eyes immediately locked on mine as soon as he sang the first line, sending shivers dancing all along my body. He kept singing, his voice rising and falling.

"Wow," Jody whispered with his gaze fixated on Stormy in amazement and awe.

His voice was even better than Jody's. An outburst of warmth burst from his lips and the cadence rose as he breathed the lines, "I only have to be good at loving you." Oakley's eyes grew wide as he looked at me, remembering those lines from the mysterious purple paper. Still, Stormy sang to me, with his eyes never leaving mine until the very last note.

When he was done, the entire room came to life with standing ovations and cheers. Stormy bowed with the largest smile I had ever seen. He was almost giggling as he pranced off the stage. Of course, I had no idea how to react.

The host, the liberal arts instructor, returned to stage to announce the winners. I didn't place, nor did Oakley and Jody, but we had suspected that would happen. However, Stormy won first place, and he stomped confidently to snatch his trophy, his large biceps finally on display in his sleeveless shirt as he held the trophy in his hand. He held his trophy above his head, and the crowd cheered. Then he disappeared backstage.

The audience disbanded, and we still sat in the front row.

"Aren't you going to go find him?" Oakley asked.

"I'll go grab him?" Jody offered.

"No." Oakley stopped him. "That song was for Pate."

"Huh?"

"He wrote that song for Pate. I think Pate needs to go find him. Alone."

Jody's face stared baffled. "Am I missing something?"

Oakley laughed. "Come on," he said to Jody, taking his hand and pulling him up. "We'll meet you and Stormy at the car," he told me as they left.

I sat frozen in my seat. I didn't know what to do. No one had ever sung a song to me. I didn't know what it even meant. The room grew empty and quiet.

"What are you doing?" a voice said.

I turned to see Stormy standing just off stage, peering at me.

"I don't know," I mumbled, sheepishly evading his eyes.

He motioned for me to come over. I stood beside him, bracing myself against the wall.

"What'd you think of my song?" he asked.

"*You* wrote those letters to me?"

"Yes." He smiled, now shyly turning his eyes away from me. "Did you like them?"

"I'm confused. Like, wait, you like me? And you write poetry. And you sing and play piano?"

He laughed. "My grandparents in Billings have a piano. My grandma taught me. I've played for years."

"I thought—"

"You thought I was some dumb ranchy guy who just spends all my time with cows?" he mused. "Yeah, I get that a lot from people. I guess folks don't really look at a tall, outdoorsy guy learning diesel as an artist, do they?"

"What about..." I stuttered. "You like me?

"Very much."

"I don't understand. Are you...straight? Gay?"

"I'm gay."

My mouth dropped. He chuckled.

"I don't get it. Why wouldn't you say anything?" I asked accusatorily. "You didn't say anything at the Badlands when I came out as bisexual to you?"

He shrugged. "It's not easy to be a six-foot-seven gay ranch hand. It's just not something I told people. Plus, I've never dated much. Never found a person who interested me. So, I never had a reason to tell people. But that changed when I met you."

"Even after I told you that Oakley and I were bisexual? You still didn't tell me?"

"I'm sorry," he replied. "I should have told you. But I guess I wasn't sure of you guys, either. Plus, I wasn't sure that you would be a friend. I don't exactly fit in with your group, you know? I didn't know you would want me hanging around. I also didn't want you to think that I was only hanging around to try to get with you."

"But you did hang around to try to get with me, right?"

"Yes, I guess I did," he admitted. "But I would have settled with just being friends, too. If I had to. I never wanted to make you feel uncomfortable with me around."

"You liked me this *whole* time?" Shock and excitement penetrated me.

"I don't take just anyone to the Badlands." He winked at me. "But I knew you were into Maybelle. But I also knew who she was and that it wouldn't last. So, I just waited. Or maybe I just hoped."

"But why *me*?"

"First, I liked your style," he responded, taking one of my hands in his. "I felt like I could be myself with you and Oakley. Honestly, like everyone else, I thought you two were gay." He laughed awkwardly. "I thought you two would get me, you know? You were nice. Then you were just everything. I couldn't get my mind off you, especially after seeing you dance. I wasn't sure if I was good enough."

"But you know I have...you know what I am. I don't have all the physical...guy parts." I stared down in shame.

He carefully turned my chin upward with his hand so that our eyes met. "Why would I care about that? It doesn't make you any less than a man. What, you think Bullet's a man because he's got a dick? No. I like you. I want you. You don't need to change anything. Not unless you want to, of course. I've seen all of you. You're all I need."

"I don't know." I sighed. "I'm trying to process all this. One minute you're one of my best friends and now—"

He leaned downward, tilting his head slightly to the side. "May I?"

He placed his hands on my cheeks and lifted my face up to kiss him. For such a large man, his kiss was passionate but soft, and all my feelings for him shifted in that embrace. Stormy was not just an awkward behemoth with dirty boots and horrific dance moves. Instead, he was a man who was gentle, passionate and romantic.

"Please give me a chance?" he whispered in my ear, squeezing me against him. "I really want a chance. I want to be your boyfriend."

"Are you sure you want me? I'm just—"

"I want you," he insisted, kissing me again.

"Okay. I'm yours, Mr. Piano man," I joked.

He laughed. "That's all I ever wanted to hear."

We made our way to the front exit, and as we started to walk outside, he took my hand.

"Are you sure about this?" I asked, gesturing toward our visibly joined hands. There were still a lot of people in the parking lot.

He proudly smiled. "Do you think anyone's going to say anything to *me*? After all, I'm the one who beat Bullet's ass!"

As we got close to Oakley's car surrounded by several groups of people laughing and hanging around, Stormy stopped.

"This is how sure I am." And he kissed me again.

That was when I knew that I could finally be myself.

Want to see more like this?
Here's a taster for you to enjoy!

Out in Austin: Teddy's Truth
KD Ellis

Excerpt

Teddy tugged at the hem of his overlarge sweatshirt then discreetly scratched beneath the band of his sticky sports bra. As far as he was concerned, breasts were disgusting lumps of fat that hoarded sweat, bounced like painful beanbags on his chest when he was busy catching a football and strained the front of any button-down he tried to wear. He couldn't understand why boys were so obsessed with them. He personally couldn't wait to get the damn things cut off.

Hormone therapy had deepened his voice and given him a shadow of patchy fuzz on his jaw. Clippers had sheared him of his blond hair and his mother's Italian heritage had blessed him with broad shoulders and narrow hips.

It was unfortunate that it had also cursed him with breasts that not even puberty blockers had been able to thwart.

He wished he could blame her awful time-management skills on their heritage as well, but he knew better. The fault lay with either Jack or John — the bottle or the boyfriend, whichever she was currently in bed with.

He'd been sitting on the hard, concrete steps of the high school for almost an hour. It wasn't like he could call her. His cell was out of minutes, and hers was probably dead on the nightstand.

Just as the final school bus trundled back onto the parking lot and Teddy was about to give up on waiting, someone stepped up beside him, casting him in shadow.

"Stay there," Teddy ordered, craning his head back until he could grin at his best friend. "Perfect. Be my sun block."

Shiloh, still in his leotard, laughed and nudged Teddy's hip with his shoe. "If you don't think I shine brighter than the sun, then clearly I'm not wearing enough glitter."

"Shine as bright as you want, but just keep standing there. Fuck, it's hot!" Teddy gripped his collar and tugged at it repeatedly, trying to stir a breeze. All it ended up doing was wafting the stench of boob sweat up into his face.

"Well, duh, it's ninety degrees—and you're in a sweater." Shiloh rolled his eyes and dropped onto the curb beside him. "And it's not even pink."

Teddy opened his mouth, his usual response dancing on his tongue—that boys don't wear pink—but he swallowed it. Shiloh was currently in a hot pink leotard and pink Chucks.

Instead, Teddy shrugged and glared down at his baggy jeans and boring blue sweater. "You know why." It was hard enough getting people to call him Teddy instead of Thea. Or, worse, Theodora.

"I'm going to make you a shirt. It's going to be pink and fabulous. It's going to say, 'Call Me Teddy'. *And* it's going to be in glitter." Shiloh threw an imaginary handful into the air, then fell back to lie on the sidewalk, his arms flung out.

"With your handwriting, they'd probably think you wrote 'Daddy'." Teddy dropped back to use Shiloh's arm as a pillow.

Shiloh shifted but didn't pull away. He just rolled onto his side, his blond hair flopping into his eyes. He left his arm beneath Teddy's head, bringing their faces close enough that their noses nearly touched. "It's not *that* bad. Besides, you're clearly not a *Daddy*."

Teddy rolled his eyes. Ever since he'd borrowed Shiloh's laptop to finish up his college application essays — and forgotten to clear his search history after falling down the rabbit hole of kinky porn — Shiloh's teasing had been less than subtle. Teddy refused to be embarrassed, though, especially since the only reason he'd stumbled onto that website in the first place was because Shiloh had left three separate bookmarks for it.

It reinforced everything Teddy knew about their relationship. They were destined to be the bestest of friends — but nothing more. They were both too attracted to the same type of man — tall, dark and dangerous.

Still, knowing his friend was into the same kinks that he was didn't mean they needed to talk about it. He ignored the leading comment and switched back to the far safer topic of handwriting. "Remember when Mr. Carmine thought you wrote an essay on *Storage Wars*?"

"Hey, Mr. Carmine also thought you wrote an essay about Quasimodo."

"I did write him an essay about Quasimodo. Well, really about how the novel by Victor Hugo helped raise the money needed to restore the cathedral, and —" Teddy felt the beginnings of a spiel on gothic architecture creeping up.

Shiloh interrupted, "Yeah, buttresses...a rose window. I remember. I still think the gargoyles are creepy."

"You said buttresses," Teddy snickered, shoving Shiloh's shoulder.

"Teddy, can I touch your *buttress*?"

"Your hand can stay far away from my *buttress*, fuck you very much."

"It's like a butt fortress. I just want to invade your buttress! Why are you so mean to me?" Shiloh rolled onto his back and kicked his feet against the sidewalk like an angry toddler, except for the smile on his face.

"No, it's impregnable!" Teddy stuck out his tongue.

"Well, duh, you're a boy. Of course you're impregnable."

"Something tells me you don't know what that word means."

Immediately, Shiloh rattled off the definition. "Impregnable. Unable to be captured or broken into. Also, unable to be defeated or destroyed. But you have to admit that it sounds an awful lot like it means you can't make babies."

"And thank God for that," Teddy shivered at the thought of being responsible for a little, squalling, helpless baby. "I might miss wearing pink, but I won't miss *that*."

Teddy froze at the accidental admission. His therapist had told him that it was normal, that gender was a spectrum and that just because he still liked feminine things didn't make his desire to transition less valid. Still, it was the first time he'd admitted it to anyone except his therapist.

Shiloh sat up slightly to face him better. "You can still wear pink. You can wear whatever the fuck you want." Shiloh's voice hardened. "And if anyone bothers you about it, I'll cover their lockers in gay porn. Just say the word."

"The poor football players won't know what to do with themselves. Think of all the spontaneous erections." The few he'd dated had been far more interested in his ass than a straight guy probably should be—not that he'd obliged, since he refused to be anyone's dirty little secret.

Shiloh sighed. "It would be a beautiful gift to all of us."

A black Mercedes pulled up to the curb, barely parking before the driver was leaning on the horn.

"Impatient bastard," Shiloh grumbled. "I don't know why he's in a hurry. He gets paid by the hour."

"Well, that stick is so far up his ass it has to be uncomfortable sitting down." Teddy sat up and straightened his sweatshirt. The Becketts' driver was a homophobic dick. He didn't understand how the man hadn't been fired yet.

Shiloh pushed himself to his feet. "I bet he has hemorrhoids. That's probably where he rushes off to every night."

"Ew. You picture him rubbing cream on his ass?" Teddy teased.

Shiloh gagged, shoving Teddy to the side. "Gross. You're such a dick. I don't know why I hang out with you."

"Because you love me."

The Mercedes blared its horn again, a demanding series of honks that only ended when Shiloh threw a hand up in acknowledgment. "I gotta go. Do you have a ride?"

Teddy shrugged. "Yeah. She must just be running late or something. I'm sure she'll be here soon." He knew she wouldn't be, but he'd rather walk than listen to the driver sling slurs. He didn't understand how Shiloh dealt with it.

Shiloh hesitated on the bottom step, looking like he wanted to say something, but all he did was give a small nod and say, "Okay. See you Monday?"

"Yeah, see you."

* * * *

Teddy dropped his backpack beside his front door and toed off his trainers. He was halfway up the stairs when he heard his mother calling from the living room.

"Boo Bear, is that you?"

Teddy rolled his eyes to the ceiling, debating ignoring her, but she'd only keep yelling until he answered. Instead, he turned back and dragged his feet into the living room. "Stop calling me that."

His mother was draped over the loveseat. She was still in the same faded red pajamas he'd left her in that morning, her hair the same twisted mess of blonde knots. She rolled her head back over the armrest and gave him a lazy smile. "You'll always be my Boo Bear, Boo Bear." She giggled. It dwindled after a second and her forehead wrinkled with thought. "You're home early." The wrinkles faded quickly, though, leaving her glassy-eyed.

Teddy moved toward the couch, cringing at the stench of stale urine. "You were supposed to pick me up from school. It's past dinner time. Have you eaten?"

"It's Saturday, Boo." She reached out like she was trying to pat his shoulder, but wobbled precariously close to the edge of the couch.

"Friday, Mom." He untangled the blanket from around her feet. "You've pissed yourself again."

His mom blinked owlishly. "No, Boo, I'm sure it's Saturday. I had a lovely talk with Mr. Thompson across the street. Did you know his daughter is coming in next week? Lovely girl. She's about your age."

Teddy sighed. Mr. Thompson was a crotchety old man whose daughter was easily a decade older than him, and even if Teddy decided to give girls a try — which he wouldn't — Heather was a bitch. He couldn't count on one hand the number of times she'd called him 'dyke'. The last time, he'd told her that if she were going to insult him, she could at least do her research.

"Come on. Let's get you to the shower." Teddy levered her off the couch.

"Don't want to." His mom pouted but leaned against him, allowing him to guide her into her bedroom and through to the bathroom. He propped her against the counter. Her mouth formed a moue as she rubbed her palm over the prickly stubble on his scalp. "You're getting shaggy, Boo. I can clean this up with the clippers." She turned too quickly, catching her elbow on the toothbrush holder and sending it scattering into the sink.

"I'll take care of it later…after your shower. Come on, Mom." Teddy urged her away from the cabinets she was rooting around in. She hadn't helped him shave his head since he had been twelve — the last time he remembered her having a steady enough hand.

"I don't want to shower." She resisted his attempts to help her out of her piss-soaked pajamas, swatting at his hands.

"Let me take them off or you're wearing them in the shower," Teddy finally snapped, losing his patience with the fight. If he searched the living room, he'd find Johnnie Red somewhere — likely nearly empty and shoved beneath a cushion.

She quieted down long enough for him to unstick her clothes and drop them in the sink. He helped her into the shower, closing the curtain partway for privacy. She pouted quietly beneath the water for the first few minutes then started belting the lyrics to *Singing in the Rain*.

"Come on, Teddy," Mom broke off the tuneless belting for a second, "Sing with me."

"Did you wash your hair?" he asked instead, tracing a small crack in the countertop.

"I can't. I'll get soap in my eyes."

"So close them."

A few seconds later, "It's too dark."

Teddy closed his eyes and rubbed them. "Fine." He tugged open the shower curtain and was immediately pelted by stray drops of water. "Turn around."

She turned away from the spray and started humming again. He poured a dollop of soap into his palm and carefully worked it through her hair, trying to untangle as many knots as possible. "Maybe we should take a clipper to *your* hair, instead," he muttered.

"We could be twins." She smiled and started swaying to inaudible music as he worked the lather around. He grimaced. She wasn't even joking. His mother had only been sixteen when she'd had him, a whole year younger than he was now. At thirty-three, she looked too young to have a kid his age. The alcohol had added wrinkles, but not enough to stop people from calling her his sister — or enough to stop the dicks at school from making crass jokes.

She reached out to touch his hair again. He cringed away from the wet fingers. "Mom, stop."

She pouted but refrained from wetting his scalp further. He helped her rinse the soap clean then grabbed a towel. She stumbled slightly climbing over the side of the tub but managed to steady herself before falling.

He got her into a pair of clean pajamas and tucked her into bed. "I'll make you something to eat."

"It's too early to eat. I'm not hungry." Mom tugged the blanket up to her chin. Her eyes slid from his, darting surreptitiously to the nightstand and away. Habit made Teddy want to snag the hidden bottle and take it to the sink to empty. He ignored the urge. He was tired of making the effort when she wouldn't, and besides, she'd just use money that should be spent on groceries to replace it.

Instead, he set her alarm and headed to the kitchen, making her a sandwich and bringing it back to her room. Maybe the bread would sponge up the liquor.

She shoved a bottle under the covers like she thought he wouldn't see it—or smell it, since she'd sloshed a good few swallows on the pillow.

"Here." He passed her the sandwich.

She took a bite then crinkled her nose and threw the sandwich, plate and all, on the floor. "Not hungry."

Teddy clenched his fists, not bothering to clean the scattered bread. "Fine."

So much for sobering her up.

About the Author

Writing has always been my passion, as well as the way that I process my own life experiences. I am an openly transgender (AFAB), panromantic asexual living in rural Montana. There are few LGBTQIA+ resources here, and I always feel there is more room needed for LGBTQIA+ literary works. I have always written fiction as a hobby and earned a B.A. in English Literature and a M.Ed. in English Education from the University of Georgia; however, I ended up earning a Ph.D. in 2013, which moved most of my writing to the academic genre in which I have published several co-authored articles in peer-reviewed academic journals.

After coming out as transgender in 2018 and as asexual in 2020, I decided to refocus my writing on LGBTQIA+ themes in which I write about my own experiences through fictional characters and stories. Writing about my experiences has been extremely therapeutic for me. I am particularly enthralled with the complexities behind LGBTQIA+ identities and highly advocate that sexuality and gender identity exists on a spectrum. This topic is highly personal because my husband married me when I presented as a woman and was adamant that he could not be with a man. He underwent his own process of reevaluating his sexuality and now identifies as bisexual with a preference for women and feminine men. I think he is a wonderful example of the true fluidity behind sexuality.

Likewise, I choose to write about what it means to be LGBTQIA+ in a rural community like my current residence in Montana. Rural communities offer their own unique challenges due to little to no existing resources in some areas and a true feeling of isolation and invisibility. I want to share my experience coming out in a rural community and choosing to live openly as a transgender person and openly in a same-sex marriage.

Additionally, I work full-time as a human services instructor and a mental health counselor at a community college. Through this work, I also educate and advocate for the LGBTQIA+ community. My work as an educator and a counselor fuels my desire to use my fiction to increase awareness and acceptance for LGBTQIA+ people. Lastly, I would characterize my writing as person-centered, a term created by Carl Rogers as a counseling therapy and later as a life philosophy. My works center around the beauty and extraordinary complexity in being vulnerably authentic.

Carey loves to hear from readers. You can find their contact information, website details and author profile page at https://www.pride-publishing.com

PUBLISHING

Sign up for our newsletter and find out about all our romance book releases, eBook sales and promotions, sneak peeks and FREE romance books!

9 781802 509625